# DIVINE RIGHT'S TRIP

# DIVINE RIGHT'S TRIP

A
FOLK
TALE
BY
GURNEY
NORMAN

*The Dial Press*
*New York*
*1972*

Library of Congress Cataloging in Publication Data

Norman, Gurney, 1937–
  Divine Right's trip.

  "First appeared, in somewhat different form, in The
last whole Earth catalog."
  I.  Title.
PZ4.N8464Di  [PS3564.O57]        813'.5'4        78–37455

Library of Congress Catalog Card Number: 78–37455
Printed in the United States of America

First printing 1972

Book design by Margaret McCutcheon

*First I want to send greetings to some men who in*
*the last ten years have been good friends, teachers and*
*brothers to me: Ed McClanahan, Ken Kesey, Jim Hall,*
*Stewart Brand, Ron Bevirt and Wendell Berry.*
    *And then I want to dedicate this book to Chloe,*
*my friend and wife and lover.*

 **Contents**

*A double-minded man is unstable in all his ways.*

*The Holy Bible*
*James 1:8*

# DIVINE RIGHT'S TRIP

## Prologue:
## Divine Right's Bus, Urge

I was a fairly straight '63 VW microbus till Divine
Right got me, a good clean red-and-white seven-pas-
senger job with five new recapped tires and near-per-
fect upholstery. The only bad thing that ever happened
to me was the Muncys' youngest kid use to puke on
my seats all the time. The Muncys bought me new in
Germany when the old man was stationed over there
in the army. He was a master sergeant in an infantry
outfit, a little old for that kind of work maybe, but he
liked it well enough to volunteer for Vietnam when
that war heated up. They brought me to the States
when the sergeant went to Vietnam, and after he got
blown up by a land mine, his wife Marie traded me in
on a Falcon.

Two days on a car lot is a long time when you're
not used to it. It was hot and damn boring, so even
though this guy Divine Right looked pretty weird, I
was so eager to get on the road again I felt grateful to
him for buying me, although it did piss me off when
the dealer let me go for only five hundred and fifty
dollars. Divine Right paid the man with cash he'd got
from a big grass score that morning, and if I could
whistle I'd have whistled when we drove away together.

Which goes to show you how much I knew about
freaks in those days. I hadn't gone five hundred miles
with that son-of-a-bitch before I'd of given my fuel

pump to be back on that parking lot. That bastard
drove me from Boston to Chicago to St. Louis to Cincinnati without once checking my oil. I found out later
he didn't even know where my oil stick *was*. Drove non-
stop too, all day, all night, the only time I got even a
little rest was when he'd slow down long enough to
refuel or buy a ratburger. If his brother-in-law in Cincinnati hadn't noticed I was a quart and a half low
I'd probably have thrown a rod as soon as we hit the
next freeway.

D.R. doesn't seem to like them much, but his sister
and brother-in-law are nice people. Doyle understands
about cars. He's a mechanic, he knows how to take care
of machines. He tried to tell D.R. about preventive
maintenance, but D.R. was too stoned to pay attention.
He was on speed that trip, out of his skull on Ritilin
and Benzedrine. He told Doyle he had to split in order
to make the Ultimate Rendezvous. Doyle said what's
an Ultimate Rendezvous? But D.R. just grinned and
started my motor and drove away.

So you get some idea of where D.R.'s head was at.
He was the kind of guy who never had the faintest
idea how he affected things. He could fuck over a nice
'63 VW microbus he'd just paid five hundred and fifty
dollars for and never blink an eye. I don't know what
was the more humiliating, having my working parts
ignored or all that stupid paint sprayed all over my
body. Inside and outside, I suffered both places. It's
one thing to go around feeling bad because you're low
on oil; but when you have to *look* like a made-up
whore it gets to be a bit much. Housepaint, Day-Glo,
fingernail polish, you name it and I got smeared with
it. Sometimes he'd pull off into the emergency lane of
some big interstate and start painting on the spot. Said
God was sending him directions how to do it. Sometimes he'd pick up hitchhikers and tell them to lean
out the window and paint while he drove. By the time

him and his weird friends got through I looked like a watercolor that got rained on. It was awful.

But I survived. I don't know how but I did. Well, yes I do know too. It was Estelle. There's no doubt about it, that little lady saved my ass from the junk-yard. She's one nice person, Estelle. There was something kind of sad about her when we were on the road together. It seemed like she cried a lot. But she sure knew how to be nice to an old broken-down bus. She'd wash me, and empty my ashtrays. Sometimes D.R. would be too stoned to drive and Estelle would take over, and it would just be so fine, just me and her cruising quietly across the country through the night. That was the thing about Estelle. She understood cruising, she understood roads, and traffic, she knew how to flow with things in motion. I never did under-stand what she saw in D.R., but it wasn't my place to have opinions about people. My job was to carry them around from place to place while they acted out their story, and although I resented it most of the time, I did my best. It was painful, but I do have to say that it was interesting, and instructive. On some level I'm sure I'm a better bus for it. I kind of wish I could have a voice in this tale to tell my side of the story, but Gurney says there's too many points of view already to clutter it up even more with a talking car. So this is the only chance I'll have to speak my mind. It ain't much, but when you've been down as long as I have, you get grateful for even small favors.

Peace,
Urge

# ONE

## St. George and the Dragon

Here comes D.R. Davenport, Divine Right he calls
himself after that incredible stoned-out afternoon
when the words *Divine Right* formed in the clouds
above the meadow where he was lying in the grass
looking up and breathing deeply in awe of how really
simple everything is when you come right down to it;
Divine Right he calls himself, D.R. for short, driving
along the highway now through a dark and rainy
night in his VW microbus, Urge.

When all of a sudden Urge's headlights pick up a
hitchhiking freak on the road ahead.

I sure don't want to pick that guy up, D.R. told
himself. I wish I didn't have to. He was into a radio
talk show out of Los Angeles. This strange woman
had called in to comment on dress styles and wound
up on the Turner thesis and the American westward
movement. D.R. was listening to her rap, even talking
back from time to time, shaking his finger, agreeing
and disagreeing (but not too loudly; Estelle was asleep
in the back of the bus somewhere and he didn't want
to disturb her). Estelle was another reason not to pick
the freak up but, out there the poor fucker was, sitting
on his backpack holding out his thumb, with a little
black dog huddled against his feet. So D.R. dimmed
the headlights and turned the radio down and pulled
off the road just past where the guy was sitting.

"Get in," said Divine Right. "We're just, you know,

rolling along, digging it, the windshield wipers, rain on the roof, this weird westward movement lady's on the radio, how far you going, how long you been sitting out there?"

The hitch-hiker hassled his gear in and stuffed it on the floor. He was a little old feller, just barely strong enough to lift his pack inside. But finally he managed it, and his dog Salvadore leaped in behind him. Salvadore didn't even bother to sniff out his new scene. He just curled up on the floor next to the emergency brake and lay completely still.

D.R. said, "Davenport's my name, Divine Right Davenport. Like, this radio guy says KCBR, sort of sings it you know, says KCBR, Wayne Dixon here may I have your name please? And I say Divine Right is my name and weirdness is my game, what's yours?"

Meaning, of course, his passenger, who was pissing D.R. off just sitting there. D.R. was a word man, you see, he liked to talk and to be talked to, and thirty seconds into their ride together his passenger hadn't said a thing. All he did was nod and grin and look at the wet highway stretching out in the long beams of light up ahead. After a mile or two D.R. was wishing he'd minded his own business and left the silent bastard sitting by the roadside, rain or no rain.

He turned the radio back up.

". . . all I mean is that genocide against the Indians was the official policy of every American President after Andrew Jackson."

The announcer was aghast. "Are you saying our government had a *policy* . . ."

"Absolutely. It's a well known, I mean you're in radio, it's common knowledge among informed people."

"It's common *rumor, maybe* . . ."

"Rumor, hell," D.R. said. "The lady's right. Every word she says is true." He turned the radio down then and leaned across to stare at his passenger. "And I'll bet if you'd say something, it'd turn out to be true too, I know it would."

When the hitch-hiker didn't answer, D.R. started slowing down. "What I want to know, fuckhead, is how you're gonna keep dry when I dump your ass out in the rain about half a mile from now."

And when there was still no reply, D.R. brought Urge to a full stop, and leaned across again to look his passenger full in the face. He was surprised to see how young the freak was. Fifteen, sixteen at the most. D.R. was only twenty-one himself, but the kid made him feel like an old man. He had a goatee of scraggly whiskers, twenty-three long blond hairs sticking out of various little blotches on his skin. His eyes were pale blue, streaked with red.

"Far out," said Divine Right. "Did you know you had red, white and blue eyes?"

No longer smiling, the kid opened the door and got out in the rain. He left his pup on the floor while he got his pack on, and settled his floppy, wide-brim hat back on his head. Finally he was ready. As he reached in to get his dog he looked up at D.R. and said, "Did you ever read about St. George and the dragon?"

D.R. said he hadn't.

"It's far-out shit," said the kid. And he closed the door and started walking down the highway toward wherever they'd just come from.

 **Looking for Dope**

Urge's wipers wiped and wiped and wiped and wiped and wiped and wiped and wiped, and still D.R. could barely see through the windshield. It hadn't bothered him the first few hours, but as the rain kept falling and the night wore on and his eyes got sore and tired, the world outside the windshield gradually turned into such a visual mush D.R. had trouble keeping Urge on the road. What Urge needed was a new set of windshield wipers, and what D.R. needed was some food and a good night's sleep. But short of that the next best thing of course was a good hit of grass to kind of bring things into focus.

Sorry old bus, he said to Urge as he felt his shirt pocket for a J.

And he meant that too. One of Divine Right's convictions was that it was possible to turn a vehicle onto dope if only the right means could be found. One time just before crossing the Canadian border he'd stashed an ounce of prime Afghan hash in Urge's crank case and Urge had obviously loved it. Within a mile Urge's headlights had started flashing on and off, his horn spontaneously bleated tones of joy. At least it had seemed that way. D.R. was pretty stoned himself at the time and it may have been that those were only things he wanted Urge to do. At any rate, the bus began to cough and choke and gasp for breath after a while, and he'd had to take the hash back out. But that's okay, Urge old buddy, D.R. said, feeling his shirt for a J. That's all right. I'm working on it. One of these days I'll come up with a formula to stone you with so fine, so right you'll think: divine.

The joint D.R. had put in his shirt pocket was gone. All he found was a tattered book of matches. He looked in the glove compartment and felt in his leather belt-pouch, but it was the same. So at a wide place at the end of a bridge D.R. pulled off the road and started to rummage around the bus in search of dope.

"What is it?"

"Shhh. Go back to sleep."

"What is it?" Estelle sat up and rubbed her eyes. She was in a sleeping bag, lying crossways on the mattress near the back of the bus. The bus wasn't wide enough for her to stretch out fully, but there was so much junk scattered around there wasn't any other place to lie. In spite of having to twist herself into an *S* to lie down, she'd slept so deeply for seven straight hours that now she was having trouble getting her eyes to stay open.

"Go back to sleep."

"No, I'm awake. Where are we?"

"Fuck, I don't know. Somewhere out west."

D.R. was on his knees next to Estelle, digging in a duffle bag. A light would have helped but Urge's overhead light was out, and D.R. didn't know where the flashlight was.

"Here, honey, light this candle," said Estelle, and she handed him a candle.

But somehow climbing through the general debris to get to the back, D.R. had lost the matches. He yelled goddamn it! as loud as he could yell.

"Shhh, honey, it's all right. What are you looking for?"

"I'm looking for the goddamn dope that I had in my goddamn hand not six goddamn hours ago. That's what I'm looking for." And he lifted the duffle bag by its bottom and dumped its contents on top of the other stuff already scattered over the mattress.

Estelle found a match and lit it. The whole wild interior of the bus came alive for a moment, but quickly began to fade. "Give me the candle," said Estelle.

"Where is it?"

"I handed it to you."

D.R. felt around his knees and legs, and in the pile of stuff he'd just dumped out. But all he could find was a broken screwdriver. He held it up, looked at it, then threw it as hard as he could toward the front. "Fuck it!" he yelled, and strangled himself on the yell. It was as if something had seized his throat and choked him. Falling onto his side D.R. grabbed the

handle of the side doors and threw them open, then
tumbled in a heap outside into the rain. Estelle was
out of her sleeping bag by the time he hit the ground.

"Honey, what's wrong?"

"I can't *breathe!*" he gasped. "That *space* in that
*bus* . . ."

"Honey, it's fine in here. Come on back in, you're
getting wet."

D.R. got to his feet and tried to wipe the mud off his
knees. But that only smeared it more. "What a goddamn mess."

"Get in, baby, lie down. I'll drive awhile, and you
can get some sleep."

D.R. did not seem persuaded, but he obeyed. Estelle
closed the door behind him, then guided him toward
the far end of the mattress.

"Where's my sleeping bag?" D.R. asked.

"Get in mine. Come on, now."

"I want mine!" he whined. "Where is it?"

"It's on the floor half full of pork and beans, that's
where. Now come on back here."

D.R. was too confused to argue. Estelle pulled off
his sandals and got his feet pointed into the sleeping
bag. He wiggled on down inside, feeling the dark
warmth of Estelle's body become his own deep in the
interior of the bag.

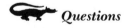 *Questions*

Did he dream about dragons? Did he dream about
deer? Did he whisper the names of friends who were
near? What songs did they play, and how far away?
Why did he whisper, why did she scream? What does
the sound of a screen door mean? Who walks in the
pasture? Who talks on the hill? Who goes to the cel-

lar, can you feel the chill? Where does the river, when will the wind? How far are the mountains? Where do they end? Why would the church? Did the service begin? Tell me who died, and tell me who cried. Help me to hide in the skin of a deer, my zippered-up bag in the mouth of a stag so swiftly I go through rows of does, it flows, it flows, it flows, it flows all over the hill where the green grass grows.

## Eagle Rock

Sometime between first light and actual sunrise Estelle turned onto a dirt road and followed it three miles to Eagle Rock State Park, where the sign said there was a campground. They really didn't have time to stop and camp. They were almost out of money and the only chance they had of getting any any time soon was in St. Louis if they could get there by Tuesday. D.R.'s buddy Eddie owed him sixty dollars. Eddie had promised to pay D.R., but Tuesday night he was splitting St. Louis for Mexico to score a big bunch of grass. If they were going to get to St. Louis by Tuesday they certainly couldn't afford to lose a whole day camping, but, as Estelle figured it, they couldn't afford not to stop either. D.R. was getting freakier by the mile and Estelle thought she felt a cold coming on. They were both wiped out and Urge was an impossible mess. Maybe if they stopped and rested for a day, straightened up their gear and got some sun they'd both feel strong enough to make St. Louis in one more non-stop push.

There was a chain across the driveway at the park entrance but it was easy enough to drive around it. If the ranger didn't come around later in the day to collect the camping fee, Estelle had just saved two whole dollars. It was a good omen. Stopping was the thing to do all right. As she cruised the graveled driveway looking among the assorted tents and trailers for a place to park, she began to feel really happy. The campground was incredibly crowded, but at last she found an empty space in the corner farthest from the river, a narrow slot between a GMC pickup with a great hulking camper rig on top, and a green Porsche parked in front of a red pup tent. There were beer cans all over the place, and someone had left an enormous turd lying crossways on the metal grill above the fireplace. But Estelle was so glad to be someplace in particular she didn't let it bother her. She picked the shit up on a piece of cardboard and buried it under some leaves. In fifteen minutes she had most of the trash picked up, which included a plastic bag with some old apples in it good enough to wash and eat. I could even cook 'em, she told herself. Cooked apples. Goddamn. Her taste buds went to work on an image of apples steaming in a pot as she walked off in search of a rest room.

 *Estelle's Shower*

It was at the Eagle Rock State Park campground that Estelle took the most delicious hot shower she'd ever had in her entire life. It was like a dream. The water pounded her neck and shoulders and folded her up in great hot clouds of steam. I'm a taco, she thought, a hot tamale cooking in a pan. The water sprayed into her mouth, the steam filled her ears and nose and seeped in at the corners of her eyes. After a night of cold rain on the open road, here she was in hot rain in a room, a steam room that at five fifteen in the morning belonged to her alone. She ran out of the shower for a minute to turn on all the other showers. In the corner stall she found a brand-new bar of Dial soap, and as the bathroom filled with steam, Estelle washed herself all over, then shampooed her hair. She stayed under the water 'til her fingers began to wrinkle. Finally she managed to draw away from the shower stall into the cloud outside, where she used her shirt for a towel. When she was dry she went to the door and looked out, holding her clothes in her hand. The camp was sound asleep. Not even the birds were stirring yet. Laughing out loud, Estelle skipped naked down the gravel path to dear old Urge, stopping off along the way to steal some firewood from a shed that was selling it on the honor system for seventy-five cents a bundle.

 ## The Lone Outdoorsman

About eight o'clock a man in a red hunting cap came out of the camper parked next to Urge and began dismounting the yellow trail bike from the front end of his GMC. He was short and overweight but you could tell by the way he wore his cap and held his pipe between his teeth that he took himself pretty seriously. His face was absurdly handsome. His face could have been in a TV ad for pipe tobacco, or a men's cologne. Probably in some previous incarnation the Lone Outdoorsman had been the best five-foot, five-inch high-school halfback in the conference. He had on a black and green wool shirt, Army boots and fatigue pants faded to a pale green. Dangling from the Army web belt around his waist were a canteen, a compass, a long sheath-knife, a first-aid kit, survival kit, snake-bite kit, sewing kit, and a kit to repair flat tires with. He banged and rattled like a mobile hard-

ware store, and yet he smoked his pipe and worked
on his bike like any neighborhood family man out
waxing his car on a Sunday afternoon.

From time to time the Outdoorsman would glance
over his shoulder and peek at Divine Right and Estelle
through the overhanging trees. They were sitting on
the ground in front of the fireplace, eating hot apples
and talking quietly. He didn't mean to pry. He was
just, you know, checking things out, looking to see
if there was any crime going on over there among the
hippies. He noticed they were both eating out of the
same dish, out of a stewpot, as a matter of fact. That
was irregular, to be sure, but not quite an infraction,
nothing to call the Lone Outdoorsman into action
yet. He glanced at the two young people every few
minutes until he got the bike dismounted. Then he
got on, started 'er up, and rode off to the bathroom a
hundred yards away.

## The Red Tent

D.R. and Estelle had finished breakfast and were into
cleaning out the bus when a woman from the red
tent and the Porsche next door came over to borrow
some sugar. She looked to be in her thirties somewhere,
a very tanned, athletic woman wearing a leather vest
and a pair of chic brown riding pants. She was European. Her accent was so thick Estelle at first didn't
understand what she wanted. But finally she heard
"shu-ger" and after they'd gone through the routine
of scooping some brown sugar out of the coffee can
Estelle kept it in, the woman began to come in a
little more clearly.

"You arrive very late," she said.

"No, no," said Estelle. "Very early. We got here just at dawn."

"You must come far."

"Very far," said D.R. "Very, very far. And we've still got a long way to go."

"We have come far too. From Amsterdam to New York, from New York to here."

D.R. asked the woman where she got her red tent.

"You like it?"

"I've never seen a tent like that before."

"Would you like to see inside? It is very lovely."

Estelle was knee-deep in the shit they'd unloaded from Urge and she wanted to get on with the work. But D.R. was fascinated by the red tent, and so he followed the woman past the Porsche over to her camping place. Another woman about the same age as the first, but who turned out to speak no English at all, was just coming out the front flap as they walked up.

"These nice people loaned me sugar," said the first woman, speaking European. "He admires our tent."

Her companion smiled and nodded and held the flap open for D.R. as he entered.

D.R.'s first hit was off the fantastic quality of the light inside. It was midmorning by now. The sun was above the tree line, shining directly into all the little clearings on the western side of the campground. It filled the red tent with the most completely restful light he'd ever seen before. A whole tension that had screwed his face tight all morning went away as his eyes gulped the quiet rose of the tent's interior. It wasn't large at all. There was only one place a person could half stand up, and two sleeping bags side by side would cover most of the floor. Yet somehow it struck D.R. as the most spacious, elegant room he'd ever been in. It was immaculate. In the corners of the tent near the entrance were two rolled sleeping bags. On top of each bag were small blue and white TWA flight bags, both neatly zippered, the carrying straps arranged just so. Except for a strip of grass down the middle, the ground was covered by two straw mats. On each mat was a rubber air mattress, deflated and folded into a perfect square and stashed in the far corner of the tent. In the middle of the far end stood a short, three-legged table with a candle on it, and a single wildflower of some kind, in a glass of water. D.R. was amazed. He hadn't smoked any dope in over twelve hours now, and yet he felt completely stoned on the perfect arrangement of the small red world around him. He glanced over his shoulder to see if the two women were watching. When he saw them through the tent flap doing something over at the picnic table, he stretched himself out on one of the mats and stared up at the slanting red roof above him.

A tent, he thought. A room of space. It starts here by my left arm, goes up then down and ends over there on the far side of the other mat. That is what this room is, and that is all it is, no more and no less. This is its total size and shape and full dimension: a room of space marked off and set aside by these walls of red canvas that weren't here yesterday probably and probably won't be here tomorrow, but they are here today and I am here too inside the particular space they enclose. This space has always been here. But it has not always been a room, at least not *this* room, because it has never been enclosed by this particular tent before. The space is here. The time is now. And they are intersecting in a way that no other tent has ever caused before. This very space where I am lying has been tented over before, closed up in other canvas rooms. And so the question seems to be: would another tent around this same space recreate *this* room, or does this room disappear forever once this red tent has been removed and taken somewhere else? And what about when this tent is pitched in another place? If you pitch it in the Blue Ridge Mountains, take it down and put it up again in the Rockies,

has the *same room* been in both places? Or is it another brand-new room every time you pitch the tent
again?

"Comfortable, eh?"

The woman's voice startled D.R. and caused him
to sit upright. But her smile was so friendly and there
was such charm in her strange voice, D.R. relaxed
again and invited the woman to come in. The idea
struck her as very funny. Giggling, she called to her
companion. Soon both women were in the tent with
Divine Right, sitting cross-legged on the other mat,
drinking tea and smiling back and forth at one another, and at D.R.

"I mean," D.R. was saying, "I mean, like, if you
take this tent down, you know, take the poles down,
fold the whole thing up, and move it fifteen yards
. . . I mean, I'm just saying, *if* you move it, if you
take it down and set it up again, where does the room
. . . I mean, like, we're in a room, right? The room
is these walls. And these walls are *here*. They're here,
and they're here *now*. And so the question seems to
be . . . the question seems to be, where does the room
go when you take these walls down and fold them up
and put them in your car?"

The lady who didn't speak English had begun to
look a little troubled, perhaps even a little afraid. But
when her friend interpreted, she began to nod. Both
women nodded and said, "Yes. Yes."

"Do you really know what I'm talking about?"

"Of course," said the woman who had borrowed the
sugar. "You're talking about space and time."

"Far out!" D.R. exclaimed. "Far out!" Suddenly he
had to get out of the red tent, and go and tell Estelle.
Hastily he mumbled his thanks and his good-byes, and
crawled to the opening. Outside, he was so excited he
tripped over a tent stake and fell on his ass.

## A Place for Everything and Everything in Its Place

Estelle, everything's by god I really believe it is. You can tell it, you can feel it, the signs are all around. This is here and we are now and the intersection of time and space is just special as hell, and I'm going to find out some things we need to know. I believe there's going to be better relations between east and west. I believe if we get organized, a place for everything and everything in its place, books in a book box, clothes in a clothes box honey you've done a wonderful, you have now, and I love you for it and take heart and determine to be better than I've been in a long time. Those women understood every word I said. When we get to St. Louis. Are these crackers any good? Where's the tape recorder? Where'd I put the cassettes? When we get to St. Louis I'm going to get some car polish and wax old Urge all over. Is this to throw away? Ain't this box any good? We need all the boxes in St. Louis I'm going to get ten cardboard boxes of identical size and label them with what they're supposed to hold. Books in one, look at this shit on my *Whole Earth Catalog*. Fuck, I was going to order some stuff out of there. Books in one box, tape shit in another, every goddamn thing we got's going to have its proper place. You've done a wonderful thing here honey, you really have. You ought to see their tent. From now on. When we get to St. Louis. Here, let me lift that for you. Wait! Don't throw that glass away. Here, I'll wash it out after while, I want to put a wildflower in it. I got into this rap about space, you know? I was afraid. But they knew exactly and I believe the world's getting to be a better place. I receive that from somewhere in my mind. I think love and gentleness and neighborliness and human harmony are going to prevail. I think the stars are moving into very particular cosmic arrangements. And we've got to do our part. I believe it all depends on everybody doing his part. Look at this bus, goddamn I bet old Urge is proud.

## Return of the Lone Outdoorsman

The birds in the treetops hushed their singing as the Lone Outdoorsman came into Divine Right's camp. But D.R. was too deep into his monologue to catch the warning. He was too deep into it even to realize that Estelle had left the camp and gone for a walk. Before he could prepare himself in any way, there the Outdoorsman was, standing above him with his hands on his hips, staring at D.R. like a teacher or a cop. As he became aware of the Lone Outdoorsman's presence, D.R. went silent as the birds. The music that had filled his head changed from harps to kettle drums, and he wondered where Estelle had gone, and why.

"Afternoon," said the Outdoorsman.

"Good afternoon," said Divine Right.

"How're you?" asked the Lone Outdoorsman.

"Okay, I guess," said D.R.

"Yeah. Well, I noticed you over there in the tent with them foreign ladies, and I just wondered if anything might be wrong."

"No," said D.R. "Nothing wrong, as far as I know."

"Yeah. Well, just checking. I noticed you over there in the tent with 'em. You never know. Cleaning out your bus, looks like."

D.R. nodded. He had been kneeling among the stuff from the bus when the Outdoorsman first came over. Now he was on his feet, and following the Outdoorsman as he walked around the bus, looking at the paint job.

"You paint all this stuff on your bus?" asked the Outdoorsman.

"Some of it," said D.R.

"How come you to do it?" said the Outdoorsman. "Messed up a good paint job. What's that there?"

The Outdoorsman was pointing at a large yellow moon on Urge's side, with a crab walking across it, leaving tracks.

"That's a moon with a crab on it," said D.R.

The Outdoorsman looked D.R. in the eye. "You say it is, hunh?"

D.R. nodded.

"How many horsepower this thing have?"

"I don't know. Fifty, maybe."

"Fifty, huh. Yeah. Well, my GMC over there's got four hundred and fifty. Of course, the rig weighs it down some, and my boat. But it'll still outrun a bus like yours any day of the week, you better believe that."

D.R. asked the Outdoorsman why he was telling him that. The Outdoorsman said you never know. Then he told D.R. to let him know if anything came up.

"What do you mean?"

"Well. You know. Trouble."

D.R. nodded. His heart was pounding. He watched the Outdoorsman light his pipe, then carefully crush the match against his knife handle.

"You remember what I told you, now," he said, and he turned and jingled off through the trees to his own camp.

### At Home with the Lone Outdoorsman

So far that day the Lone Outdoorsman had motorcycled to the toilet and back, and hiked around Section B of the Eagle Rock State Park campground. His plan had been to stop off at his camper for a beer and a bar of pemmican, and then go hunting over in the park amphitheater with his new AR-15 semiautomatic double-barrel over-and-under. But after he'd noticed the hippie queer bothering the two foreign ladies in the red tent, he decided he'd better hang around the campsite just in case.

He wanted a beer really badly by now, but as an act of discipline he kept his cooler closed, and satisfied his thirst with the warm water in his canteen. He considered foregoing a beer as an act of sacrifice for the ladies. As women, alone in the wilderness, they had a right to expect that much of him. He owed it to them, to the cause of westward settlement and civilization in general, to keep alert and ready until the threatening element among them had been dealt with in some sure and final way. Maybe it had already been dealt with. Maybe that little show of force right there in the hippie queer's own campground would be sufficient to keep him from running amok. The Lone Outdoorsman hoped it would. He sincerely hoped it would.

For he was a peaceable man. He'd fought the war to make the peace. It was his most fervent hope that peace would in fact endure, so that women and children could be safe in their homes, to grow and learn and become good citizens, so that people like those two foreign ladies could come to America and witness the magnificence of this great land from sea to shining sea in freedom and safety. Let the foreign people come to America, he thought. Let them experience our great mountains, our flowing rivers, our abundant wildlife, our historic monuments, our magnificent parks, both state and federal, and our majestic canyons, deserts, plains and lakes, both fresh water and salt. Let peace reign, he thought. Let the people come, and enjoy, and be free. And let the freaks and queers and Jews and motorcycle gangs be goddamn careful when they fuck with the Lone Outdoorsman.

The Lone Outdoorsman took another pull from his canteen. As he holstered it again he peered through his curtains and saw a suspicious thing: the threatening element next door was trying to sneak away, to rendezvous with a band of confederates over by the river. The Outdoorsman reached for his AR-15 semiautomatic double-barrel over-and-under and prepared to fire. But then he lowered the weapon and through clenched teeth muttered, "I think I'll follow that son-of-a-bitch." He hung the rifle on the wall and got his .357 magnum pistol out of a drawer and hitched it to his web belt.

As Divine Right disappeared into the trees in the rear of Section C, the Lone Outdoorsman stealthily trailed behind him.

## By the River

The rock Estelle was on was one of several boulders near the river, all of them gray and half as big as houses. It was already dark on the ground around the rocks, and cold enough to make you want a sweater. But the sun was still shining in the trees, overhead, and as D.R. climbed he thought: climbing for Estelle is climbing for the sun. It warmed him to think that. And he was warmed all over again when he saw Estelle lying on her bright Mexican serape on the broad, flat surface of the rock.

Estelle had her shirt off, rolled under her head for a pillow. Her skin was naturally dark, a sort of pale olive that was always consistent in its tone no matter how much or how little sun she got. Estelle's hips and her thighs were too thick for anyone ever to call her figure "beautiful" in that plastic sense that Miss America is considered "beautiful." And her face was too much the face of the average girl in a crowd for, say, a TV camera man to ever zoom in on and freeze as something special. And yet Estelle was a truly beautiful girl. She had dark hair and very large, dark brown eyes. Her breasts weren't especially big, or little, or round, or pointy or any of those magazine-writer tit-fetish clichés. They were just nice boobs on a nice woman, absolutely real like everything else about her. Goddamn, D.R. thought. Tears came into his eyes. He could hardly believe the loveliness of the moment his painful walk across the campground had led him to. The sun was just going down behind the cliffs across the river, shining orange through the trees and across Estelle's naked skin. Shielding her eyes with her hand, she looked up and smiled at D.R., then patted the rock beside her with her hand. D.R. lay down and snuggled his face in her hair.

"I've been having the loveliest visions," said Estelle. "I've been seeing wonderful feathered horses, flying through the sky. And wheat fields that would turn to wings and fly away."

D.R. asked Estelle what she thought the visions meant.

"Nothing," said Estelle. "At least I hope they don't mean anything. I like them just exactly as they were."

They lay quietly for a while. The sky was full of light and still a brilliant blue. But the rock and the river valley and the cliffs on the other side were all in shadow now, and it was getting cool. Estelle turned on her side and moved closer to D.R., laying her arm across him. Her breast tumbled precisely into D.R.'s hand, and for a time the reality between them was simply hand on breast, hand folded in the flesh of breast, pressing and rubbing and smoothing like patting down a pillow. Then their mouths came together in a long and dreamy kiss.

## Falling

Estelle and D.R. hadn't had many times like this one lately. They fucked a time or two coming down through California, but it seemed like there just wasn't enough leisure on this trip for any real love-making. Exhaustion was the theme so far. Exhaustion had been catching up to them for a long time now. In a way their whole experience together since Altamont had been a steady descent into exhaustion, a drop that gained momentum as they went along, like falling. When D.R. felt particularly tired, and dirty, and locked up in his mind, it was like he was the one who was falling, with Estelle being dragged along behind. That wasn't accurate, of course. That was just stuff in D.R.'s head, a product of the same weary fever that produced the sense of falling in the first place. There was a way in which Estelle had already fallen further than D.R. had, already knew stuff that he had yet to learn. In a way, she was coming up as he went down, and reaching out a hand to save him from what she already knew. The thing that overwhelmed D.R. when he thought about it that way was how utterly generous that was of her, and how dangerous for her. Danger was everywhere, it seemed, and in more guises than he could account for. Sometimes D.R. felt like he had some kind of disease that Estelle was sure to catch if she stayed with him long enough. As a matter of fact, he'd given her the clap the very first week they were together. As a man who dealt heavily in signs and omens, he had seen that as a forewarning, a metaphor of other and worse things yet to come. It hadn't bothered him all that much at the time. In the beginning, Estelle had been just another cunt by the roadside as likely to give the clap to him as the other way around. But that was a couple of months ago, or three, or four, he wasn't sure any more just how long ago it had been. His sense of time was all internal now.

The only things he measured were miles and micrograms, and even then he had little use for precision. But however long ago it had been since he'd first found Estelle, it was long enough for him to come to depend on her so much it threatened him. He hated depending on someone as much as that, and the fact that she depended just as much, or more, on him only made it that much worse.

But it wasn't a thing that he could choose by now. It was like there was a power over his life that wasn't his to wield, a power so large and mysterious all D.R. could do was yield.

Wield to yield, now there's a nice play on words for you. I'll have to work on that. Wield and yield. Shield and dealed.

"I've just written a poem," said D.R.

"Tell it to me," said Estelle.

"Wield and yield and shield and dealed."

Estelle laughed and rolled onto her back so she could take her pants off. "That's a good poem."

D.R. started undressing too. When they were naked Estelle pulled D.R. on top of her, and for almost an hour they made love.

 ## The Humanity of the Lone Outdoorsman

There were at least three things the Lone Outdoorsman could have done in response to the filthy crime he saw happen on the big rock by the river. He could have shot big holes in the young couple's arms and legs and heads and backs with his .357 magnum pistol. Or he could have gone to his camper, got his rubber life raft out of his fourteen-foot Cris-Craft motorboat, launched it a mile upstream and staged an amphibious assault upon the little beach near the rocks and captured them before they knew what was happening. Or—and admittedly this is a big or; it's big because, as it turns out, the Lone Outdoorsman is far from your ordinary, everyday one-dimensional heavy; the thing that redeems the Lone Outdoorsman is a refreshing mental complexity of a kind you don't ordinarily run into in folk tales. All mixed in with his gory mental images of bullet-riddled bodies and heroic assaults upon beachheads was a commendable impulse to be nice to these kids, to befriend them and hopefully influence them in some constructive way. In short, the Lone Outdoorsman could either shoot these kids, assault them from the river and take them captive, or else be a good neighbor and invite Divine Right and Estelle over to his place for supper.

And so when D.R. and Estelle had finished balling, had dressed and folded the serape and walked back through the darkening campground to their own scene, they found the Lone Outdoorsman leaning against Urge's front, waiting for them.

### The Invitation

"Well," he said, "how are you young folks this evening? Feeling all right? What I thought was the two of you all might like to come over and eat supper with me, I mean it looks like you all have been traveling pretty hard, and maybe not eating too well, and since I've got these steaks, yes sir, four of the juiciest steaks you ever sunk your fangs in, buddy, that ain't no lie. And I'd be mighty pleased to have your company, you know I've got a niece and a nephew about your age, my brother's kids, the wife and me, we had a kid but he died, but my brother's kids, now, I tell you, they're all right. They come out from Little Rock about once a year, and we appreciate seeing 'em, I declare we do. You know, a lot of the older folks now, they ain't got much patience with young people these days, they object to the way they behave. And I guess in some things I do too. But my grandfather was a big influence on me, and what he believed in was giving people a second chance. I take after Granddaddy in that repect. I guess when it comes to being with people and judging 'em, I'm what you'd call a liberal. For I find a lot of good in young people nowadays, I declare I do. Why shit, all the young people need is to get out in the hills and romp around some. I grew up on the land and I know how good it is for you. Why when I was a kid I could hunt and track, why I'd go out by myself for days at a time when I was ten and twelve years old. I loved it, there just wasn't anything greater than getting off to myself in the hills with my gun. I've always said I was born a hundred years too late. I ought to of been a pioneer. The wife, she don't like to get out much, so two or three times a year I just cut loose by myself and go live out in nature a few days. As my granddaddy would say, nature's good for what ails you. Ain't that what you all say?"

Estelle mumbled that that was what she said too. Divine Right said something and the Lone Outdoorsman said something else. But five minutes later they didn't have the faintest idea how the conversation had ended. The vision of steak crowded everything else out of their heads except the smoke from the horrendous joint D.R. rolled, in celebration of the party. Giggling, tumbling around in the bus trying to get dressed and smoke dope and hug and kiss all at the same time, D.R. and Estelle were ecstatic. Every kink in them had been ironed out by their wonderful hour on the rock. And now here they were, getting all dressed up and stoned, about to go eat free steak with their neighbor. Steak! Goddamn. It would be their first real meal since they'd left the Anaheim Flash's house in California.

When they had their outfits on, Estelle in her ankle-length gingham dress and D.R. in his pioneer outfit of leather pants and shirt and coonskin cap with tail, they paused long enough to hold each other tightly for a moment. Then D.R. took the last drag on the joint, ate the roach as the first hors d'oeuvre of the evening, then set out with his lady to call on the Lone Outdoorsman.

 ### *The Lesson of the Deer*

Divine Right and Estelle were sitting in folding chairs drinking beer and eating cashew nuts while the Lone Outdoorsman grilled steaks over a charcoal fire. Like Estelle and Divine Right, he had dressed for the occasion too. He had on a cowboy hat and cowboy boots, a pair of Levis, a flannel shirt with a vest and, while he cooked, a knee-length apron that was white everywhere it didn't have bloodstains on it. Now and then a breeze would swirl the smoke up in a cloud around his head, momentarily decapitating him so that it appeared that there was only his wide, round body in cowboy clothes tending the slabs of meat on the charcoal fire. It was a surreal scene all right, but D.R. and Estelle were both so stoned it struck them as the most ordinary of domestic occasions. It was dark by now and so far there wasn't any moon. The trees around the camp framed the entire universe, as far as they were witness. What they saw was all there was anywhere in all creation, and for heads as awash with dope smoke as D.R.'s and Estelle's, that was quite enough.

"I'm a Cancer," D.R. suddenly called out to the Lone Outdoorsman. "My sign is the crab. I get where I'm going by walking sideways."

The Lone Outdoorsman nodded as he turned the

steaks. "Yeah. I'm in the Fin, Fur and Feather Club myself, great buncha guys."

"Got him!" Estelle exclaimed, swatting a fat mosquito on her arm.

"Yeah," said the Outdoorsman. "They're pretty bad tonight. We'll go in soon as these steaks are done. Time for 'Westward, Westward' anyhow."

"You got TV?" Estelle asked.

"Sure. It's a little one, but you can see it all right."

"Far out! Can we watch it too?"

The question pained the Outdoorsman. He turned to look at his guests. "Of course you can. You're my guests, ain't you?"

"Fantastic!" Estelle and D.R. were so excited by the prospect of TV they leaned their chairs together and gave each other little hugs.

"We haven't seen TV since we left Oregon."

"How long ago was that?" asked the Outdoorsman.

"I don't know," said D.R. "When did we leave Oregon?"

"Three weeks ago tomorrow."

"Three weeks ago tomorrow," D.R. said to the Outdoorsman.

"Shucks. I drove here from Phoenix in a day and a half."

"Yeah, well, you see," said D.R. and he got out of his chair and walked closer to his host. "You see, I'm a Cancer, my sign is the crab, I get where I'm going by walking sideways."

"I plan to take a different route back to Phoenix myself," said the Outdoorsman. "See some new country. That's the great thing about America, there's always some new country to see."

Estelle asked the Lone Outdoorsman if he lived in Phoenix. She'd come over to the fire and was holding a plate while he piled the steaks on. Hungry as she was, she was already plotting in her mind to stash part of their supper in her bag so they'd have something to eat the next day. She'd already scored a can of beer and a handful of cashew nuts. What she wanted now was half a steak and at least one baked potato. She would have scooped a potato off the platter then and there if the Outdoorsman had given her a chance. But he said, "I'll help you with that," took the platter and led his guests around the truck and through the narrow door of his camper.

"Yeah, I'm from Phoenix," the Outdoorsman said. "My grandfather helped settle that place in the seventies. Came out with the United States Cavalry, chasing after Proud Person, the Apache renegade."

"Did he catch him?" D.R. inquired.

"Well sir," said the Outdoorsman. "As a matter of fact, he did."

"Far out. What did he do with him?"

"Took him to jail. Made him promise to quit bothering people, then let him go."

"Did Proud Person keep his promise?" asked Estelle.

"He did. Proud Person was a good Indian from then on. My grandfather was proud of that. He used to talk about it a lot. He got out of the Army and settled there in Phoenix as a grocer. Proud Person used to come in from the hills about once a year and trade with him. They became lifelong friends. My grandfather was a tough old codger, but that's one thing you can say for him, he was always a believer in giving folks a second chance."

The Outdoorsman was quiet then as he chewed a bite of steak. When he'd swallowed he set his plate aside and got up to turn the TV on.

The television set was a little portable with a four-inch screen. It sat on top of the refrigerator toward the rear of the camper. Estelle and the Outdoorsman were seated on bunks on either side of the little room, with Divine Right between them sitting on a stool at the end of a table that folded out of the wall. Behind and above D.R. was a sleeping space that ran cross-

ways of the cabin. On either side of the entrance to
that space were the mounted heads of two small deer,
both of them does. D.R. noticed them as soon as he
came in. He didn't want to sit under them but he
didn't want Estelle to have to either. Somehow the
two does reminded him of Estelle, and he didn't like
the thought. If he hadn't been on the crest of a good
mood at the time, the two sad-eyed deer would have
depressed him terribly. But Divine Right was about
two steps back from his ordinary responses now, and
the two mounted deer were no more than a minor
weight upon his consciousness. He was even able to
laugh when he asked the Lone Outdoorsman where
he'd bagged the deer and the Outdoorsman said he'd
run over them with his truck.

"Both of 'em at once?"

"No. But within a week of one another. It was the
strangest thing. Soon as I got my truck fixed from
hitting the first one, I was out in the hills again, and
I'll be damned if another one didn't crash right into
my fender."

D.R. laughed. "Sounds to me like those deer were
trying to tell you something."

"Could be," said the Outdoorsman. "Cost me four
hundred dollars to get my front end fixed."

## Westward, Westward

On the TV screen the world's tiniest wagon train
began inching its way across what was surely the
world's smallest prairie, and Divine Right and Estelle
cracked up immediately.

But the Lone Outdoorsman didn't see anything
funny about it.

"What do you mean?" he argued. "Look at it, why

it's two miles long or more. Count the wagons. I see
fifty right there."

"No! No! No!" D.R. cried. "The screen itself's only
four inches wide."

"But this is a *movie,*" the Outdoorsman protested.

"I *know* it's a movie," said D.R. "That's the point!"

To settle the argument, Estelle got up and held her
finger against the TV screen. "I officially pronounce
this wagon train we see before us worming its way
across the west as being precisely one and three-fourths
inches long, no more and hopefully no less otherwise
it will disappear altogether."

D.R. was in hysterics. He laughed so hard he fell
over backwards off his stool. And even the Lone Outdoorsman was amused now. He didn't know why,
exactly. He was a little put out by the irreverence of
his guests, but their mirth was contagious. He grinned.
And then he laughed as hard as D.R. did when the first
line of dialogue on "Westward, Westward" turned out
to be the wagon master saying "Shut up and sit down,"
to a lady wagon driver.

"Stuff it up your ass," Estelle replied. When the
wagon master started to answer, Estelle turned his
volume down so low nobody could hear what he said.

"Turn it up, turn it up!" D.R. and the Lone Outdoorsman yelled. Estelle turned it back up and sat
down to eat her steak as the lady wagon driver said
to the wagon master, "Have you no *feelings?* Don't
you care about *any*thing except your stupid westward
movement? I hate the westward movement. I wish I'd
never left St. Louis."

And the lady wagon driver began to cry.

The wagon master was moved. Behind the stern set
of his huge jaw his face showed real emotion. He
stood above the weeping woman, trying to figure out
what to do. Finally he thought of something. He took
off his hat. But the woman cried on as before, and
the wagon master showed more and more real emo-

tion. At last he sat down beside her and picked up a stick and began drawing in the dirt.

"Aw shucks, ma'm," he began. "I didn't mean tuh make yuh cry. It's just that, well, out here on the trail, it seems like there just ain't no time much for payin' attention tuh people's feelings. Life's hard out here, ma'm. And it makes a man hard. Whatever good comes out of this westward movement's going to have to be carved right out of the dust, and it ain't a gonna be easy. People get hurt, and people get bitter, and some people get killed. But I believe a great thing will come out of it all someday, ma'm, a brand new world where folks 'll stand tall and be free and independent. Every day more people are headin' west, ma'm. And once you set out, there ain't no turnin' back. They've got a vision, ma'm. They're a very special kind of people, almost a new kind of people, you might say. People that want something more outa life than just comfort and security and money. This wagon train's made up of people like that, ma'm, people willin' to work and sacrifice and give up the old things so they can learn how to do what the new world requires 'em to do. That's the kind of person you are, ma'm. And I mean that. It's people like you who're gonna make this new world into what it's going to be. And I'm proud to help out some. I know I make a lot of mistakes, ma'm, mistakes that a woman like you is bound to notice and get upset by. So I apologize, ma'm, for upsettin' yuh. I'll try to keep it from happenin' again. If we don't run into any redskins, we'll be in Fort Leary in a couple of days. Everything'll be all right then."

The lady wagon driver dabbed her eyes with a hanky. Then she looked up and managed a smile through her tears. "I don't know why I'm telling you this," she sniffed, reaching to take his hand in hers. "But after what you just said, I feel compelled to. Tom, I've admired you greatly, ever since we left St. Louis. I know

I haven't shown it. I know that I've been silly, and a nuisance. I've been confused, but now I think I understand, and I must speak my heart to you. All these weeks on the trail together, long days of dust and thirst and the ever-present danger of Indians, and these cold nights when the wolves howl and the moon lights up the emptiness of the lonely prairie, all the long, hard weeks since we left St. Louis, Tom, I've believed that I was in love with you. And the thing I realize now is that I'm not. I admire you too greatly for that. To love you would only be to tie you down. You've got a great work in front of you, Tom Ginsberg, a great role to fill on behalf of all the people who are to follow you west to help build the new world of freedom and opportunity you spoke of. It's not people like me who keep alive the promise of the westward movement, Tom, it's people like you. You've got dragons to slay, great heroic deeds to perform. I know that now. And knowing it somehow fills me with the deepest peace I've ever known."

The wagon master didn't know what to say. He just sat there scratching in the dirt with his stick. Finally he reached over and shook hands with the lady wagon driver. Then he went over to the chuckwagon and told the cook to fix her a buffalo steak.

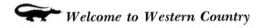 *Welcome to Western Country*

"Welcome to Western Country," said a fag in a cowboy suit as he held up a package of cigarettes. "Welcome to the clean, fresh taste of the great outdoors." As the fag took a Western out of the package and lit it, the camera pulled away to show a bunch of guys branding calves and generally horsing around the corral. Then the camera closed in on the fag again as he took a deep drag on his Western. He filled his lungs, and then without exhaling he seemed to fill his lungs again. Two, five, ten seconds and more went by and still he didn't exhale. As his face turned red and his eyes began to bulge he looked straight at Divine Right and grinned. D.R. laughed and gave him the V-sign. At last the fag blew the smoke out and holding up the cigarettes one more time he said, "Won't *you* have a Western?"

"Thanks," said D.R. "But I just had one."

Laughing, Estelle said, "Them Westerns is all right cigarettes."

The cigarette commercial was followed by one about Stud pickup trucks. The picture showed a new Stud pickup rolling across the prairie chased by a herd of wild mustangs. A close-up showed how the independent front suspension absorbed the shock of the rocks and holes while the passengers rode in total comfort. "The Stud," said an unseen baritone. *"Everybody wants one."*

The Lone Outdoorsman asked Divine Right if his VW had independent front-end suspension. D.R. said he didn't know.

"It's a good thing to have if you're going to do any cross-country driving."

"I guess it is," said D.R.

"We're driving cross-country," said Estelle.

The Outdoorsman turned and looked at her. He was on his feet now, looking for some ketchup in a cabinet near the TV set. "No kidding? You all drive around in the boonies?"

"No," said Estelle. "We stay on the highway. But we're driving across the country."

"I've driven across the country fourteen times in the last two years," said D.R.

"Oh," said the Outdoorsman. "That's not what I mean. I mean out in the boonies, where you'd take a trail-bike, or something. You know. Cross-country."

Divine Right asked the Outdoorsman if he'd ever driven across the country.

"Well now," said the Outdoorsman. "Do you mean cross-country, or across the country?"

"I mean across America," said D.R.

"The nation, in other words," said the Outdoorsman.

"But the nation is the country," said Estelle.

The Outdoorsman wrinkled his brow and thought about that as he spread ketchup on the remnants of his steak. "The nation is America," he said. "What the country is is all the land, and the rivers and things."

D.R. had stopped eating altogether. Leaning toward the Outdoorsman, and emphasizing with his fork, he said, "Do you mean you don't think America and the country are the same thing?"

"Of course not," said the Outdoorsman. "Ain't you ever read any history?"

"I've read history," said Estelle.

The Lone Outdoorsman swallowed some more steak and went on as if Estelle hadn't said anything. "Now you take these people on the wagon train. They're traveling across the country, right?"

"Right," said D.R.

"Okay. They're traveling across the country, but they're *not* traveling across America. Because the country where they're traveling hasn't been taken into the nation yet, if you see what I mean. There's no statehood there on the plains yet, therefore that country they're in isn't part of America. Now if where they are was a *state*, say Kansas, or South Dakota, then you could say they're traveling across America. But since they're not, why then they're traveling cross-country."

"So you mean the people on 'Westward, Westward' are not traveling in America, but just traveling in the country, because America and the country are two different things."

"Something like that. America, you see, is yet to

come on 'Westward, Westward.' Of course by now it *has* come. 'Westward, Westward's' just a story, don't you see. It's about something that's been over a long time. I mean, the westward movement is something my grandfather helped do. Him and the others took the *country,* and turned it into *America,* if you see what I mean."

"Well, I don't, actually," said Divine Right.

The Lone Outdoorsman chewed the last of his steak, and sopped up the gravy with a piece of bread. "Well," he said. "You're young yet. You will one of these days."

## *Tom Ginsberg's* I Ching

By the time the Outdoorsman and his guests had finished their steaks and cleaned the table off for desert, the wagon train had been surrounded by about a thousand Indians, and Tom Ginsberg had been wounded twice. He could still shoot a pistol but the lady wagon driver had to load for him. She loaded while he shot and he shot while she loaded, and the bodies made a little border around the circled wagons. Now and then the camera panned around the circle and showed other people firing at the Indians. But it was clear that the outcome of the battle really depended on how well Tom and his lady friend did with their guns. And in spite of the stack of bodies beyond the wagons, you could tell by the desperate expressions on their faces that they didn't think they were doing very well.

"Poor old Tom looks sort of undecided, don't he?" said the Outdoorsman.

Estelle laughed. "Maybe he ought to throw the *I Ching,*" she said.

D.R. leaped to his feet. "Perfect!" he yelled. "Perfect!"

The Outdoorsman asked what was perfect but D.R. was moving too fast to answer. He bolted past Estelle, stumbled out of the camper and ran through the dark to his own campsite where Urge was patiently waiting. Half a minute later he was back in the Outdoorsman's camper, carrying his battered, leather-covered copy of the *I Ching*.

"What are you doing?" asked the Outdoorsman.

"We're throwing Tom Ginsberg's *I Ching*," said D.R.

"What's an *I Ching?*"

"Never mind," said D.R. "Just toss these coins."

Quickly they tossed the coins, two times each, and Estelle drew the hexagram.

Chien.

Obstruction.

Trouble.

"Uh oh," said D.R. "It looks heavy."

Indeed it did. Nearly everybody in the wagon train was dead now except Tom and the lady. Indians had penetrated the inner circle and were systematically scalping the slain white folks while still other Indians battled the remaining survivors.

D.R. began to read Tom's *Ching* aloud: "The hexagram pictures a dangerous abyss lying before us and a steep, inaccessible mountain rising behind us. We are surrounded by obstacles."

As D.R. said that, an arrow pierced the lady wagon driver's heart.

"Difficulties and obstructions throw a man back upon himself," D.R. went on. "While the inferior man seeks to put the blame on other persons, bewailing his fate, the superior man seeks the error within himself, and through this introspection the external obstacle becomes for him an occasion for inner enrichment and education."

The screen was filled with the face of a hideous
savage, advancing on Tom with tomahawk upraised.
Tom shot him with his pistol but instantly two more
savages appeared, armed with knives and tomahawks.

"When threatened with danger," D.R. read, "one
should not strive blindly to go ahead, for this only
leads to complications. The correct thing is, on the
contrary, to retreat for the time being, not in order
to give up the struggle but to await the right moment
for action."

"Retreat, Tom!" yelled Estelle. "Crawl back under
the wagon!"

"Retreat, hell!" shouted the Outdoorsman. "Stand
your ground, Tom. Die with your goddamn boots on!"

The camera closed in on Tom's tense face. In spite
of the blood oozing from the gash in his forehead his
eyes blazed with courage and determination. Gritting
his teeth, Tom struggled to get to his feet. Leaning
against the wagon wheel, his left arm dangling useless
at his side, Tom raised his right arm and pointed his
pistol at the advancing Indians. Then he disappeared
and was replaced on the screen by fifteen Dalmatian
pups gorging themselves on Fido dog food.

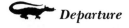 *Departure*

If D.R. had done what he wanted to do right then he
would have leaned across the table and turned the
television off.

If he had done that, and the Outdoorsman had then
done what he wanted to do, he would have leaned
across and turned the TV on again, which very likely
would have resulted in an argument between him and
D.R. about the difference between stupidity and
heroism.

If there's to be a fight, D.R. reasoned, the coura-
geous thing is to retreat before it begins, as the *I Ching*
so wisely advises.

And so D.R. stood up, held out his hand to the Lone
Outdoorsman and announced that he and Estelle were
leaving.

The Lone Outdoorsman took D.R.'s hand.

Then, realizing what D.R. had actually said, let it
go again and began pleading with them to stay for
dessert and the rest of "Westward, Westward."

No, said D.R. We must continue our journey to the
east. We have to be in St. Louis by Tuesday in order
to meet Eddie. We have a long, hard trip ahead. But
we sure thank you for the food and the hospitality.

Estelle told the Outdoorsman thanks, and good-bye,
and stepped out the door, with D.R. close behind.

From the ground D.R. turned to shake hands with
the Outdoorsman again, and again to tell him thanks
for the food and the very pleasant evening.

The Outdoorsman said that they certainly were
welcome, and urged them again to stay on for dessert
and the rest of "Westward, Westward."

But D.R. said no, they had to be on their way, that
it was going to be hard to make St. Louis by Tuesday
as it was.

The Outdoorsman said he understood, and walked
with them to their bus.

As D.R. and Estelle drove away the Lone Outdoorsman stood in the empty campsite, waving until Urge's
red tail lights were swallowed by the night.

Then he went back to his camper and wrote this
letter to his wife, while drinking a beer:

Dear Lucille,

How are you? Fine I hope. I'm having a good
time in the big woods. Ha. There are not as many people at Eagle Rock this year as last year but at Pine Point
there were more people this year than last year. Rig

doing fine. Tell Charley he was wrong in all his predic-
tions of mechanical failure and he owes me five bucks.
Ha. Food good tho not like you can cook it. Ha. Met a
young traveling couple here at Eagle Rock, nice kids.
Lucille you take care of yourself call Wanda any time
necessary, you be sure to call her if you have to. I'll be
home a week from Monday.

Sincerely yours,
William F. Dixon

# TWO

## The Fisher of Men

About two o'clock in the morning Divine Right and
Estelle passed through a little town that was absolutely
unlit except for a light shining on the front of a funeral home, and a neon sign in front of a church
across the street that said, "Dope Is the Only Answer.
Surrender Now." Actually the sign said that Christ
was the only answer, but somebody had crossed out
"Christ" and with a crayon written the word "Dope"
just above. It was crude lettering but the message
was clear enough for D.R. to dig it, and he took three
hundred micrograms of acid on the spot.

Half an hour later, the first messages from God
began to float up through his soul. Feel good, God
said. Feel what your eyes can see as smooth and soft
and rounded. Let all the world around you sigh, let
go and start to breathe. Let the steering wheel melt
to bread dough and bake a donut in your hands.
Guide Urge around the curves by leaning with your
body, go with Urge as a sighing sleigh, riding high
and far away, beyond the desert, behind the moon,
you won't be coming back anytime soon.

An image of D.R.'s grandfather chopping kindling
flashed on the movie screen of his mind as Urge's
headlights caught the gleam of animal eyes on the
road ahead. D.R. blew the horn so hard and long it
turned into a roar, then whooshed on out of hearing
like a jet plane passing by. The plane became a bug

that flew into his ear, but when he probed his finger punched on through and scratched his brain instead, causing sparks to fly out of his eyes and turn to dragon-flies. The flies swarmed, flew apart all over the inside of the bus, then came together in a cloud of smoke above a burning world in front of D.R.'s eyes. Fire was everywhere. Urge's headlights were darts of flame, the center strip down the highway was a stream of molten red. In every grate in every room of some old house he'd lived in fires hissed and licked and brooded like inflamed sick eyes of some old ancient man. Water, D.R. yelled, someone bring some water! He leaned and guided Urge from room to crowded room, swaying with his body steering Urge past people singing hymns on Sunday mornings as they warmed before the fires in grates in all the separate rooms. He rode into a kitchen where someone was making donuts in a coal stove. He wanted one, and took it, but his mother jerked it from him saying, "Honey, no, come on now, you'll have to let me drive."

D.R. tried to say no, but his tongue ignored his mind and babbled stupidly on its own like a baby's. He was crying like a baby now. Crying was the only words he had and D.R. had oh so much to say. He wanted to say the kitchen, and his grandfather build-ing fires. He wanted to say the river he had been baptized in, and swimming in that river with other people who had not lived. He was on a riverbank now, casting far out in the stream. The sun was shining on him, he was naked in it, but a shadow lay upon the water from a bank of tall sycamores on the other side. D.R. reeled in and stuck another dragonfly on his hook, and cast again, upstream this time near an old snag of a tree where the water seemed to spin a little as it flowed. The hook sailed through the sun-light and plopped into the water a few feet from the snag. Instantly a giant catfish took hold and pulled so hard D.R. fell on the muddy riverbank and slid

into the water, where an unseen current sucked him
far into the river and dragged him down below. Air!
he tried to call, Breath, give me breath! But his lungs
were full of water now and he could make no sound.
Deeper and deeper he sank in the dark and murky
river. Nothing he could do would help him rise again.
Nothing he could think would give him air. The chill
of death entered at his fingertips and toes and slowly
flowed up through his body to his throat to gather in
a pool. D.R. was drowning in the pool that filled his
throat and choked him. He felt his life go out, and
turn into a fish with gills and scales and fins and tail,
tempted by a powerful light that dangled from his
brain. The light scared him but he nosed around it,
lured and terrified. Against his will he nibbled at its
edges. As soon as his lips touched the light a three-
pronged hook snagged his throat and yanked him up.
Blood filled his throat and ran out of his gills and
eyes and asshole and spilled upon the sand. He
struggled to ease the pressure of the hook against his
flesh, but the fisherman only laughed and dangled him
up and down. At last when he could stand no more
the fisherman gave the line a jerk and ripped D.R.'s
tongue out by the roots and dropped him bleeding
to the sand. Words rose up inside him to protest but
they could get no farther than his throat. Words that
started deep inside him lifted through his system to
collide and fall apart in heaps of jumbled *a b c*'s.
Words he'd said in childhood came charging into
words he'd heard old preachers say in sermons long
ago, words of preachers, words of teachers, words
mysterious kinfolks uttered over Sunday chicken din-
ners into words he'd muttered to himself in saying
who he was and might become all crashed against the
roadblock and piled up in a grave of words as dry and
hard as bones. D.R. picked up a bone shaped like the
letter *W*. He smelled it, licked his tongue across it,
and held it to his ear. He tried an *O,* and *R,* and a

broken *D,* but they were all the same. Dead. Dead.
All the words were dead, not one had lived to tell
what happened, none survived that knew the tale.
Tell it! said the fisherman, but all he could do was
cry. Tell it! said the fisherman, but all he could do
was cry. The fisherman cursed and roughly kicked
D.R. back into the river. The water scalded his wound
as it mixed with blood and made a soup for bones of
broken letters D.R. clutched at for support to keep
from drowning.

### When Morning Gilds the Skies

When morning gilds the skies      my heart awaking
cries out the night sky      light blossoms yonder
where the roll is called out to a weary traveler looking for his home      among the desert sand dunes
stained glass pictures of holy desert ground      pale
cactus set against an earth of waving blond      up
toward the sun about to rise behind Mount Sinai
so vast and barren      yet something lush about it
something cool      promises to satisfy whatever thirst
it causes weary travelers looking for a home among
the desert sand dunes      rolling up as wings and fly
away      What building is this window in      Would
it hurt if I would touch it      Would it shatter into
pieces      Would the artist ever know and if so would
he mind      How heavy walk on holy ground
how far      burlap by my face      a burlap bag of
knitting stuff to carry Estelle's in      burlap weaves of
pieces full of burlap holes around the seams of burlap      weave together for a bag of knitting stuff to
knit together into things that keep you warm      and
dry      and hold together parts of wholes      a million
teeny holes to smell leather through      leather smell

old gloves in someone's pocket      smell leather har-
ness over mule sweat      smell sweat and miner's
leather belt flashing on your ass smell leather in my
nose of leather rows of leather doeskin smell and feel
the leather strap get tightaroundmyhead.


## Signs

Signs along the freeway, rolling selling telling messages from someone's head to mine. Someone wrote
them, someone hoped and sent them to the billboards
and stuck them to the walls of everybody's memories
down old forgotten halls. Eat somewhere and sleep
somewhere, we plead for you to eat and sleep and buy
our gas and oil. You love us and we'll love you, the
town of Lone Oak up ahead invites you to its food
and sleep and oil and gas and friendly hospitality
from Mayor Andrew Hess.

   Welcome said the Civitans, welcome said the Lions.
Welcome said the J.C.'s, there's room in all our inns.
Pioneer Ho-tel, Frontier Mo-tel, Dizzy Burger French
Fries Cole Slaw Blue Skies, Tumbleweed and Dragon-
flies, we've got it all in Lone Oak, Welcome to Our
Town.


## Flipping the Dial

Estelle turned the radio on and began to flip the dial
MICHELLE MY BELLE IN THE FIRST GAME
OF A WEEKEND DOUBLE-HEADER with the vol-
ume up ONE MILLION NINE HUNDRED THOU-
SAND JOYS AWAITING ALL WHO SUFFER

WITH CHRIST ON SALE NOW FOR ONLY NINETEEN NINETY-FIVE SINGING BLUE MOON OF KENTUCKY SHALL BE DIFFUSED BY PRESIDENT NIXON AT A PRESS CONFERENCE WHO SAID THE MIDDLE LETTER IN THE WORD SIN IS "I" but she couldn't find anything she liked so she turned it off.

 *Oasis*

Estelle had been driving since about two in the morning and by ten she was exhausted. She might have been able to go another hour or two if she hadn't drunk the beer she'd swiped from the Lone Outdoorsman the night before. But she did, and it wiped her out completely. Divine Right had been in a trance for over an hour now, but she couldn't spare the energy to worry about him yet. She felt it was a major achievement just to get Urge off the freeway into the little town of Lone Oak before she passed out at the wheel. Her neck and back were killing her, and she could barely keep her eyes open to look for a Chevron station. She had to find a Chevron station because they were traveling on the Anaheim Flash's credit card, and they only had three dollars and a quarter left out of the twenty dollars they'd set out with. Lone Oak was just a one-street spot on a two-lane road, but if it had a Chevron station it would be an oasis indeed. Estelle held her breath as she slowly cruised the street. At last she saw the blessed red white and blue sign, and gratefully pulled up under the canopy.

"Good morning miss, how are you today?"

The service station man was an older fellow who walked with a limp, but he gave off the nicest vibe Estelle had found at a station in more stops than she

could remember. As soon as he got the gas pump
going he went right to work scraping bugs off the
windshield and checking Urge's tires. Estelle was so
used to taking crap from service station people the
old fellow's manner made her want to just stop the
trip and hang around the station all day. Or even just
live here, she thought. God, would I ever like to have
a nice, clean service station to call my home for ever,
ever more. Her sense of welcome, and relief, was so
complete she decided to celebrate and blow fifteen
cents on a Coke.

"Don't drink that stuff," a man's voice behind her
said. "Try some of this."

Estelle turned around to face two freaks, a man in
a Greek athlete costume and a girl in a drab outfit of
dirty jeans and work shirt with the tail hanging out.
Her expression was very spacy. She looked a little
older than Estelle, but her eyes were so weird it was
hard to read anything very definite in her face. After
she'd looked Estelle up and down, she turned and sat
on the curb in the lotus posture and stared off into
the east. The Greek, however, stayed right there with
Estelle, looking into her eyes very intensely, smiling
broadly as he held out a small brown bottle of stuff
for her to drink. Estelle glanced at the bottle, then up
and down at the guy's costume. He had on a white
toga, a leather thong for a belt, leather sandals that
laced up to his knees, and a leather band around his
upper arm. Estelle disliked him immediately, although
she wasn't exactly sure why.

"What is it?" she asked.

"This, my dear, is acidophilus," said the Greek,
taking the lid off his bottle.

Estelle asked what acidophilus was.

"It's the source of everything good for your tummy.
People have been drinking it since before recorded
history. You really ought to try some."

Estelle asked if it got you stoned.

"Absolutely," said the Greek. "It stones you on health, vigor and enthusiasm for the pure-food way of life."

Estelle nodded and said no thanks and turned around to buy her Coke. The Greek pleaded with her not to buy the Coke, and when she went ahead and bought it anyway he lectured her on its evil properties as she drank it. To hush him, Estelle asked if they were traveling.

"Oh yes," said the Greek. "By all means, we are traveling. We are traveling along the Middle Way enroute to a land where nothing has a name. And we'd also like to get to Oklahoma City, if you happen to be going that way."

"Can you drive?"

"Drive like a champion," said the Greek. "I have many talents for the many circumstances, situations and occasions one encounters as he journeys along The Way. I've also got some good food in my bag here, in case you happen to be hungry."

Estelle positively disliked the Greek by now, but she knew she was going to give the people a ride and so she tried to come on to him as neutrally as she could. If he would drive and let her rest it would probably be okay. Ideally Estelle would have liked to simply pass out and wake up in St. Louis some time during the night, but she knew that was too much to hope for. An hour or two of sleep while they made a few more miles was the realistic prospect, but it was enough. She told the people to go on over to the bus, that she'd be there as soon as she went to the bathroom.

"Who's that in back there?" asked the Greek when Estelle got back to the bus.

"My old man. He's a little strung out right now, but he'll be all right. You ready to drive?"

"Who painted this thing?" asked the Greek's girl-friend. Her name was Frieda. It was the first time she had spoken. There was something belligerent in her tone, and for a second it pissed Estelle off. But when she looked at Frieda again her anger went away and turned to something close to pity. Something about her eyes, what was it? She looked so lost, so far away in her mind. As gently as she could, Estelle replied, "Different people."

"Different people, huh."

"Yeah. You know. Friends."

"Friends, huh."

Estelle nodded and said yeah, and turned to pay the man for the gas and oil.

"Good-bye," Estelle said to the Chevron man. "I really enjoyed your station."

"Stop in again," said the man. "All of you, come back and see us, you hear?"

The Greek started Urge's motor. Estelle crawled in back and stretched out next to Divine Right. By the time they were on the freeway again, she was sound asleep.

## The Greek's First Rap

As soon as the bus began to roll the Greek launched into his first monologue of the day. It was actually his tenth one, but the first that Divine Right had heard, and it blew into the middle of his acid high like a rock band showing up for supper unannounced. Estelle was so sleepy the words merely pricked her awareness, like flies flitting about on her skin; but the words were like sudden good music to D.R.'s mind. They energized and charged him up at the same time they smoothed out his waking, day-long dream. D.R. had never heard a voice like the Greek's before. He'd never heard anyone speak that confidently that rapidly. The rap was two or three minutes old before D.R. even realized that a strange man and woman had taken over the bus and were driving them away. If it had been a silent fellow mysteriously behind the wheel, acid-paranoia would have overwhelmed and terrified D.R. But this was a talker, a speaker, and D.R. trusted him implicitly. For a long time he lay there next to Estelle, taking in the Greek's words as he would a song. But then D.R. felt like moving around some. He felt like getting closer to this Greek. D.R. was weak and shaky, but slowly he made his way to the front of the bus and situated himself on a box of stuff just behind the front seats.

"What I envision," the Greek was saying, "is a world entirely free from mucus. I'm convinced that if mucus can be overcome then everything else will fall into place. War. Poverty. Racism. All second-level stuff in the gross dimension, and absolutely avoidable if people would only give up their attachment to mucus-making foods."

"F . . . f . . . f . . . f," D.R. stuttered, trying to say food. His tongue felt like a big wad of sponge. His silly *F* sounds tickled him and made him grin. The Greek eyed D.R. in the rear-view mirror, and talked on.

"Now I know a lot of people are on a dairy-protein trip. You hear a lot about yoghurt, cheese, eggs, and brown rice these days. And it's true that protein is essential. But what's got to happen is that people must quit accepting mucus as the price of protein in their bodies. As anyone who has studied the sex and dietary habits of the ancient Sumerians can tell you, there's lots of protein available in non-mucus-making foods. But the thing about people in the west is, nobody's interested in what he eats, now, let alone people in ancient cultures. Since the industrial revolution, people have become mere spectators of their own lives, eating what's sold to them, thinking what's told to them,

never giving a thought to life after the arbitrary
cut-off point the mucus propagandists have established
as natural. That's why eighty is considered extremely
old in places like the United States. It's due to nothing
other than the American mucus conspiracy, business-
men, capitalists, money-mongers of the lowest order,
out to make money peddling food that causes people
to die when they're about seventy-five or eighty."

"D . . . d . . . d . . . d," D.R. stuttered. He was
trying to say ". . . that causes people to die." But only
foolishness came out, and the Greek hardly slowed
down for D.R.'s interruption.

"Now I realize that not very many people can dig
on this," the Greek went on. "But it's actually an
established fact that our national leaders are dedicated
to the pro-mucus ethic. They consciously and mali-
ciously *intend* people to get hooked on mucus-causing
food as a means of keeping them in bondage and servitude, so they'll buy anything that promises to keep
the specter of age eighty at a safe distance. You take
the Food and Drug Administration. Big-time outfit,
right? Big federal scene up there in Washington.
They're into mucus like the State Department's into
hydrogen bombs. It's like the President's got these
two big heavy numbers he's laying on people, hydrogen bombs and youth-cult mucus promotion as a
means of subjecting the world to a mucus-loving
servitude. That's what's behind the eighteen-year-old-
vote shuck. And the Peace Corps. Big youth-cult mucus-
oriented shuck.

"It's like these friends of mine. I had these friends,
used to be in the Peace Corps, over in Africa, trying
to turn the spades onto mucus. Stayed over there two
years pretending to help the people, and all the time
they were trying to get 'em hooked on mucus. And the
poor people in Appalachia, down there in Kentucky,
and West Virginia, and in the slums, giving away
all those food stamps that won't buy anything except

a lot of pasty mucus-making food. And the Middle East. What do you think all that friction over in the Middle East is really about, if not mucus? A whole big goddamn mucus plot run right there in Washington, D.C. by the Food and Drug Administration. Trying to stop drugs that might help enlighten the people about the evils of mucus-making food, and promote mucus-spreading foods all because our national leaders are determined to stamp out health and spirituality, and because they're against people getting old naturally and gracefully."

"N . . . n . . . n . . . n," said D.R. "N . . . n . . . n . . . n."

"Look at the state of old people in America," said the Greek. "Look at what America reduces old people to. People in the western world are absolutely terrified of getting old. That's because instinctively they understand, although intellectually they reject it, that man's true sexual possibilities don't even begin 'til around the age of ninety. It's a fear of sex, and for sex read natural health and vigor, disguised as a fear of death. Do you know what the average life span was among the ancient Sumerians?"

The Greek was looking hard at D.R. in the mirror.

"Do you?" the Greek repeated. "Do you have *any* idea?"

"Ide . . . ide . . . ide . . . ide," D.R. stammered. And before he could quit the "Ide" turned into "Die . . . die . . . die . . . die."

"A hundred and sixty-two years," said the Greek. "And that's the *average,* mind you. Their elders lived well over two hundred years, and death at a mere hundred was considered tragically premature. Those people knew, man. They knew about everything. Western people can't even conceive the kind of sex trip those dudes were into. Western people are fuck-gluttons just like they're food-gluttons. Got to have it, got to have it, and it's all just one big energy-wasting, mucus-oriented sham, shaped and defined and made into policy, as I say, by the American federal government, with the Food and Drug Administration as the principal architects. The western idea is to get people to ball two or three times a week, and eat a lot of mucus-producing food so their minds won't ever wonder how it would be *without* all that mucus. The Sumerians knew better. All they ate were walnuts, and they only fucked once a year. Once a year, that was all, but it was enough, you see.

"Because what they had were these fantastic folk rituals where everybody over ninety got together in the temple at the summer solstice and balled, seventy-two hours non-stop. It was far out. Of course the younger people did it a little more often than that. But even they knew, at incredible young ages, like nine and ten and twelve, that there were laws in life, and that if you learned them and obeyed them, learned how to *orchestrate* your impulses properly within the limits set by Sumerian law and folk custom, you became capable of genuine spiritual enlightenment.

"Yes sir. The Sumerian line of nut-eaters remained unbroken right on up 'til modern times. That's a little-known fact, but it's true. There's a good book about Sumerian nut culture by a guy named Agolt you ought to read. *The Happy Sumerians* is the title."

"Ag . . . ag . . . ag . . . ag," said D.R. "Olt . . . olt . . . olt."

"Agolt," said the Greek. "Dr. F. Wong Agolt. Fantastic book. It really changed my life."

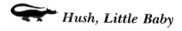 **Hush, Little Baby**

Estelle resisted the irritation of the Greek's rap for perhaps a hundred miles. But gradually she moved into a thinner sleep dimension which his voice pierced like claws. When she absolutely couldn't stand any more she leaned up on her elbow and yelling asked the Greek please to hush awhile.

"Hush, you say," said the Greek, also yelling so Estelle could hear him above the VW's whirring engine. "Hush. Now there is one of the more peculiar words in all the English language. Hush. Notice how simple that word is, yet how loaded with implication, and strange music. Hushhhhh. Hear that whisper? Hear that sigh? It's like wind through sycamore trees. It's the audial equivalent to wheat swaying in a Van Gogh painting. Hushhhh, little baby. There's only one vowel in hush, but notice how the whole word hangs on it, sort of pivots on the *U,* how it seems to clutch at either side of the *U* and just hang there in perfect balance. Notice, too, how the word is at once imperative, *hush your mouth, hush that noise,* but also a noun. *A hush settled over the audience as the maestro walked onto the stage.* Hush. Hush, now. A marvelous word, hush."

When the Greek had finished, Divine Right broke into applause. "Br . . . br . . . br . . . br," he stammered, trying to say "Bravo!" But he was so stoned, his tongue so uncontrollable, the word came out as a kind of growl, like some moron's, or an ape's. The nonsense of his sound caused D.R. and the Greek both to break into hysterical laughter.

"Stop the car," said Estelle. She had left the bed and scooted forward to sit next to D.R., just behind the Greek and his girlfriend Frieda.

"What?" said the Greek.

"What?" D.R. tried to say. But it came out so goofy he and the Greek roared with laughter again.

"Excuse me, honey," said Estelle to Frieda as she elbowed past D.R. and crowded into the little space between the two front seats. When she was situated she told the Greek once more to stop the car.

"Stop," said the Greek. "Now there is truly one of the interesting words in our language. When you analyze the word stop . . ."

Estelle grabbed the steering wheel and jerked Urge violently to the right.

*"Are you crazy?"* yelled the Greek, and he fought to keep the bus from going off the freeway. Estelle said nothing. She waited 'til the Greek had the vehicle under control, then grabbed the wheel and yanked Urge toward the edge again. When she did it two more times the Greek at last got the idea and began slowing down. A mile or two later they left the freeway and pulled up at a roadside rest area.

## Onward Christian Soldiers

Oh joyous joy of wondrous joys, look at the lovely world.

The sky, the clouds, and feel the wind whipping little dusts against your skin.

A minute ago I bent over to pick up a rock the size of a nickel, but when I touched it it scurried away on the tiniest little footprints I ever saw.

A beautiful intrusion quadruples the illusion.

Confusion.

Confucian.

Ha!

What I'm trying to do is get from here to over there but it's a long, hard way of going, let me tell you.

Oh joyous joy of wondrous joys, look at the lovely world. The world has a blue ceiling and no walls anywhere to be seen.

And a sandy-colored carpet with a parking lot painted on it.

The bright sand is painful to my eyes, and wondrous to behold.

I've got some sunglasses, but who knows where they are?

Estelle would know, but where's Estelle?

Playing in the dunes.

If I were to call to her she couldn't hear me, because of the constant wind, blowing through my mouth to take my breath away.

Trudge, trudge, trudge. Onward Christian soldiers, over the wasted land. Through heat, sun and wind, in spite of loneliness, fear, isolation, and a twisted tongue he goes on, on, forever on toward the Concrete Picnic Tables, ancient relics of a culture long forgotten, buried by the desert sand.

"I'm coming, you guys. Wait for me, I'm coming!"

### Ritual

"I'm coming, you guys, wait for me, I'm coming!" is what D.R. tried to say, but only garbled idiocy came out. And even if it hadn't been garbled idiocy the people he was calling to could not have understood what he said, because of the ceaseless wind. They were in a paved rest area just off the freeway, a hard, tree-less place with white lines marking off the parking places, and concrete picnic tables permanently estab-lished beyond a curb. At the far end of the paved area a big trailer truck was parked parallel to the curb across a couple dozen diagonal parking lines. Near it a family surrounded a picnic table, eating food. The Greek had established himself seven or eight tables down the line from the family, where he was pre-paring to do his daily food ritual. He usually did the ritual at sundown, but since they had stopped, and because everybody's nerves seemed a little on edge, the Greek felt a soothing ceremony was called for, to cool the vibe a little, and bring everybody together.

When they first stopped Estelle wandered off by herself among the dunes, but when she heard D.R.'s yell and saw him having trouble negotiating his way from the bus to the table, she went back to help him along. His arm around her neck, carrying him like a drunk, she staggered up to the table with him in time to observe the Greek setting up his scene.

It was a simple scene to set up because the only food involved was walnuts and water, and no dishes or utensils were involved. The Greek carried his walnuts, already hulled, in a leather bag about the size of a woman's purse. The water was in a gallon plastic jug with a label on it that said, "Pure-O Artesian Drinking Water. Rich in Natural Minerals." The Greek unfolded a black cloth about the size of a pillow case and spread it on the table. He set the jug on the eastward corner of the cloth, and placed the nut bag diagonally across from it with the open top laid out toward the west. As he picked up his first walnut the Greek bowed three times to the east, and then three times to the west as he picked up the jug and drank from it. When he'd chewed and swallowed the walnut he closed his eyes and held his palms together in front of his face in an attitude of prayer.

"F . . . f . . . f . . . f," D.R. stammered. "F . . . f . . . f."

The Greek opened his eyes to see who was speaking. Although he'd only been praying about five seconds he frowned as if he'd been disturbed from a deep sleep.

"What's he trying to say?" the Greek snapped.

"He's probably trying to say far out," said Estelle. "D.R. says far out a lot."

"Why doesn't he go ahead and say it, then?"

"I don't know," said Estelle. "Ask him."

"Hey," yelled the Greek. "Get away from those walnuts."

D.R. had turned away from the Greek and was grooving on the leather walnut bag. The rough side of the leather was out, so that when you rubbed your finger across it, it made a pattern that seemed to D.R. extraordinarily beautiful. He heard the Greek tell him to stay away, but it surprised him when the Greek took him roughly by the arm.

"You're not supposed to get into the walnuts until we've prepared our hearts and minds," said the Greek. "Kindly wait."

The Greek closed his eyes and folded his hands and began again to prepare their hearts and minds to receive the walnuts. Stoned as he was, D.R. felt like his heart and mind were already prepared, but he certainly did not want to disrupt the ritual. The ritual was beautiful to D.R. The Greek was beautiful, the walnuts were beautiful, all the world around was beautiful, beautiful. Inhaling deeply, D.R. folded his hands and closed his eyes, and listened to the Greek's prayer.

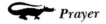 **Prayer**

The Way is uncharted. The map cannot be spoken. Names are in words, but nature lives only in nature. The source of creation is nameless, but the matrix of all is named. The secret eludes eyes clouded by longing. Prejudiced eyes must stop cold at the surface. The secret is self-contained.

May we be mindful of these truths. May we become pure enough to pass through the gate to the root of the universe.

**Love**

"Amen."

The Greek bowed to the west and he bowed to the east, and came up filled with love for everything in the universe. When he saw D.R. leaning against the picnic table with what he took to be a forlorn look on his face he felt apologetic for coming on to him so hard during the ceremony. To make amends he went over and hugged him.

"I *love* you, man," said the Greek. "I love you, and you and you too, you're all just lovely, and I love you. I love the bus, I love those people down there at the other table, I love that big truck, and its driver, and the drivers of all those cars going by. I love the desert, I love the sky, I love the mountains in the distance, the oceans beyond the mountains, and all who dwell in the lands beyond the oceans. I love all sentient beings everywhere, regardless of their race, color, creed, species or place of national origin."

While to herself Estelle was thinking, "And I hate *your* goddamn guts."

The Greek looked at Estelle and grinned. It was a condescending grin, sly and malicious, sharpened by its brevity as the Greek let his eyes slide right on past Estelle as if she wasn't really there, to D.R., who was sitting at the picnic table now, trying hard to say "love."

"Lve," D.R. grunted, pushing against his palate with his tongue. *"Lve."* The Greek smiled at D.R., patted him gently on the head, and talked on:

"Now perhaps you wonder how it is that a mere mortal such as myself has become capable of such boundless love for everything in all creation. I mean, how is it, do you suppose, that a single individual is able to sustain a feeling of love for absolutely every-thing, twenty-four hours a day, every day, all his life?

The answer, my friend, is simple: I have lost my name."

"N . . . n . . . n . . . nme?" asked D.R.

"I've lost it," said the Greek. He was sitting down too now, cross-legged on the bench of the picnic table, facing D.R. "It's gone, lost in the mists of time, I hope forever. And it's the most wonderful sense of liberation a human can feel."

"Uve lst ar nme?" D.R. asked.

The Greek nodded. "It's like rebirth," he said. And before he spoke again he reached into the leather bag and brought out a handful of walnuts. "What it's all about you see, is death."

"D . . . d . . . d . . . *dth?*" said D.R.

"Spiritual death," said the Greek. "Death as a kind of cleansing agent, to make way for true illumination. You know about the ego. How it develops out of the formless void that is the childhood psyche and then, through ceaseless practice of the various yogic disciplines, it is at last obliterated, so that that which was torn asunder by the trauma of leaving the mother's womb has been reconciled and made whole again in eternal union of individual consciousness with the cosmic life force. You know about that. Well, namelessness and death are closely bound up in that idea. For one must suffer many deaths on the road to true illumination. Some are actual, some are only symbolic. Giving up your name is only a symbolic death, but for many people it is so painful it could well be likened to an actual death. But what those people fail to understand is that after death there comes the resurrection. The experience of resurrection is available to every individual on one level or another, on planes both gross and subtle, if the individual is truly committed in his quest along the Ultimate Way. It's available to me, it's available to that truck driver over there, it's available to each person in that family at that other table. And it's available to you, my friend. This profoundest of all experience is available just for the asking."

There was a little silence then while the Greek placed both hands on D.R.'s head and uttered a brief prayer. "The Way is uncharted," he said. "The map cannot be spoken. May we become pure enough to pass through the gate to the root of the universe."

"U . . . u . . . u . . . *un*-vrse," D.R. said.

"Hey!" the Greek exclaimed. "That's *very* good," and he took a walnut from the bag and handed it to D.R.

"What I need," said the Greek as D.R. chewed, "is to know your full name, your place of birth, astrological sign, your height, weight and rate of heartbeat. Since you've got that little frog in your throat, perhaps you could just write that information down in this little notebook here, and then we can get started."

The Greek handed D.R. a worn notebook with the yin-yang symbol drawn on the front in blue ink, and the word "love" written about fifty times on the back. The book had about a hundred pages in it, and nearly all of them were full of writing and drawings and weird little scribbles too obscure to make out thumbing through. The book excited D.R. tremendously. He would have loved to read it, but he was much too awed by the Greek to ask. He flipped to near the end where the blank pages began, and with the Greek's ball-point pen wrote: "Divine Right (David Ray) Davenport. Born, Finley County, Kentucky. Cancer. Five feet, ten inches tall. 158 pounds. I don't know my heartbeat."

"A close estimate will do," said the Greek. And sliding closer he took D.R.'s wrist in his hand, located his pulse, and began to count it as he watched the seconds tick off on his wristwatch.

 *Estelle's Complaint*

As desperate as she was for someone to help her drive, and generally hassle the whole bummer of a scene on to St. Louis, Estelle wished she was by herself again. The girl Frieda seemed okay, actually. At least she was cool enough to simply settle into the motion of the journey and keep whatever trip she was on to herself. But the Greek was such an asshole Estelle could not bear to stay in hearing of his voice. What Frieda saw in the Greek Estelle could not begin to imagine, but whatever it was, she hoped she did not hear about it. Frieda was a sad, forlorn little chick, obviously in need of some sort of help, but Estelle just did not have the psychic energy to go messing with her head. Maybe later, if things cooled out a little, they could manage a little chit-chat, but for the time being the only thing Estelle could think about was getting as far away from the Greek as possible.

At two o'clock on a hot afternoon in the middle of the desert she didn't have much appetite for walnuts. But if walnuts were what fate was serving up that day she guessed that was what she'd have. She reached into the Greek's leather food bag, got a handful of nuts, and eating them strolled off toward the dunes she'd walked on awhile ago.

The thing that particularly bugged Estelle was the way Divine Right was zapping on the stupid Greek. There he'd been in a stupor for eight hours, sometimes huddling in her arms like a baby, and as soon as he comes out of it what does he do but fall in love with the first wise man to come along and lay a heavy word trip on him. They were only a few minutes into it together, D.R. and the Greek. But Estelle had seen it happen so many times before she knew exactly what was coming down, and it was a drag. In her mind she saw the next five hundred miles unfolding in a stream of blather from the Greek while D.R. sat beside him doting on his every word.

Oh D.R., Estelle thought. You're such a goddamn child.

When he was right, when he was clear and cool and up and unhassled, D.R.'s mind was as beautiful to see in operation as anybody's that she knew. And yet he craved other people's words about "truth" and "life" like some poor junkie craving dope. If it was a habit D.R. had, there certainly wasn't any short-age of junk on the circuit they traveled in. As far as Estelle could see there were at least twice as many wisdom pushers as dope dealers in the world, so how come the cops never got uptight about them? If she'd kept notes on all the philosophies, theories, schemes and plans to bring the world to a state of grace and love and enlightenment she'd heard in the last eighteen months she'd have enough recorded bullshit to fertilize the cosmic compost pile. There'd been a time when she was young, way back there a year or two ago, when other people's enthusiasms could excite her a great deal. But because enthusiasm was all it usually amounted to, Estelle didn't get much out of it any more. Because D.R. still did, because he was so willing to devalue what was already in his own head and credit fast-talking assholes with some sort of superior wisdom, it divided them, and left them in different places. If she could have believed that he was over there at the picnic table grooving on the food freak simply because he was stoned on acid and *everything* he saw and heard seemed groovy, it would have been one thing. But Estelle knew that wasn't what it was. D.R. would have homed in on this dude stoned or sober and that was why it bothered Estelle so much. She knew that left out a lot about D.R. She knew there was a lot more to it than that. But right now she wasn't able to consider much that was in his favor. She was pissed and jealous and weary and depressed. If D.R. had any virtues that redeemed him she preferred not to think about them right now.

### Frieda's Name

So everybody around the old picnic table has something to do now except Frieda. The Greek is teaching D.R. how to do alternate nostril breathing, and Estelle is off brooding among the dunes. That leaves Frieda to entertain herself, and so what she decides to do is work some more on letting go of her name. As we know, the Greek has forgotten his name completely. It took him six months of concentrated effort, but he made it. Frieda is not as strong in the mind as the Greek. She has been at it over nine months now, and where she is at is that delicate halfway point between being totally identified with her name, and forgetting it all together. She has managed to forget how to spell it; it means nothing to her to see the word "Frieda" written down. But when she hears it, the imprint is restored in her mind and her effort is set back a frustrating distance. Becoming nameless in a world where everything is named is a complicated process requiring the utmost diligence and perseverance, but she is committed now. That is the legacy of being the girlfriend of the Greek for over a year.

The only thing wrong with that legacy, though, is that now she is known as the girlfriend of the Greek. Where is that at? she asks herself. How is that better than being known as Frieda? It has slowly been dawning on her that it isn't better, that, in fact, it is a good deal worse, and suddenly she is resolved:

She stands up, dusts off her pants with her hands,

glances at the Greek who is busy teaching D.R. the bellows breath, walks with great dignity over to the picnic
table where the family is eating, and asks if she can
ride away with them when they go. At first the family
is a little uptight about this strange request, but when
the girl explains to them that she has been kidnapped
and held for ransom, they understand. The big fat
momma of the family especially understands. She was
never kidnapped, but she was an orphan as a child,
and in her heart she carries a vast reservoir of love,
pity and protective concern for all waifs and strays.
She is also one very tough big fat momma. She offers
to go over and beat up on the poor girl's tormentors,
and take them before the law. But Frieda says no,
that merely to escape will be enough. So the family,
the Willitts family, of Oklahoma City, abruptly begins to pack up the food and load into the two-tone
green and white Pontiac nearby. Momma shepherds
the whole gang in before her, the Greek's former girlfriend, two boys about eleven years old, a little girl
about six, an old grandfather, and of course Poppa
Willitts, who drives. It's crowded, but they manage.
Momma Willitts gets in last, and the Pontiac, sagging
drastically, eases out of the rest area onto the freeway,
headed west.

*Family Reunion*

When Estelle saw the girl go up to the family at the
picnic table she figured something weird was going
on. And when the girl got in the car and drove away
with them Estelle decided she'd better go back to the
rest area and find out what was wrong.

   D.R. was sitting on the picnic table, gurgling and
groaning with his eyes closed. The Greek was peering

into D.R.'s open mouth like a dentist, trying to see why he couldn't say "OM." Estelle came up behind the Greek and watched him operate for a minute or two. Then she walked around so he could see her and asked him if he had seen Frieda leave.

"Just a minute," said the Greek. He probed D.R.'s throat with his finger till he gagged. "Now try it," said the Greek. "Just sort of hum it, go OMMMMM-MMMMMMM." As D.R. swallowed and warmed up for the try the Greek looked up at Estelle and said, "Yeah, I saw her. Looks like she's headed west again."

"But didn't she *say* anything?" asked Estelle. "Do you know *why* she left?"

The Greek shrugged. "'Everybody splits sooner or later," he said. "This was just her time, I guess."

"Awwww," D.R. intoned. "Awwwwrrrr."

"*Me*llow," said the Greek, stroking D.R.'s throat. "Make it mellow. It's a prayer, not some sort of challenge."

The Greek turned toward D.R. again, but Estelle leaned and stayed in front of him. "But how do you *feel* about her going," she said. "Don't you care? I mean, doesn't it make any difference . . ."

"I'm very happy for her is all," said the Greek. "It was time she went. I'm pleased she was clear enough to recognize it."

"She didn't seem very clear to me."

"And what is that supposed to mean?" asked the Greek.

"Nothing. I just feel a little more concerned than you seem to. She seemed very fragile to me."

The Greek laughed. "I'm sure she did."

"And what is *that* supposed to mean?"

"Well, it's obvious, isn't it? You see Frieda as this helpless little creature who couldn't possibly get along on her own. And I'm sure you think you might have been able to do something for her if she'd stayed around."

"That's bullshit."

"Of course it is. It's all bullshit."

"No it's not," said Estelle. "It's not all bullshit."

"And I would agree with that, too. It's not all bull-shit."

"Jesus," said Estelle. "You are really full of shit, did you know that?"

The Greek smiled. His white teeth were as big as thumbnails. His blond hair glinted in the sun. "Of course I know it. Do you realize that you are full of bullshit too?"

"Yap yap yap," said Estelle. "That's all you do."

"Awwwrrr," D.R. gurgled. "Awwwrrrr."

"*Mel*low," the Greek said to D.R. "Make it mellow. Make it a prayer."

But "awwwwrrrrr" was the best D.R. could do.

"Poor old D.R. Do you realize he can't make a single vowel sound?"

"I've seen him in worse shape," said Estelle.

"You really are a bitch, aren't you?" said the Greek.

"You're a son-of-a-bitch," Estelle hissed. "A god-damn phony superguru son-of-a-bitch."

"Right on," laughed the Greek. "God, is that ever right on. You're a bitch, and I'm a son-of-a-bitch. Hello, Mother. Welcome to the family reunion."

## The Key

Estelle was so furious she went to the bus intending to just get in and drive away and leave D.R. and the Greek to their stupid games. Leave leave leave was all she could think about. Go. Go. Go. Same old story. Same old broken record. Same old thorny point on the never-ending cycle.

She was crying now. That seemed like a broken

record too. God, she thought. Do I ever cry a lot.
Am I ever one whiny tearful bitch.

Cry. Cry. Cry.

Go. Go. Go.

But Estelle couldn't go because the Greek had
taken the key.

"You son-of-a-bitch, give me that goddamn key!"

She was about fifty yards from the Greek, and the
wind was still blowing.

"What?" called the Greek. "I can't hear you."

Estelle ran a few yards toward the table. "I said
you've got the goddamn key!"

The Greek grinned and nodded his head vigorously.
"I know it," he called back. "I've always had the key."

"You slimy bastard!" Estelle screamed. She glanced
around the ground for a weapon of some kind to kill
him with. But her eyes were too full of tears to see.
She blanked out for a moment then. The whole
world went black as night and Estelle forgot everything she knew. When she came to again she was in
the bus with the pillbox in her hand, looking for a
downer.

## Coming Down

Maybe D.R.'s acid trip ain't so groovy any more.
Maybe he wonders where Estelle has gone, and why. It's
funny stuff, acid. It'll make you laugh, it'll make you
cry. It'll make you wonder where your woman is, and
why. It'll give you something new to say, but take
away your words to say it with if you're not careful.
D.R. tried to say "Estelle!" but it came out as a moan.
He tried to say, "Forward, on to St. Louis!" but his
tongue flapped useless in his mouth.

If in the beginning was the word and the word was

with God and the word was God, what are you when you're speechless?

Pretty fucking depressed, if you want to know.

Depression is a rocky land-ing. Depression is your parachute not working after a weird reentry.

Wham.

Grounded.

And it's stony fucking ground.

She's not there to know you're hurt, you can't call for help because your tongue won't work, he don't see your signals because he's talking all the time.

Maybe D.R.'s acid trip ain't so groovy any more.

Maybe that steel band around his head's a headache after all.

Maybe that stained window of the countryside's an actual desert after all.

Maybe the wind is really blowing, maybe the sky is actually overhead.

Maybe Estelle was really crying.

Maybe the time had come.

"Has the time come?" asked D.R.

"*Me*llow," said the Greek. "*Me*llow."

## When the Time Came

When the time did come, the Greek did not delay. He put the items he'd used in the food ritual back in the leather bag, and carried it and the jug of water to the bus, D.R. following behind. D.R. started to get in the back where Estelle lay sleeping, but the Greek directed him to sit in front with him. D.R. obeyed, although he was uncomfortable in the front. He was close to true distress now. He was confused because he didn't know how stoned he was; he didn't know how far to trust his mind's version of things. He felt a little afraid of the Greek now, but he didn't know if that was just paranoia or his straight mind picking up real warnings from actual stimuli. He very definitely felt threatened, but he could not be sure what by, and that made the moment seem more sinister than ever. His mind was very neatly divided in two. Half of it was clear and half of it was muddy, but it was hard to keep up with which side was which because both sides claimed to be clear, and each denied that it was muddy. The sense was that of being surrounded and infiltrated by enemies, within and without. But the enemies were all unseen, and the clear half of his mind understood that very likely he was imagining the whole thing.

If Estelle had been awake she would have cooled D.R. in an instant. She would have seen that he was feeling freaky, and told him it was okay, to go ahead and feel freaky, that she would remain there before him as a living, concrete presence in a weird and abstract world. But Estelle was asleep and the sound of Urge's motor didn't disturb her. D.R. didn't learn until later that Estelle had dosed herself heavily on downers, but just looking he could tell that her sleep was very deep, that that was only Estelle's body lying there, that her life and soul and spirit were somewhere far away, and unavailable to him. D.R. felt a powerful urge to go to her, though for whose sake, his or hers, he wasn't sure. But every time he so much as glanced back at Estelle the Greek looked at him out of the corner of his eye in a strangely intimidating way, and froze D.R. in his seat.

## And Down Some More

So this was the situation in the bus as they drove out of the rest area: Estelle was asleep in the back seat,

Divine Right was some sort of psychic prisoner in
the front beside the Greek, and the Greek, in charge
of the bus now, driving east across the barren, windy
plain toward Oklahoma City, was talking on and on
about health, truth and beauty as destinations along
the Ultimate Way. His rap had begun as soon as they
hit the freeway again with a final lecture to D.R. on
breathing and the holy sound of OM, and continued
into an explanation of the concept of karma and ways
in which images like the Third Eye reconcile Zen and
the mystic point of view with all modern psychology
from Freud through Reich to Jung. Within fifty miles
the Greek had ascended into a description of the
physiology involved in the experience of Unitive Consciousness, and within a hundred miles of that he had
called D.R.'s attention to the I–Thou theme in the
Secret Songs of the Hindus and analyzed the personal
aspects of the relationship between Ouspensky and
Gurdjieff, which amounted, of course, to a kind of
rambling introduction to the Greek's abbreviated version of his own life story.

We'll get into that life story a little later on. But
before we do it's important to understand what was
happening with Divine Right as he told it. The Greek
said, "The problem, of course, is that young people
have grown up oriented to a twentieth-century Einsteinian concept of unitive time while their elders
remain stuck in nineteenth-century industrial time,
which is fragmented." D.R. nodded and gurgled some
nonsense sounds of agreement. But his real attention
was on Estelle now, asleep on the mattress behind
them. When he could manage it without the Greek
noticing, he would glance over his shoulder at Estelle
and long to be back there with her. He had a splitting
headache, and in his stomach a wad of half-chewed
walnuts lay like rotten cork.

The Greek said, "Some say that God is merely a
compromise between the time it takes light to travel

across the Einsteinian universe, and the time it takes light to cross a neutron, that space is merely a snapshot of time, and time is space in movement."

D.R. nodded and mumbled, but he wasn't listening to the Greek. He was seeing himself coming down, down, down from high above in a parachute through heated air onto stony ground that turned to muddy water as soon as he touched it. And in the water Estelle was sailing away on a raft while D.R. struggled to keep from drowning. D.R. was desperate to reach Estelle. He tried to swim toward her, but words from the Greek's incessant talk filled the sail and pushed the raft farther and farther away. He called to her, he yelled for her to wait, but Estelle couldn't hear him. *Things are going to be a lot better from now on!* he yelled. *As soon as we get to St. Louis! As soon as we get with Eddie!*

"Eddie!" D.R. yelled in the car. "Eddie!"

The Greek looked at D.R. sternly and asked who Eddie was.

"Wh . . . wh . . . what?" D.R. stuttered.

"You said Eddie. I was wondering who that was."

D.R. cleared his throat and worked his tongue inside his mouth. "Ed . . . Ed . . . Ed," he began. "Eddie's m . . . m . . . my p . . . p . . . p . . . *pal*," said D.R. "He's m . . . m . . . my f . . . f . . . *friend.*"

When the Greek asked what kind of friend, D.R. answered, "G . . . g . . . g . . . *grand.* He's a g . . . g . . . g . . . *grand* friend."

The Greek was plainly irritated. He told D.R., "Well, you ought not say his name out loud like that. If you're going to forget your name, you've got to give up your friends' names too. If you go around pronouncing them out like that you'll never erase the imprint from your mind."

"I'm s . . . s . . . s . . . sorry," said D.R.

"Don't apologize," the Greek snapped. "Don't say

people's names, and don't apologize when you forget and say them anyway. It's bad karma."

D.R. nodded. The Greek changed the subject then, and during the next three hundred miles he told D.R. his life story.

**D.R.'s Scheme**

"Before I tell my life story I want to explain where I'm on my way to," said the Greek. "I'm going to Norman, Oklahoma to destroy a manuscript I wrote and left in the University library when I was a student there some years ago. That manuscript has to be destroyed because the story of my life from nineteen hundred thirty to nineteen hundred fifty-five is told on its pages. If it ever happened that I accidentally got a glimpse of what's written there, all the personal history that I've worked so hard to forget these last years would come flooding back into my mind, and my entire life work would be destroyed. Except for that document, which I stupidly wrote and left on deposit in the library, the whole early phase of my life is totally lost to memory. I'm so haunted by the possibility of suddenly remembering it again that I'm going to Norman now to destroy that manuscript once and for all. I just wanted to explain that to you, as a kind of preface, so you wouldn't think the story I'm about to tell you is too weird."

Oh, don't worry about me, D.R. thought. He didn't try to say it out loud, he just thought it: don't worry about me. D.R. had decided he wasn't going to speak to the Greek any more. He wasn't even going to try. He didn't want to speak to the Greek, and didn't want to hear him either if he could find some way to avoid it. Don't worry about *me* thinking your story is weird, D.R. said to himself. I'm not even going to listen to you tell it if I can help it.

For D.R. was working on a scheme. It was a hard thing to do because the Greek's voice kept running through his brain like a rusty wire and shorting out his mind. If he had been as stoned as he was earlier his mind would have been so vulnerable the pain of the Greek's rap would have been more than he could bear. But D.R. was coming down now. His head still hurt, and the fatigue was nearly overwhelming, but slowly his mind was becoming capable of its own defense again, and D.R. was working on a scheme.

The idea was to somehow get the tape recorder into the front seat to listen to the Greek, so D.R. could escape to the back of the bus and lie down beside Estelle. One side of D.R.'s mind said that it was a stupid idea; but the other half was convinced that once the recorder was in the front seat, listening, the Greek wouldn't know the difference, and that's the side that D.R. was listening to now.

The problem was maneuvering the recorder to the front without attracting the Greek's attention. All he needed was three seconds. The recorder was on a pile of stuff right there behind the seat, not twelve inches from D.R.'s shoulder. All he had to do was edge off his seat, lean and reach and he would have it. Two seconds, even. Two seconds would be plenty.

The Greek said, "The personal history that's still alive in my memory begins when I was twenty-two. When I was twenty-two, I thought that what I wanted more than anything in all the world was to be a student of literature."

Nodding as the Greek talked, D.R. eased his ass to the edge of his seat, then slowly turned until his eye was on his tape recorder.

The Greek said, "Scholarship seemed like such a *gentle* thing. The library, the English department,

the lectures, all were images of utmost quiet and tran-
quillity to me then, and I wanted nothing more than
to be quiet, to read and write and think, to live the
classic life of the mind right here in the twentieth
century."

D.R. nodded and scooted a little farther off his seat.
He paused there, waiting his opportunity. And a moment later it came. As the Greek was about to pass a
Rambler going slow in the right-hand lane, suddenly
a big semi came up from behind in the outer lane so
fast the Greek had to dart back behind the Rambler,
and as the Greek braked and fought the wheel, D.R.
deftly reached around, grabbed the recorder and
straightened up in his seat again. After that it was a
simple matter to turn the recorder on and tune it in
to the Greek's voice, and then steal away to the back
and join Estelle on the mattress while the Greek talked
on, suspecting nothing.

### Failure

Sad to say, however, D.R.'s clever maneuver did not
have the result he was so desperate for. He wanted
Estelle to know him, to open her eyes and see him and
include him in her world again. He wanted her to
soothe his headache, to make the fatigue and subtle
nausea in his stomach go away. But when he lay
down beside her, Estelle rolled away. Even in her sleep
she would have nothing to do with him. In the front
the Greek was saying, "The problem with my career
as a scholar was the Master's thesis." I *love* you, D.R.
thought, trying to reach directly to Estelle's mind with
his mind. I *need* you. But the Greek said, "I got my
Bachelor's degree easily enough, and I did well in the

lecture courses and seminars," and Estelle moaned and frowned and drew away to the far side of the mattress when D.R. tried to hold her in his arms.

"But I just couldn't hack that thesis," said the Greek. "And the reason I couldn't hack it was I really didn't want to write a thesis. I'd sit down and try to write about the metaphysical poets, but every time, I'd wind up saying personal stuff about myself."

D.R. sat up on the mattress and pressed his hands against his head to keep his skull from breaking into pieces. That's how it felt: the Greek's voice was in his head, grinding and prying like some evil dentist of the mind, gouging loose great hunks of brain while Estelle slept on as if nothing else was happening.

"I worked over a year on that paper," said the Greek. "But when I finished, all I had were three hundred pages telling my life story from birth through graduate school."

"*Al rgt!*" D.R. screamed. "*Al rgt!*"

All right.

He gave up, he yielded.

With tears streaming down his face, D.R. crawled off the mattress and made his way back to his seat in front where he rode beside the Greek throughout the night, listening to the story as he cried.

## The Greek's Life Story

"Of course I knew the professors wouldn't accept the manuscript as a thesis," the Greek went on. His voice was a low monotone now, but it was so intense that D.R.'s return to the front seat had no effect on it whatsoever. "So what I did was have it typed up professionally, and bound to look like all the other theses on the shelf. Then one day I sneaked into the stacks and when nobody was looking I slipped it up on the shelf and left it there. A few weeks later I left the university, I left Norman altogether and entered the next phase of my life's adventure.

"It was a period of the loneliest wandering I had ever done before. I traveled in all the states, in Canada and Mexico, and deep into Yucatan. I even went to Japan, thinking I would enter a Zen monastery. But they denied me. The *roshi* there spoke with me for five minutes, then told me I was crazy and to go back to America. I was hurt by that, but beneath the hurt I knew the *roshi* was right, and I knew that I had to return to America. So I came back, and landed in San Francisco.

"In San Francisco all the talk was of earthquakes, earthquakes. Earthquakes and Edgar Cayce. Everyone was convinced there was going to be an earthquake any day, that California was going to tumble into the sea. And my trip was, I wanted that to happen. The *roshi* was right in calling me crazy. I was a madman. I wanted California to fall into the sea, and I wanted to fall in with it, to be swallowed up by a thing so big, so huge, so utterly enormous that I would disappear into absolute nothingness. I wanted to see California heave and slide and fall with the greatest roar and rumble the world had ever known. And I wanted to go down with it, because once I went down with it I wouldn't have to think about how scattered were the fragments of my life, and mind. If the fragments wouldn't come together and function for me, then let them fly apart, scatter and be gone weightless through the universe. Let freedom reign! Let nothing matter! That was my belief.

"Well, of course, as we all know, there wasn't an earthquake. California didn't fall into the sea. I was disappointed but sobered a good deal by the months I spent in anticipation of it. My head felt clearer. I quit wanting California to sink into the sea. I began to be interested in the idea of things rising. As if in reaction to all my brooding over things collapsing, I began to get interested in things rising, and before long I found myself fascinated by Atlantis, wondering what I could do to help that lost city rise from her dark grave. I thought about Atlantis so much it became a kind of project for me, and one day I sat down and wrote a little pamphlet called, "What To Do When Atlantis Rises." It was a good little pamphlet, and I decided to have a few hundred copies printed up, on brown paper. I tried to sell the copies, and when no one would buy them I started giving them away to people passing on the street.

"And then one day a very strange thing happened. I was walking through that little park on Clay Street in San Francisco, that steep one with all those old Victorian houses around it, and I gave away a copy of my pamphlet and wound up in conversation with the guy who took it, this young kid who had the most intense brown eyes I have ever seen. And before long a couple of other people came up and joined us, and there I was, sitting on a park bench with six or eight people around, some of them on the ground, some of them just standing with their arms folded, listening to me come on about Atlantis, and about my experience with the earthquake that never came. When I tried to quit talking they wouldn't let me. And finally we all went over to someone's pad, and I kept on talking. I have no idea now what I said, but I talked all night. By morning when someone served tea and toast, there must have been fifty people in that apartment, and it was as if we'd come through a magnificent thing together. I didn't know what I was saying myself, half the time. It was as if the Lord had taken my tongue and used it Himself, as if I was but a mere vehicle for His message.

"People began to come to me individually for advice, and I advised them to do incredible things. One

fellow, a black man who had suddenly come into a
good deal of money, came to me just fraught with
worry and asked me how he should spend it. I asked
him where he had grown up. Dothan, Alabama, he
said and I said good. Take that money and hire five
hundred other black men, and all of you go rent or
buy the finest black suits, with black hats, black canes,
and black top coats and black sunglasses, and starting
on a Monday morning begin drifting into Dothan one
at a time, every hour or two another one of you just
sort of amble in and walk down the street, and just
kind of look in the windows as if nothing much is
going on, and don't speak to each other. Act as if the
town is not slowly filling up with five hundred well-
dressed spades, a few at a time, maybe seventy or
seventy-five a day. Do that for a week, until by Saturday there's all five hundred of you there on Main
Street, walking around. And this spade *did* that. He
actually did it, and when I saw him some time later
he came up and shook my hand and said Man, you
are fantastic.

"By then, of course, I began to believe I was. People would come and listen to me, and later pat me on
the shoulder and say to me, trust it, man, whatever far-
out thing it is that you've got going, trust it. And
that's what made the difference. I got so I could trust
it. It was like help from some source you never had
counted on before. It was like getting access to some
demon that's always scared you so bad you've kept a
tight lid on his cage door. And then somehow you go
crazy and lose your grip on his cage door and out he
comes, ripping and snorting, only instead of eating
you up or beating your ass, he's your friend, and off
you go, the two of you, side by side, heading down
the road looking for some action.

"One time in Seattle this kid comes up to me and
says his family has kicked him out because they
thought he was queer. He asked me what I thought

he ought to do. Without hesitation I told him I thought he ought to go and read *Finnegan's Wake* into a tape recorder, then call his family up long distance and when they answer, turn the record on and walk away and leave them to deal with it. And that kid did that, and I saw him some time later and he shook my hand and gave me this big grin and said *thank you man, thank you.*

"It's a far-out thing, having people come up to you and say thanks for helping them. I guess one of the reasons my life went sour again was I got to liking that part of it too much. I got so I waited for it to happen, and when it didn't it would bug me. There was a recognition I wanted from people that was almost like having a name again, and sourness was the only possible consequence of craving to be named. That wonderful period of my life went away, and was followed by another time of despair. It was that despair that drove me on into a truly committed effort to forget my name, to forget everything I could recognize myself by. It's painful, laborious work to lose your attachment to identity, but I believe that once I destroy the manuscript telling my early history, I will have gone past the last serious obstacle to becoming infinitely Nameless. I don't want to say that categorically. To say it categorically would be a speculation upon the future, and the future is of no concern to one who is truly nameless. I can say, and this is a confession, that I have got this close to destroying that manuscript twice before, and each time I was unable to go through with it. In nineteen hundred sixty-two I got to the front entrance of the library and couldn't go in. In nineteen hundred sixty-six I made it to the very stacks where the Master's theses are kept, and turned around and left empty-handed. So it's not for me to say how this new effort to burn the manuscript will turn out. All I know is that I'm

on my way to the University again, that I'm still trying, and that I believe that if one perseveres in a
righteous cause, he must eventually succeed."

## Instant Replay

Some time past the middle of the night Estelle felt
the bus slow down and come to a stop by the side of
the road. She heard the motor fall suddenly quiet,
and in the quiet she heard the Greek bidding D.R.
farewell. It was completely dark outside and she
couldn't see either one of them, but she heard the
Greek plainly. "Farewell, old friend," he said. "And
remember one thing: *persevere*." There was the sound
of the door opening and closing, and then of D.R.
shifting over to the driver's seat and starting the motor
again. She felt the bus jerk forward, then roll smoothly
as they began to pick up speed again. And instantly
Estelle was filled with a marvelous feeling of lightness
and freedom. It perked her up so much she sat up and
would have gone to the front of the bus to be with
D.R. if the Greek had not suddenly started yelling at
her at the top of his voice. I WAS A MADMAN. I
WANTED CALIFORNIA TO FALL INTO THE
SEA. The force of the words literally knocked Estelle
over backward and took her breath away. AND I
WANTED TO FALL IN WITH IT, TO BE SWAL-
LOWED UP BY A THING SO BIG, SO HUGE, SO
UTTERLY ENORMOUS THAT I WOULD DIS-
APPEAR INTO ABSOLUTE NOTHINGNESS. Es-
telle crawled to the farthest back corner of the bus
and huddled there terrified until she finally realized
that it was only an instant replay of the Greek and
not the Greek himself. I WANTED TO SEE CALI-

FORNIA HEAVE AND SLIDE AND FALL WITH
THE GREATEST ROAR AND RUMBLE THE
WORLD HAD EVER KNOWN, the Greek yelled.
AND I WANTED TO GO DOWN WITH IT, BE-
CAUSE ONCE I WENT DOWN WITH IT I
WOULDN'T HAVE TO THINK ABOUT HOW
SCATTERED WERE THE FRAGMENTS OF MY
LIFE, AND MIND.

Estelle's fright was replaced by simple heartache
then, that old, lost lonely feeling she knew so well
but which she had hoped she would never have to
feel again. The world became just too drab a place
to endure when she felt that way. It was worse than
D.R. behaving crazily. It was as if he wasn't even there,
as if that was just some anonymous shadow in front,
driving the bus. Estelle lay down again and covered
her head with a sleeping bag. And there inside that
dark within a dark, she began to cry. She didn't know
it but tears were rolling down D.R's cheeks then
too as the Greek said, IF THE FRAGMENTS
WOULDN'T COME TOGETHER AND FUNC-
TION FOR ME, THEN LET THEM FLY APART,
SCATTER AND BE GONE WEIGHTLESS
THROUGH THE UNIVERSE. LET FREEDOM
REIGN. LET NOTHING MATTER.

THAT WAS MY BELIEF.

# THREE

## Eddie's Funeral

The mourners were lying around the room on mattresses, smoking hash between hits on nitrous oxide. Nearly everybody there was a St. Louis dealer, and since Eddie had been a dealer the Native thought it would be nice if samples of everybody's stuff was done, in honor of Eddie's passing. Somebody do grass. Somebody else do acid. Somebody else do DMT. Somebody else do IT-290. Somebody else do STP. Somebody else do peyote. Somebody else do mescalin. Somebody else do psycilocybin. Somebody else do reds, and everybody share the laughing gas to tie the whole thing together, in honor of Eddie's passing.

But that was just the Native coming on, just the Native doing his usual thing. The Native got his name because he was always talking about how nobody's a native any more. Nobody lives where he was born, nobody's got real roots any more, and that's why people are so unhappy. The Native grew up in the Ozark Mountains of Missouri. He was so homesick most of the time, all he ever talked about was his family and his old home place back in the Ozarks. People at home have got identity, said the Native. They've got a history, and their lives are full of the most beautiful rituals. The Native loved rituals, and he wanted Eddie's funeral to be one, an elaborate ceremony where everybody would take a different kind of dope and then do communal things like chant and sing and mourn poor Eddie's passing.

But none of the others were up to it. There were eleven people at the funeral, besides the Native. Blue Ox was there, and Gilded Lilly, Chuck, Friendly Persuasion, City Girl and the Crosstown Rivals, plus Reed and Winston and Divine Right Davenport and his chick who had just blown in from somewhere. They had all been Eddie's friends, and they were all just as sorry as the Native that Eddie was dead. But the hash and the nitrous oxide and three TV sets all going at once were all that they could handle right then.

"Give me the hose," said Bert of the Crosstown Rivals. Bert's rival, Norton, had been sucking on the laughing gas almost two minutes now, and Bert was getting antsy. His last flash had been all about time, it had taken him down the passageway to the very door of the rose garden, but as he was about to go in the flash had started to wear off. Against his will he'd come reeling up the same passage he had taken down, and that was a disappointment. If he could have gotten the gas hose when he was supposed to, he could have made it back down in time to keep the dream intact, for even though he'd become conscious again the footprints still echoed clearly in his memory and showed the way back to the garden. But stupid Norton had the greeds and wouldn't let go of the hose.

"Give me the goddamn hose!" said Bert. He reached to take it out of Norton's hand, but Norton, although he was unconscious by now, held it in a slobbery death grip, and Bert was too stoned to fight him. As usual City Girl had to mediate. Gently she worked Norton's hands loose and gave the hose to Bert as Norton fell over in City Girl's lap. Bert put the hose in his mouth and inhaled until he flashed. He wanted the rose garden again, but all he got was Billy Graham silently rapping at him on the top left television screen.

The three TVs were in the corner of the living

room opposite the entrance to the kitchen. The big set on the bottom was a brand new color one that Eddie had bought only a week before he was killed. The other two were black and white, and small enough to sit side by side on top of the big set. The sound on the top left TV was torn up, but that's the one Billy Graham was on, and nobody wanted to hear him anyway. He was okay to look at, but the picture everybody wanted sound to was the quiz show on the big TV, in which newlywed couples got a lot of free stuff if they knew the right answers.

The competition on the newlywed show was between three young couples, the Morrisons of Buffalo, New York; the Littons of Oneonta, New York, and the Baileys of Maryville, Tennessee. The funeral party was instantly unanimous in its hatred of the Baileys, because it was so obvious that their highest aim in life was to get to Knoxville where Charles would run for city attorney, and Rita would be an active Vol booster. As Rita pointed out when she introduced herself, she was a graduate of the University of Tennessee, where she had been very active in extracurricular affairs. When she mentioned "extracurricular affairs," the audience laughed. Rita blushed but laughed too. "I didn't mean it *that* way," she said. Every time Rita and Charles said anything the people at the funeral hissed and booed and called them stupid motherfuckers.

Everybody was kinder to the Morrisons. They dug Mrs. Morrison especially because she was so straightforward and upfront in her manner. Her manner said: okay, by God, I'm on TV now, and I'm going to win every goddamn thing I can while I've got the chance. The people at the funeral liked Mrs. Morrison for that, and until the mid-program commercials Blue Ox, Gilded Lilly and Winston rooted hard for her and her husband to win.

As the program went on, however, the group senti-

ment slowly shifted to the Littons of Oneonta, and by
the end of the program everybody at the funeral was
solidly behind them. They were the truly engaging
couple. Roger Litton was short and, at twenty-seven,
a little jowly already, and Betty was having her weight
problems too. They were handsome enough in the
face, but there wasn't any getting around it, the
Littons of Oneonta were fat, and because the Morrisons and Baileys, particularly that prissy Rita, were
trying to come on so chic and "now," the people at
the funeral loved the Littons all the more. They were
fat, and they were modest, and they were also damn
clever. The subject of the day was World Religions.
The Littons weren't theologians or anything, but they
knew that Buddha was enlightened under a bodhi
tree, and that it was Jesus who'd said, "Straight is the
gate, and narrow is the way, which leadeth unto life,
and few there be that find it." The Morrisons and
the Baileys didn't know shit about World Religions.
When the question man asked Mr. Morrison what
country was most closely identified with Zen, he
guessed Persia. When he asked Rita Bailey who was
the author of the Bhagavad-Gita, she said, "Mahatma
Gandhi?" When the scores were added and Roger and
Betty Litton pronounced the winners of a new Mav-
erick, fifty cartons of Marlboros, a fur coat for the
Mrs. and a set of golf clubs for the Man of the House,
plus a year's supply of parakeet food and a forty-
eight-hour vacation in Barcelona, everybody at the
funeral applauded except Divine Right and Estelle,
who had sort of withdrawn from it all and were sulk-
ing quietly in separate corners of the room. Roger and
Betty hugged each other. As the program credits
streamed across the screen they walked arm in arm
off the stage into their new life together.

"Turn to channel four," said Chuck. "It's time for
the hypnotism man."

## The Hypnotism Man

The hypnotism man was a little old sawed-off Jew with a goatee who stood with his hands folded at his chest like a teacher about to say "now children." He spoke in a wonderfully deep and resonant voice, but he wasn't nearly as handsome and pleasant to look at as Billy Graham. So the Native, ritual freak and prank-ster that he was, decided to rearrange things a little. What he did was fuck up the picture image on chan-nel four so that you could hear the hypnotism man without seeing him, while you looked at Billy Graham on channel three of the top-left TV. As a kind of sub-plot, some bulldozers were hacking down a mountain in a strip-mining operation in Kentucky on channel seven of the TV next to Billy Graham.

"Far out," said Reed.

"Groovy," said Bert of the Crosstown Rivals.

"Move your fucking knee," said Bert's rival, Norton.

After some stirring and shifting around and some goings and comings to the bathroom, everybody settled back onto the mattress for another half hour of good funeral.

"Good afternoon," said Billy Graham. "And wel-come to today's session in self-hypnosis. I hope you've done your homework since yesterday, because today's lesson will require considerable strength of mind if you are to complete it successfully. You will remem-ber that yesterday I asked you to practice being very quiet, all by yourself, for at least half an hour. I hope that most of you did that, for you will find, as you continue in self-hypnosis, that several minutes a day of simple quiet will add greatly to your capacity to count yourself into a trance. Being quiet for a few minutes each day is like planting a little seed in your mind that can grow and grow all through the day, and help you to stay calm and alert. So if you did not practice since yesterday's session, I urge you most strongly to sit quietly for at least half an hour before tomorrow's session.

"Now. Today we are concerned with time expansion. A lot of people have different notions of what time expansion is, and they approach the phenomenon in a variety of different ways. But the thing that all the ways have in common is that time expansion implies a more intense experience of the present, the here and now. I'm sure that many of you sitting there listening to my voice are still not actually *here* in this moment, with me, *now,* as I talk to you. Your minds are filled with thoughts of other people and other places, of experience that has already happened or that you are waiting on to happen, or that you wished had happened or would happen. This is very common. Indeed, it is the way most people go around in their minds all the time. And it is a most wasteful, and actually harmful, destructive way to conduct your mental life. What we are going to do today is play a little self-hypnosis game that, once you master it, can be useful to you in helping you to learn how to live in the present in a natural, vital way.

"So, if you will, lie down now, and make yourself comfortable on the floor, or on a mat, or mattress, or whatever you are lying on. Let your body sink and relax into the floor. Feel the relaxation begin in your toes and flow up through your legs, into your thighs, feel it flood your mid-region and swell on up through your chest. Relax your hands, relax your elbows, and your arms and your shoulders. And let the tensions go out of your neck, and your jaw muscles, let your entire face relax and settle naturally against your bones. Feel the relaxation flowing through you from your toes right up through your scalp, and feel your breath going in and out evenly and without effort.

"As your body has settled into deep rest, your mind has been relaxing too, emptying itself until now it is cool and clear and free of all images except those I

will suggest to you with my voice. Your mind is like
a wall with absolutely nothing on it, no shape, no
form, no color. It is empty and at rest, ready to receive the image of three boxes, three simple boxes sitting side by side in the middle of the empty space of
your mind. The boxes are all the same size, and they
are sitting in the same positions, with their fronts
toward you, so that you can read the words written on
the front of each box. Except for these words, the
boxes are just alike, three neat boxes, very simple
and clean of line, sitting next to each other in your
mind. On the front of the box on the left is the word
'Past.' The box on the right is labeled 'Future,' and
the box in the center is labeled 'Present.' Keep seeing
all three boxes sitting there together, now, but pay
particular attention to the box on the left, the 'Past'
box. Think about that box a minute, and think about
the word 'Past.' And as you think about the word
'Past,' begin to put into the box all those things in
your mind that you ordinarily associate with the word
past. All your memories, all your recollections, all your
backward longings, everything in your mind that has
anything at all to do with the past put it into the box
on the left, and when you have done this, close the lid.

"Now you have closed the lid on the box marked
'Past.' Continue to see all three boxes in a row, but
turn your attention now to the box on the right, in
particular, the one marked 'Future.' Think about the
word 'Future,' and as you think about it, begin to fill
up the box on the right with all those elements in
your mind that have anything at all to do with the
future. All your ambitions, all your plans, every forward longing, every expectation, the very concept of
the future, put in the box now, and when you have it
all in, close the lid. The past and the future are now
closed. You don't have to think about either of them
again. The three boxes are still there, side by side in
your mind, but the only one you are interested in

now is the one in the middle, marked 'Present.' Turn all of your attention to the box in the middle marked 'Present.' Concentrate your entire mind on everything you can grasp that belongs to this particular present moment of your life. Everything that is, *now,* put in the box marked 'Present,' and watch, notice how the box in the middle is beginning to grow in size. You continue to put in it everything that you can possibly get hold of in this moment, this *now,* but as you do the box is growing, getting larger, it is swelling in length and height and breadth. You continue to put in it all the elements of the here and now that you can get hold of, but as you find them and put them in, you discover more and more of the present that should be included in the box.

"And as the middle box grows, the other two boxes on either side get smaller and smaller in proportion. They get smaller and smaller as the box in the middle gets larger and larger. And gradually the box in the middle begins to crowd the other two boxes out of your mental picture. Their place is being consumed by the box in the middle, which you continue to fill with every stray possibility out of the world of here and now. The two boxes on the sides are so small now you can barely see them. And now they are gone.

"Now there is only the box in the middle, the 'Present' box, still swelling, still growing, getting larger and larger with every breath you breathe.

"And now the edges of even this box begin to disappear into the limits of your picture. It is beginning to lose its form, its identity as a box, it is turning into pure space now, pure light, and inside it is every aspect, every particle of *now,* of *here,* of this single, living, breathing, ongoing instant of your life."

## Divine Right's Boxes

I get the boxes all right but they won't stay shut. I
get 'em set up in my mind side by side and just alike
and I get the labels on. But they won't stay shut. I
put stuff in the past box like saying sometimes I go
whole days at a time and never even think about Estelle. But it never has been in my mind as a concept
that we'd split up 'til I put her in the future box. I
mean, I depend on knowing how a thing's going to
come out and that's a terrible, I mean that's really a
limitation. I put that kind of thing in the future box
and close the lid, and I put past stuff in the past box,
about Eddie being dead, about taking acid with Eddie
in the Grand Canyon when we did. But Eddie's body
comes crawling out of the future box, two bodies dead
and rotten out of past and future boxes swarm all over
my present box and mix in with me hating that we
ever went to look at Eddie's body in the funeral home.

His face looked like a wax apple. They'd cut his
hair beyond all recognition, so I try to stuff the hair
and the apple in the past box but the lid won't stay
on. It flies off and stuff swarms out and mixes with
me calling up my sister in Cincinnati and asking her
for money swarming out of my future box and all I
see is poor old Eddie dead Eddie dead Eddie dead.

When we got to St. Louis, I called Eddie from this
shopping center at the edge of the city and City Girl
said hello. I said hey Eddie, Divine Right is my name
and weirdness is my game what's yours. And City Girl
said Eddie's dead. She said he's dead. She said they
shot him in an alley two blocks from the bus station
and I said who? She said Eddie. Two blocks from the
station in an alley. She said for me to come on over if
I wanted to. That some of the others were going to
spend the weekend together in Eddie's apartment and
mourn. And so we went, Estelle and me, and it was
Eddie's apartment all right. It was in City Girl's name

or the cops would have busted it yet Eddie was all over
that apartment, you could feel him in it you could
smell him you could see him in those weird dragons
he drew on the wall, and that big color TV. That TV,
God was it ever Eddie. Was the whole scene ever
Eddie, Eddie dead.

Ah, the mystery of it all, the questions gone unan-
swered. Where is Eddie's spirit now? What's happening in his cold body? What box does *it* belong in?
Lying there in his high-school graduation suit, hands
all folded and a stupid rose in his lapel and dust upon
his rose and half a crewcut on his head. Goddamn
Momma, give him a crewcut rather than half of
nothing. Why did you go halfway? He's dead, let's
give him the full cosmetic treatment and be satisfied.
Eddie wouldn't give a shit. He dug you, Momma, and
it's very sad to see you standing here so sad like this,
weeping over the body of your darling baby boy. If
you wanted it short you should have cut it short, you
should have given the boy a crewcut like you wanted
because you're the one whose living now. You should
have pleased yourself before anyone else, how long
has it been since you've been pleased? Now nobody's
pleased but it's not too late to do something about it.

I swarm out of my future box with a foot-long
pair of scissors right into the funeral parlor to open
Eddie's box, his last and past and present future box.
And give him a good short haircut like his Momma
wants. Let's do it Momma! It's not too late. Right
there it sits, right there it is, what's left of Eddie's in
that box and we could do it if we tried.

But City Girl opens the door and says Eddie has
been shot dead in an alley not far from the Greyhound station, and then slams the lid on the box.

### Reincarnation

One by one, the people at the funeral sat up and rubbed their eyes. The hypnotism program was only half an hour long, but everybody had the feeling that two or three hours had gone by. The TV sets were off now. The cool, blank tubes were as much a surprise to whoever had turned them off as they were to any of the other mourners at the funeral.

"Who turned the TVs off?" asked Winston.

"I don't even remember them going off," said Norton.

"I think you turned them off," said Norton's rival, Bert.

"No, man," said Norton. "I don't know who turned them off."

"We have a mystery in our midst," said City Girl.

For a little while the room was quiet, except for the sound Estelle made as she flipped the pages of a book on Etruscan art.

M . . . m . . . maybe it was Eddie's g . . . g . . . ghost," D.R. stuttered.

Everybody in the room except Estelle turned to look at Divine Right. It was the first time he had spoken since the night before. His silence had become such a fixture in the room it was as if a piece of furniture had been moved out when he spoke.

"I can dig that," said Chuck.

"I can dig reincarnation," said Winston. "But I don't believe in ghosts."

"It's all the same shit," said Reed.

"No it isn't," said Gilded Lilly. "Reincarnation is an established fact."

"I had a dream once about reincarnation," said the Native. "I dreamed I was a lizard in a previous life."

Friendly Persuasion asked the Native what that had felt like.

"It was pretty weird. I mean, I liked it. I liked crawling around that close to the ground. I liked the point of view. When I die, I hope I'm a lizard the next time around."

Bert shook his head. "It don't work that way," he said. "You're never the same thing twice."

"Bullshit," said Norton. "Sometimes you're the same thing three or four times in a row."

Bert started to argue with Norton. But as he was about to speak, his energy suddenly failed him. Arguing with Norton about reincarnation just didn't seem worth the trouble right then, so he kept quiet. For a while everybody kept quiet. Finally City Girl got up and went to the kitchen. For a moment it seemed as if her departure might produce some kind of conversation. But it didn't. Ten or fifteen minutes went by. The only sounds in the whole apartment were Estelle shuffling pages and City Girl clinking dishes in the kitchen.

## Grand Canyon

Again it was Divine Right who broke the silence.

"The first t . . . t . . . time I ever had acid was in the G . . . G . . . Grand C . . . C . . . Canyon with Eddie," he stuttered. "We were d . . . d . . . driving from L.A. to Shockey's p . . . p . . . place in Taos and stopped off at the C . . . C . . . Canyon and Eddie said let's go down in the fucker and drop acid. We called it our G . . . G . . . Grand Canyon trip. About every half hour Eddie'd say, what k . . . k . . . kind of canyon trip you having, D.R.? And I'd say g . . . g . . . grand, man, g . . . g . . . grand."

Friendly Persuasion was rummaging in her bag for a cigarette. Without looking up, she asked D.R. what was grand about it.

D.R. had to think about that. And his thoughts

grew until they were much too thick to say. If his tongue had been healthy he would have said we're near the center of the earth with the goddamn Colorado River flowing by. And over there is Eddie lying naked on the sand. I'm feeling nervous about taking my clothes off, but finally I do, and I remember how the sand felt against my skin, and the kind of hit it was to see the impression of my body in the sand when I stood up. Like a shadow, like a mirror image of someone trying to arrive there in the Canyon. I was nervous about being naked and I was also nervous about the load of shit I'd carried down the Canyon with me. Eddie stuck a peanut butter sandwich in the pocket of his field jacket and that was his supplies for an all-day, all-night acid number in the Canyon, seven of the fiercest miles, straight down from the rim. I held us up half an hour, sorting through my shit, loading cans of food and pots and pans and lengths of rope and waterproof matches and emergency signal mirrors into an Army cargo bag I'd rigged out as a pack. I lugged it down seven miles of trail to the banks of that amazing river, and then sat there all stoned out feeling guilty about carrying so much shit when all Eddie brought was a peanut butter sandwich. Him over there on the sand so cool and into it, me sitting beside my shadow in the sand, feeling guilty and blaming myself because the moon wouldn't finish coming up over the eastern rim of the Canyon.

I knew it was me that was stopping it. I knew damn well it wasn't Eddie, the Canyon couldn't tell Eddie from the little birds that flitted among the willows along the bank. It had to be me, and it was a terrible burden to carry. How old is this Canyon? I asked Eddie. He said aw, I don't know, few billion years. I said I bet this is the first time the moon has refused to come up over it in all that time. It does seem kind of stuck, he said. I said I think it's my fault the moon

won't rise. It's because I carried all this shit down
here with me. Eddie said why don't you throw it away?
I said throw what away? He said all your shit. I said
throw it *away?* I paid good money for this stuff, I'm
not going to throw it away. Eddie grinned and
shrugged and went back to grooving on the little
eddies of the river around the rocks where he was
sitting.

But of course I knew I had to. I reached into my
pack and took out a can of pork and beans and threw
it in the Colorado River. And I'll be damned, if the
moon didn't rise another notch above the rim. I found
a can of sausages and threw it in the river too, and
sure enough, the moon came up some more. I threw
my rope away, and an old candle I'd been carrying
around for years. And then all of a sudden with an
enormous whoop I grabbed my whole camping rig
and heaved it pack and all into the river. And instantly the full, round moon rose into the sky above
the rim and filled the evening Canyon with its light.
Yelping and leaping I ran to the rocks where Eddie
was and for the next five minutes danced and pranked
about in joy. He just grinned at me, and leaned back
on his elbows to stare up at the moon, old Eddie did.
Old friend, old teacher.

Eddie.

If D.R.'s tongue had been healthy it would have
been easy to rattle off that story as a monologue. But
his tongue was not healthy. He had his voice back
now, but he had to take it easy, spend words carefully,
or else stuttering would take him over completely
and reduce his speech to mere babble again. He took
a long time to decide the answer to the question
Friendly Persuasion had asked him. Finally, speaking
slowly, he said, "Because we were d . . . d . . . deep
in the earth, b . . . b . . . by that river."

Friendly Persuasion thought about that for a minute. Then she said, "Anybody got a cigarette?"

## Trips with Eddie

"I've got some, wait a minute," City Girl called from the kitchen. And she came into the living room carrying a tray loaded with cups and milk and honey to put in tea. She set the tray on the floor in the middle of the room and went back to the kitchen to get the teapot. Before she sat down she got a package of cigarettes off a shelf behind the TV sets. As she settled cross-legged on the floor by the tray, Blue Ox got a clear look up her dress at her pubic hair.

Blue Ox poured himself some tea. "One time me and Eddie and Winston were stoned on peyote, out in the desert," said Blue Ox. "And the goddamn stars attacked us. You remember that, Winston?"

Winston nodded and grinned a little as he dipped a spoonful of honey into his tea.

"I mean," said Blue Ox. "I mean, like, where do you run to when the whole fucking Milky Way is after your ass, answer me that?"

"You could close your eyes," said Bert.

Norton snorted. "Close your eyes. That's exactly what you'd do is close your stupid eyes."

D.R. leaned across the mattress and touched Estelle's shoulder. "You want some tea?"

Estelle shook her head and flipped another page.

"One time over in Afghanistan," said Reed. Reed was wrestling with a pillow, trying to fold it so it would support him as he drank his tea. "One time over in Afghanistan, me and Eddie had gone over there, to be big-time dealers. We had four thousand dollars between us, and the plan was to score this incredible amount of hash, bring it back and sell it for a million dollars and retire from this fucking shit. So there we are fucking around goddamn Kabul, and who do we run into but this really spaced-out American cat who says the best hash deal in the country is in this other town about fifty miles away. So he turns

us on and shows us around a little, and tells us how
to get to this other town. Of course we're all hot to
go, but the thing is, his directions are pretty fucking
weird. Like, I don't know how many roads there are
going out of Kabul, but the one he put us on was this
fucking dirt trail going north across this totally empty
country. Not a house, not a road sign, not a goddamn
thing except this fucking rut they call a road going
north into the country out of Kabul, just me and old
Eddie bouncing along in this old taxi this other friend
of Eddie's had scored somehow and left it there for us
to use because he was going to be gone, some shit like
that, I never did understand that car and I was too
stoned at the time to care. So anyway we're on this
dirt trail, bouncing along looking for this fork in the
road see, and this guy who's supposed to be out there
giving directions. That was his job. He was a road
sign. Every day this guy goes to the forks of the road,
and he sits there, and people coming by ask him which
road to take to wherever they want to go, and this
guy tells them. The government pays him and that's
his job. Only when me and Eddie get there see, the
guy ain't there. He's gone. We're at this crossroads
out in the middle of nowhere, three roads going three
different directions and the guy who's supposed to be
the road sign ain't around. We hang around all day
waiting for him to show up, but he never does. It
blew me out. That fucking Eddie wanted to toss a
goddamn coin, or throw the *Ching* or something, and
just *take* a road and see what happened. But it was
too freaky for me, man. It pissed Eddie off but I
couldn't help it. I mean, I was really counting on that
guy being there and when he wasn't, the first thing I
thought was nark. Maybe even CIA. I didn't want no
part of that shit. We wound up not even buying any
hash in Afghanistan, except just some to have around
and smoke. It was heavy shit."

Reed sipped his tea as everybody laughed at his

story. Most of the people at the funeral had heard it before, had heard Eddie tell it, in fact, and so the laughter was muted, very gentle and low-keyed. Reed lifted the teapot to refill his cup, but nothing came out.

"I'll put some more water on," said Gilded Lilly. She got to her feet and tiptoed through the people to the kitchen.


### What Would You Have Done?

"What would you have done?" Friendly Persuasion asked the Native.

"What do you mean?" said the Native.

"At the crossroads. What would you have done?"

"Do you mean would I have gone with Eddie?"

"What would you have done, Winston?" asked Friendly Persuasion.

"I would of gone with Eddie," said Winston.

"I would of thrown the *I Ching* first," said Chuck. "They should have thrown the *Ching* and gone with it."

"Not me, man," said Norton. "I would of gone with Reed straight back to Kabul and got my ass out of there."

As people began to talk about what they would have done or not done in Afghanistan, Divine Right looked around the room for a copy of the *I Ching*. Chuck's mention of it gave him the idea to throw it, then and there. He didn't have anything in particular he wanted to ask. He just felt like it would be a good idea. When there was an opening in the conversation he asked City Girl if there was a copy of the *I Ching* in the house.

"There's Eddie's copy," said City Girl.

"You going to throw the *Ching,* man?" asked Reed.

"Yeah," said D.R.

"Groovy," said Gilded Lilly as she came in the room with fresh tea. "Let's ask it which road they should have taken in Afghanistan."

"I'd rather ask it what Eddie's been reincarnated as," said Chuck.

"I'd rather ask it how you get a job like the road sign guy had," said Chuck.

"Oh man, wouldn't that be far out?" said Norton. "Wouldn't that be a fan*tas*tic job."

'Shit," said Gilded Lilly. "Just sit out there and give people directions, send them this way, send them that way."

"Yeah," said the Native. "And people you didn't like you could send them the wrong way. Have a whole network of your buddies in charge of all the intersections, fucking cops come up and say, which way is Kansas City? and you'd say that way, motherfucker, and send 'em to Gallup, New Mexico."

'Yeah," said Chuck, "but good dudes, send them to the grooviest places there is. Have this big farm, see, have this incredible big spread in fucking Oregon, or Colorado, or someplace. And when a really good cat would come along, that's where you'd point 'em."

"I'd rather ask who killed Eddie," said Norton. "Some son-of-a-bitch killed Eddie and we don't even know who it is."

"You can't ask shit like that," said Bert. "You can't ask specific questions."

"The fuck you can't," said Norton. "I ask it specific questions all the time."

"If you're not going to ask which road to take in Afghanistan, I don't want anything to do with it," said Gilded Lilly.

"I'm going to watch TV myself," said the Native. And he rolled across the floor and turned on the color television.

As the sound of television began to grow in the room

and people quit talking about Afghanistan and the *I Ching,* City Girl motioned for D.R. to follow her. Together they stood up and picked their way across the people scattered around on the mattresses and disappeared behind the bedroom door.

 *Bedroom Scene*

City Girl lay down across the mattress and reached for some books on a little stand next to the far wall. She straightened up again with Eddie's *I Ching* in her hand.

"I don't want to throw it right now, but if you want to, this is Eddie's."

And she held the book out to D.R.

D.R. took it, but his mind was on City Girl now. Without having anything in particular to say, he felt like he wanted to talk to her, or at least to sit there in the room with her a little while. Something like that was on her mind too, because when D.R. sat down on the mattress beside her, City Girl put her arms around his neck and hugged him. They sat holding each other a moment. Then they fell over on the mattress and lay together a long time locked in a very tight embrace. It wasn't a sexy embrace. It was, actually, but the sex was only one element of something else that was going on between them. City Girl didn't have on any underwear, and D.R. could feel her plainly against him. His leg more or less on its own wedged in between her legs right up into her crotch, and her great breasts pillowed roundly against his chest. And yet it was all just a part of this other, larger thing between them that was going on. City Girl kissed D.R. two or three times on the mouth, and once he kissed her very deeply with his tongue. But nothing led to anything. It was just a crushing physical hello between two people who had a special bond between them, and when they'd said that hello they drew apart and lay on the mattress looking at each other.

Finally City Girl sat up and pushed her hair back and leaned on a pillow propped against the wall.

"I guess we're going to talk about Eddie being dead," she said.

"I g . . . g . . . guess so," said D.R. "Is that what you want to d . . . d . . . do?"

"Fuck, I don't know what I want to do. All I know is Eddie's dead, and that's just the farthest out thing I ever heard of in all my life."

"How sad d . . . d . . . do you feel?" D.R. asked.

City Girl shook her head. "I don't know. Not very, I guess. I don't get sad much."

"I'm fucked up in the head m . . . m . . . most of the t . . . t . . . time," said D.R.

"Are you sad now?" asked City Girl.

"Yeah."

"You look sad. You look damn beat up, if you want to know the truth. And that chick, what's her name?"

"Estelle."

"Jesus. Where'd you get with her?"

"Altamont."

"I was at Altamont."

They didn't say anything else for a minute, and in the silence D.R. looked around the room. The room wasn't much bigger than the mattress on the floor, but it had so much shit on the walls it looked like an infinite universe. Eddie had only lived there with City Girl a couple of weeks, but in that time he had painted serpents and dragons on every wall and ceiling. Behind a tall, skinny plant of some kind in the corner Eddie had painted a jungle of green leaves on the wall, with a vine running through them and little orange and purple dragons crawling up and down the vine. There was a red dragon on the ceiling. On the wall opposite the window a long yellow snake stretched from the corner near the floor to a corner near the ceiling, diagonally across. Light streaming through the strings of colored beads hanging down over the window made the whole place seem like an exotic tent in a curiously happy and benevolent jungle. The pictures were recognizably Eddie's, but something about them was very different from other stuff of Eddie's D.R. had seen. There was a precision in them, an order in the general arrangement of things. The place said something about Eddie that was not familiar to D.R. It looked as if Eddie had intended to stay in this apartment awhile, and D.R. could not get used to that idea. He wanted to ask City Girl what she and Eddie had had going, but he couldn't bring himself to. What he wound up saying, without actually deciding to say it, was that he had gone to look at Eddie's body in the funeral home the night before.

"You said you might do that," said City Girl.

"Yeah. M . . . m . . . me and Estelle went."

"How was it?" asked City Girl.

"A bummer."

City Girl asked D.R. how Eddie had looked.

"F . . . F . . . Fucked over."

"Did he have a ring on?" asked City Girl.

"I d . . . d . . . didn't see one."

"I guess his mother took it off."

"The undertaker m . . . m . . . m . . . might have t . . . taken it off."

City Girl shook her head. "No. It was her. She wasn't going to bury little Eddie-boy with that ring on his finger."

"D . . . D . . . Did you give it to him?"

City Girl nodded.

"I m . . . m . . . might b . . . b . . . be able to get it b . . . b . . . b . . . b . . . back for you," said D.R.

"Nah," said City Girl. She scooted across the mattress

and stood up. "Nah. Fuck it. It was just a ring. You got the book?"

"Right here."

"You can have that book if you want it," said City Girl.

"D . . . D . . . Don't you want it?" said D.R.

"I think you're the one ought to have it," City Girl said. "Eddie told me about you. Eddie talked about you a lot. Hey, you want something to eat? I'm hungry."

D.R. shook his head.

"Okay," said City Girl. As she left the room, she leaned over and touched D.R.'s face with her fingertips.


*Estelle Again*

D.R. started to throw the *I Ching* by himself when City Girl went out, but he didn't have any coins on him. He was focused so well on what he was about to do he didn't much want to interrupt it to go outside to ask somebody for some coins. But then he considered that maybe that was part of it, that maybe his not having any coins on him was crucial to the reading somehow, and so he yielded to that and went into the living room.

The scene had changed a good deal since he and City Girl had left. Everybody except Estelle was drawn up in front of the TV to watch an old Charlie Chan movie called *The Big Secret*. Friendly Persuasion and Winston had a joint going back and forth between them that nobody else seemed much interested in. They were all into the number Charlie Chan was doing with the Door to the Mystic Palace. The door was about twelve feet high, and made out of some kind of shiny metal, with a big dragon embossed upon it. You could tell just by looking at it that a tank would have a hard time breaking it down. And yet, by fiddling around with the eyeballs of the dragon, old Charlie was about to spring the whole thing and enter the Mystic Palace. Everybody was so into the program D.R. didn't want to disturb them so he did the next best thing and went over to Estelle in the corner.

'Have you got any coins?" asked D.R.

Estelle looked up at D.R. It was the first time their eyes had met in what seemed like days. D.R. and Estelle had been waging some kind of silent combat ever since his acid trip and the business with the Greek. Neither of them knew what the issue was, but they both knew that it was serious, whatever it was. Except for the four hours D.R. worked at the Save-More Store they had stuck close together ever since they got to St. Louis, but their minds were in separate, and hostile, galaxies. They had only been in St. Louis thirty-six hours, but that, too, seemed like days. Eddie being suddenly dead had lifted St. Louis out of time onto a plane where each moment is forever. Death is an infinity, and so are thirty-six hours of life in St. Louis when you're not speaking to someone you ostensibly love. I ostensibly love you, Estelle, thought D.R. And ostensibly I love you too, thought Estelle. The meeting of their eyes was filled with cold, ostensible love and both thought *what in god's name is happening.*

*Going through Changes*

The *I Ching* was what was happening. Estelle took three pennies out of her bag, handed them to D.R., then turned back to her book. The way she did it, the way she fished in her bag for the coins and handed them to him as if he was collecting for the Heart Fund or something, infuriated D.R. He came close to throwing the coins right in her face. His next impulse was to jerk the book out of her hand and fling it across the room.

Fuck it! he yelled inside his mind. Fuck it!

In the bedroom with the door shut D.R. took his place on the mattress again and worked at cooling his mind with some of the breathing exercises the Greek had taught him. He tried to do alternate-nostril breathing but he was so stirred up he didn't have enough patience to hold his breath for sixteen counts. Bellows breathing was easier. Huffing and puffing, doing them in sets of twenty, then twenty-five and finally thirty-five, D.R. stoned himself on breathing, his mind joined him on the mattress and at last he felt cool enough to toss the coins.

He didn't feel that way long. The first goddamn throw came up fucking Stagnation and he didn't want to read about it. He knew it was a sin not to accept the reading but he didn't give a shit. He threw the coins again. It came up Adversity and Weariness. He threw them again. It was the Estranged this time. Opposites. Fuck opposites. He threw them again. It was Ku, Decay, with changes in the third, fifth and sixth nines which gave him Abysmal, the Abyss. Fuck it. It was Eddie's *I Ching*, it was Eddie's room, fuck it, Eddie's dead and Divine Right threw the book across the room, then burst into the living room and told Estelle to get off her ass, they were going to the Western Union office.

Estelle looked up at D.R., half expecting to be afraid. But she wasn't. She got up and went out with him, but she definitely wasn't afraid.

## Angel's Farm

The money from D.R.'s sister turned out to be twenty-five dollars instead of the fifteen he had asked for. At some earlier point in their trip together such a delightful surprise would have sent D.R. and Estelle into little dancing ecstasies and racing to the nearest candy store to buy a bag of jelly beans. But they were so far from joy right then that ten times that amount could not have given them pleasure. D.R. put the money in his pocket and went outside where Estelle was waiting, leaning against a telephone booth.

"I want to call Gail," she said.

"C . . . c . . . c . . . call?"

"I want to call Gail. Give me a dime."

D.R. felt in his pocket. The Western Union lady had given him some change but it was all in quarters.

"Give me a quarter, then. I'll get it back. I'm calling collect."

D.R. handed Estelle a quarter. She went in the phone booth with it and slammed the door. A few minutes later D.R. saw her bang the receiver on the hook and storm furious out of the booth.

"Shit!"

"Wha . . . wha . . . wha . . . what . . ."

"Her old man answered and refused to accept the charges. Shit."

"Let's p . . . p . . . p . . . pay for the c . . . c . . . c . . . call. We can af . . . f . . . f . . . f . . . ford it."

"Fuck it," said Estelle. "Let's go."

"Let's c . . . c . . . c . . . call the Flash," said D.R. "He'll accept it."

Estelle shrugged. She was leaning against the bus now, her arms folded across her chest, looking at the sidewalk. "Call him," she said. "I don't care."

D.R. went in the phone booth and asked the operator

to connect him with the Anaheim Flash in Anaheim, California. He listened to the phone ring, he listened to the Flash tell the operator he would accept the charges. He heard the Flash's soft, laconic voice say, "Hey man, what's up?"

"N . . . n . . . n . . . n . . . nothing," D.R. stammered. "N . . . n . . . n . . . nothing's up. We just wanted to call somebody. We're in St. Louis."

"What's wrong, man?" asked the Flash. "You sound like you got epilepsy or something."

"N . . . n . . . no," said D.R. "It's this th . . . th . . . th . . . *thing,* it's my t . . . t . . . t . . . tongue. It's getting b . . . b . . . b . . . . b . . . better. Listen, d . . . d . . . did you hear about Eddie?"

"Yeah," said the Flash. "Fucking bummer."

"We g . . . g . . . g . . . got here after it happened. We b . . . b . . . b . . . been in St. Louis t . . . t . . . t . . . two days."

"That's two days too long for me," said the Flash. "You better get back out here to the land of sun and fun. Where's Estelle?"

"Right here," said D.R. "You want to sp . . . sp . . . sp . . . speak to her?"

"Sure. Put her on. I've got a message for her from Angel."

D.R. stepped out of the booth and handed the phone to Estelle.

"Hi baby," said the Flash. "How's your life?"

"Fucking miserable," said Estelle. "How's yours?"

"Better than yours, obviously. What's going on?"

"It's too long and too weird to tell," said Estelle. "What's happening in California?"

"Angel bought a farm in Oregon," said the Flash. "Two hundred acres. Her and Speed. They're into goats and bee hives."

"Far out," said Estelle. Suddenly she was smiling, and there was genuine cheer in her voice. "Far fucking out. They really did it."

"Two hundred acres," said the Flash. "I was up there the other day, it's really a neat scene. She was asking about you."

"Fan*tas*tic! Tell 'em hello, okay? Tell 'em I'll come see 'em."

"Will do," said the Flash. "Any other news, comments, hits, reports or flashes from the hinterlands?"

"It's grim," said Estelle. " 'Nuff said."

"Well," said the Flash. "Every cloud has a silver lining, and the darkest hour is just before dawn, and such like bullshit."

"You're stoned," said Estelle.

"Ah, yes, the blessed state. As a matter of fact, the old fire is waning a bit, I better go stoke it up a little. But listen you guys, call me again, you hear? I'm interested in your fate."

"Sure," Estelle laughed. "We'll give you a weekly casualty report. Listen honey, it's nice to talk to you. Take care, okay?"

The Flash said he would take care. Estelle hung up then, and as soon as she did the smile vanished from her face. Without saying a word to each other, D.R. and Estelle went back to City Girl's apartment to get their stuff, and to tell everyone good-bye.

*Leaving St. Louis*

Gilded Lilly and the Crosstown Rivals had split while D.R. and Estelle were gone, and the others were asleep or half-asleep in odd places about the room. City Girl had gone into the bedroom by herself and closed the door. The only person who was on his feet was Reed, long, rangy Reed, bent over peering in cabinets, looking around the kitchen for stuff to make a sandwich out of.

"Get your money?" Reed asked.

D.R. nodded. "I g . . . g . . . guess we'll t . . . t . . . take off now. Anybody want to go to Cincinnati?"

"Somebody going to Cincinnati?" said a voice in the living room. It was Friendly Persuasion. She'd been asleep in the corner where Estelle had sat earlier. She was sitting up now, yawning and scratching herself through a hole in her sweatshirt. "Somebody going to Cincinnati?"

"We are," said Estelle. She was in the living room, looking around to see if they were forgetting anything.

"Far out," said Friendly Persuasion, and she leaned over and shook the Native, who was stretched out next to her. "Hey. Wake up. You want to go to Cincinnati?"

The Native opened his eyes long enough to say sure. Then he closed them again and turned over. Friendly Persusaion got to her feet and went to the kitchen where D.R. had joined Reed scrounging for food.

"Hey," said Friendly Persuasion. "No kidding? You got room? You got room for the Native too?"

"Sure. We g . . . g . . . got a b . . . b . . . bus."

Friendly Persuasion looked at Reed as he licked something sticky off his fingers, then wiped his hands on his Levis.

"Do I want to go to Cincinnati?" she asked.

"Nah," said Reed. "You don't want to go to Cincinnati."

"But I do! I know a lot of people in Cincinnati."

"You don't want to see those people," said Reed.

"Don't I? No shit?"

"Nah. Go on back over there and go to sleep."

Reed had made a sandwich out of rice and some old chili. He took a bite, then held the sandwich out for Friendly Persuasion. She took a bite, and went back to the living room to talk it over with the Native.

"Hey, wake up," she said. "We got to decide."

"Decide what?" mumbled the Native.

"Are we going to Cincinnati or aren't we?"

"Sure," said the Native. "We're going to Cincinnati."

"I don't think I want to go," said Friendly Persuasion. And suddenly she knew for sure that she didn't. "Hey," she said to Estelle. "Hey, honey. Thanks, but we're not going, we changed our minds, okay?"

"Whatever's right," said Estelle.

"Yeah. I was just there a month ago. Fuck it." And Friendly Persuasion lay down on the floor beside the Native and soon went back to sleep.

Estelle snapped the duffle bag shut and set it beside the door. D.R. and Reed came in from the kitchen, eating chili and rice sandwiches. D.R. handed one to Estelle, then picked up the duffle bag and threw it over his shoulder.

"Well, see you around," D.R. said to Reed.

"Good-bye," said Estelle.

"Yeah, wow, man," said Reed, and he wiped his hand again and held it out to D.R. D.R. set his duffle bag down to shake hands with Reed. "Good to see you guys," said Reed. "Carry it on, okay?"

"We'll see you around," said D.R.

They left then.

Reed closed the door behind them.

# FOUR

 **Balance**

In Vincennes, Indiana, Estelle said, "Why don't we get a motel for the night?"

"What do you want with a motel?" D.R. asked.

He was fumbling with the radio dial, trying to tune in a talk show out of Indianapolis, where people were discussing the word "balance." There was an electrical storm south of Vincennes that had been interfering with the radio signal, but they were moving outside its range now, and the static was gradually going away.

"Oh," said Estelle. "To take a good shower. And sleep between some clean sheets for a change. Just get a good night's rest is all. I feel like I haven't really *rested* in about a year."

"Get in the back and rest," said D.R.

"I don't know," said a man's voice on the radio. "Balance just means when everything's . . . *balanced*."

Estelle leaned forward and turned the radio off.

D.R. leaned forward and turned it back on again.

"That's not a definition," said the talk show host. His name was Dewey Carbo. He spoke with a New York accent, but a little slower than most New Yorkers speak. Obviously, Dewey's life and work in the Hoosier State was having its subtle influence upon his speech, but he seemed satisfied for that to be. Dewey talked and laughed like one of the world's few truly satisfied men. "You can't use the word you're trying to define within the definition itself. Sorry, but thanks for trying and hel-*lo* there, KNAT Word Quiz, Dewey Carbo here, may I know who's calling, please?"

Estelle leaned forward and turned the radio off again. "That shit really fucks up my head," she said.

"It straightens mine out," said D.R. as he turned it back on again.

Evelyn Pughe of Terre Haute was talking about balance. "It's when opposite and equal forces are in accord," she said.

"That's very good," said D.R.

"That's very good," said Dewey Carbo. "Congratulations, Evelyn, you're our third winner of the evening, and KNAT is going to send some nice things out your way. Dinner for two at the Starlight Lounge. The country music album of your choice free from Cowtown Records, and any hardback book at half-price from Shirley's Books in the Southland Shopping Center. Thanks for playing Word Quiz, Evelyn. After a quick station break we'll be back for round four of Word Quiz."

"Did you hear what that woman said?" D.R. asked.

"I don't give a *shit* what she said," Estelle hissed.

"It was really good. Balance is, how did she say it? Opposite and equal, how did it go?"

"I don't give a *goddamn* how it goes."

D.R. looked at Estelle. In a genuinely surprised tone he said, "How come you're such a sourpuss all of a sudden?"

*"It's not all of a sudden!"* Estelle screamed. And before she could stop herself she hauled off and slapped the shit out of D.R., she really whammed him one flush on his left cheek with her right hand, so hard D.R. lost his vision for a moment. By the time he could see again, and had the bus under control after nearly going off the highway, Estelle had disappeared into the back of the bus somewhere.

 *Accord*

As D.R. drove on through the night to Cincinnati he entertained a very complex little drama in his mind, rather like a movie an airline might show its passengers while in flight. It went like this: a few miles out of Vincennes D.R. stopped at a pay phone along the road and called up Dewey Carbo to rap about the word balance some more. There he was, standing in the pay phone, rapping with Dewey Carbo, and there in the bus outside was Estelle, utterly charmed and thrilled as she listened to their conversation on the radio. It was such a vivid picture that he saw, and the dialogue was so convincing, that D.R. was tempted to believe the little drama was actually happening, for he surely felt more like its audience than its author. But deep down where it counts he forced himself to remember that it was all a fiction, that he was only making it up in his mind for something to do as he drove through the night in a bus.

D.R. said, "Dewey, what I'm calling about is that lady from Terre Haute, who had that good definition of balance a while ago."

"Right you are," said Dewey. "That was one of the best definitions we've had in a long time here on Word Quiz."

D.R. said, "Yeah, well, what I was wondering is, do you remember how it went? I mean, exactly how it went. Something about opposite forces equalizing . . ."

"Being in accord," said Dewey. "Opposite and equal forces being in accord."

"Accord," D.R. exclaimed. "That's the word I missed. *Accord.*"

"It's a great word all right," said Dewey. "I've already decided to use it here on Word Quiz some night."

"That would be great, Dewey," said D.R. "I really like your show a lot."

"I'm glad," said Dewey. "Where did you say you were calling from, Mister . . . ?"

"Davenport," said D.R. "Divine Right Davenport. I'm calling from just a few miles out of Vincennes."

"Great town, Vincennes," said Dewey. "How long have you lived there, Mr. Port?"

D.R. started to tell Dewey he had got his name wrong, but at the last second he changed his mind. "I'm actually just passing through, Dewey, Estelle and me, we're on our way to Cincinnati, to see my sister."

"Great town, Cincinnati. I want you to give my regards to Fountain Square, Mr. Port. And keep listening to KNAT, thirteen thirty on your dial."

"I will, Dewey," D.R. said. "And thanks a lot for that word accord."

D.R. waited for Dewey to say something else to him, but he had already signed off for the evening. By the time D.R. got back in the car a disc jockey had come on with the Big Band Sound, featuring Tex Beneke and his orchestra. D.R. had never heard of Tex Beneke before but he kind of liked his music. He would have listened to it as he drove if Estelle had not been in back asleep. She's tired, D.R. thought. She needs to rest. D.R. turned the radio off and drove the rest of the way to Cincinnati in silence.

*Cincinnati*

At the edge of Cincinnati D.R. pulled into a Gulf station and parked around the side by the tire rack. Since their argument the night before, and the cryptic statement over the radio by the guy who didn't feel very balanced, D.R. had been into balance as a con-

cept. About to enter Cincinnati, he wanted to stop at
the station and spend some money so his wealth would
align with the inner grammatical logic of the city he
was coming to. D.R. had lived in Cincinnati, and in
the smaller towns north toward Dayton—Middletown,
Hamilton, Franklin, Miamisburg—the last ten years of
his life, and yet this very day was the first time he had
ever really flashed on the word Cincinnati. There he
was, driving along, considering the concept of balance
while Estelle slept furiously in the back, when suddenly the word "Cincinnati" popped up on a highway
sign. Fantastic, D.R. thought.

Cin
Cin
Nat
I.

How balanced, how smooth the word Cincinnati.
Both in form and content. Content equals sin two
times, add one natty. Natty sin. Four vowels in Cincinnati, three *i*'s pierced by a single *a*.

Cin
Cin
Nat
I.

Four syllables. Four vowels and four syllables, ten
letters in the word all together. Four and four are
eight, plus ten is eighteen. I've got eighteen dollars
and eighty cents, an imbalance of eighty which it won't
take me a jiffy to rectify if this old boy will wait on me.

"Excuse me," said D.R. "How much are those fuses
there?" He was looking at a sign above a box of fuses
that said, "Why be helpless when fuses blow? A few
cents spent for a box of fuses will save you possible
delay or danger later on."

"Do which?" said the attendant in a high, nasal, hillbilly whine. He was busy making coffee on a hot plate
over by the road maps.

"Those fuses. How much are they?"

"Twenty cents apiece," said the attendant.

"Good," said D.R. "I'll take four."

The attendant picked out four fuses and stepped with them to the cash register, yawning as he rang them up. It was about five in the morning, barely sunrise. It was hard to tell if this was an all-night station or the start of a brand-new day.

As the attendant pecked the various keys, D.R. felt a deep sense of well-being glowing inside him. Eighty cents from eighteen eighty left eighteen exactly. How perfect, how balanced, how lovely the word *exactly*. Ex. Act. After the act. It reminded D.R. of the *I Ching* hexagram called After Completion, the one about the importance of tuning the flame beneath the kettle exactly right, so that it burns with a precise intensity. Precision, D.R. thought. Precision and intensity. Those are the keys.

"That'll be eighty-three cents," said the attendant, yawning again.

D.R. looked at him. "How much?"

"Eighty-three cents."

"Why the three cents?" D.R. asked, and when the attendant said sales tax D.R. thought: fucked in the ass by a tax.

D.R. was not enlightened by any of this experience, but it edged him a little further along the way.

 *The Coach's Pants*

D.R. didn't feel like going out to his sister's place 'til things got a little more balanced, so they drove into downtown Cincinnati and parked around the corner from the Greyhound bus station. They figured that would be a cheap place to eat, and besides that, D.R. wanted to change clothes and wash up some. He

didn't want to disguise himself in cleanliness for his
sister's sake, and her family's, but he didn't want to
scare anybody either. He looked pretty freaky for Cincinnati. He and Estelle had been drawing stares since
the streets began to fill with people going to work.
What D.R. really wanted was for his appearance to
not be a factor one way or another. That wasn't very
likely, considering his hair, but maybe a change into
more or less straight clothes would at least keep the
whole how-you-look thing at some low plane out of
everybody's way. If that could happen he figured he
stood a good chance of bringing this day into balance
after all.

D.R. fished around in his duffle bag for the shirt
and pants he'd bought at the Goodwill in California.
The shirt was gray with little blue pin-stripes up and
down it. It had wide, french cuffs and a button-down
collar, although when he put it on he didn't button
it down because the button on the left side was gone.
The pants were brown, frayed at the pockets and shiny
at the ass and knees. They'd probably been part of a
suit worn by the manager of a discount store, or perhaps by a small-town high-school coach about to leave
athletics and go into administration. Probably he
coached about four sports. Leaving it to go into administration would mean going back to college, of course,
and finishing up the old M.A. Probably he would do
it in summer terms. Ten or twelve summer terms, ten
or twelve more football, basketball, baseball and track
seasons and he'd be all set. Maybe he would even get
a new suit somewhere along the way and build his
wardrobe again, after the loss of his brown pants.

Suddenly it occurred to D.R. that the reason the
pants had wound up in the Goodwill on sale for
twenty cents was that the coach had died. A heart
attack, most likely, maybe cancer. D.R. didn't like to
think about the coach being dead. The thought of
him being dead put things out of balance again. To

keep from thinking about the coach D.R. read the graffiti on the walls of the toilet stall as he rolled his old dirty clothes up in a wad.

*Suck on this one, Hard Hat America,* someone had written in ink. *I'm over thirty, college educated, liberal, have long hair, and make $45,000 a year.*

Next to it someone had replied, in crayon: *When they aren't sucking a big dick, all Long Hairs are skin divers for Roto-Rooter.*

Above the toilet paper container someone had scratched with a knife: *If you've got it all together, what's that all around it?*

And then as D.R. was leaving the stall he read on the door: *There are times when the wolves are silent and the moon is howling.*

That one sort of got him. He stood there looking at it a long time, wondering if it would make things more balanced or less for him to write something on the wall. Finally he took a stub of pencil out of his pocket and wrote: *I am a balance freak in a dead football coach's pants.*

## Terminal

As D.R. came out of the men's room he was flashing on the word *terminal.* T-E-R-M-I-N-A-L. I am in a terminal. The end of a line. Three vowels, an *e,* an *i* and an *a.* And three syllables, three very neat and pungent syllables each with a vowel nestled in its middle like a jewel. How balanced. How very balanced is the word terminal, in content as well as form. At a terminal people arrive and depart, they begin new journeys even as they are ending old ones. Both things happened at a terminal, it goes both ways. It's like calling graduation *commencement.* Commencing as you end. Indeed, because you end. Like living because you die. That's a very religious idea. Bus terminals are very religious places when you think about it. Old rituals happened here, old ceremonies of farewell and return.

D.R. had been coming and going through the Cincinnati terminal as long as he could remember, although most of his recollections of those old times were recollections of feelings rather than events. As a child he had waited there for buses to or from Kentucky with his father, and his mother, but it was funny: he could not remember ever traveling with the two of them together, anywhere. He surely had, but in his memory there was no picture, no trace of the three of them, or four of them counting Marcella, ever being on the road together, going somewhere. There was the *feeling* of it, there were lots of feelings alive and working in D.R. like old evidence, but hardly any pictures of how those old times were. He remembered how it felt to say good-bye to his father and his sister when he was leaving with his mother to go become a Davenport, way off in Illinois. He remembered how it felt to wait in that big room at three A.M., twelve years old and traveling alone from Illinois to Kentucky. He remembered how it felt one time when someone stole his suitcase in that station, while he was buying an orangeade at that very refreshment counter across the way. The sudden sense of *gone*. His suitcase *gone,* a brand-new one his aunt had given him for making good grades in school. Someone *evil* right there *near* him had taken it away, and no amount of tearful pleading with the drivers or the ticket agents would bring it back again.

Ah, how the feelings accumulate in terminals and churches. The places of the weddings and the funerals, the comings and the goings. How they do accumulate and never stop, and there's another one in the works today. Here I am again in this old place, this old familiar room inside my head, and it's all still going on.

Look at this room. A waiting room. People gathering in off the streets to wait together for the next thing in their lives. A place to come and wait. Waiting is a form of worship, sitting in these pews. Estelle is there in a pew. She could very well be praying. Praying and waiting, waiting and praying, how balanced, how in accord.

I wonder if she'll like my outfit.

"How do you like my outfit?" D.R. asked Estelle.

He had come up from her blind side, down the lane between the rows of pews, and his voice startled her and made her jump. She looked around at him, and smiled. But it was a feeble smile. Estelle seemed confused. Then D.R. noticed there were tears in her eyes. He sat down and put his arm around her shoulder and asked her what was wrong.

Estelle shrugged his arm away. "Nothing's wrong," she said.

"But you're crying."

"I'm not crying," said Estelle.

"But you are, honey. I see the tears in your eyes."

"Please don't say I'm crying when I'm not," said Estelle. "I'm all right."

"But honey . . . "

"Oh!" she exclaimed angrily. And she got to her feet and moved several seats away.

D.R. followed her and tried to put his arm around her again.

"Estelle, something's wrong."

"You're *hassling* me is what's wrong!" Estelle turned to look D.R. in the face then, and when she did the tears spilled over and she really began to cry. She looked awfully sad to D.R. then, quite weak and helpless and worn down, and he wanted more than ever to take her in his arms. But the same pleading that had been in her voice was in her eyes now. She truly wanted to be left alone. D.R. leaned back in his seat and gazed around the room. A minute or two later he leaned over and whispered that he would be right back. Then he got up and walked to the row of telephones by the wall on the far side of the room.

## Telephone Call

D.R. dropped two nickels in the pay phone and dialed his sister's number. But as soon as he heard it ring he hung up and took his nickels back when they came clanging down the shoot. Then he was so pissed at himself for not completing the call he hit himself on the leg with his fist. As the force of the blow spread outward through his thigh and turned to pain it made him feel so one-sided and imbalanced he had to hit himself on the other leg to keep it all from toppling over.

There weren't many people in the bus station that hour of the morning, and no one was using any of the other booths. So D.R. stayed in his booth after his aborted call to think things over. He guessed that was what Estelle was doing too. Thinking things over. Her pose even resembled that of the Thinker. D.R. saw her through the window in the door of the phone booth. She hadn't moved since he left her. She sat turned to one side, one hand propping up her forehead, her elbow on her knee. She looked very unbalanced sitting like that, very awkward and unnatural. To balance it, D.R. sat up very straight in the phone booth, with both feet flat on the floor and his hands on his thighs, palms down. That did it for a minute or two. But then D.R. realized that his left nostril was stopped up, and that his breathing was very unbalanced as a result. His solution was to move his right foot until the heel was off the floor, getting the right foot out of phase as compensation for his malfunctioning left nostril. That felt pretty good. He held the position the next few minutes as he tried to think things over.

What in the goddamn hell's going on? In the long run I really couldn't say, but in the short run, to tell the absolute truth about it, what's going on is I want to leave Estelle here and go on out to Marcella's by myself. To check things out, you dig? I want to go see where it's all at with them, see what kind of vibes I get, sort of break the whole thing in easy-like, and bring Estelle out later. Marcella doesn't know about Estelle. I didn't mean to hold the information from her. I just more or less didn't tell her I was traveling with a chick. And I don't want to go busting into their house with a lot of weirdness and heavy vibes and freak everybody out, that's all. It's very simple.

D.R. eased his pose then, and slumped over, relaxed. His little rap with himself wasn't at all conclusive, but somehow he felt better for it. The thing to do was call Marcella and tell her where he was and that he'd be coming on out after a while. That was the thing to do.

Encouraged, and determined this time, D.R. put the nickel in the phone again and started to dial. He put his finger in the hole, he felt the cold metal of the thing you dial against his finger, he put his finger right up there in the old hole and started to dial. And then didn't. Instead he placed the phone on the little metal shelf, ran to the next phone booth to get that number, then came back to the first booth and dialed it. When the phone in the next booth rang he went around and answered it.

It was for Estelle. "Hold on a minute, please," said D.R. and he went over to the seats and told Estelle she had a phone call. Slowly she lifted her head to look at him. She wasn't crying now. Her eyes were red, but they were dry, and very clear. When D.R. took

her by the hand and tugged, she did not resist. She
followed him to the phone booth and went into it as
he directed. Then D.R. went to his booth, picked up
the receiver and after clearing his throat said, "Hello,
Estelle? This is Divine Right Davenport. I want to
talk to you."

## The Conversation

D.R. said, "Estelle, we've got to talk."

Estelle didn't reply immediately. She was looking
out her window at an old lady buying something at the
magazine stand. She was the oldest-looking person
Estelle had ever seen in a place like a bus station and
she was fascinated. The lady had on a long winter
coat and a furry hat with two white feathers on the
side. She carried an umbrella on her right arm, an
enormous pocketbook on her left, and leaning against
her leg was a large shopping bag running over with
stuff. She'd been standing at the counter long enough
to buy reading matter for a year but when she turned
away, after going through a very complicated money
routine with the clerk, all she had was a candy bar.

"Hey, Estelle? You there?"

"I'm watching a lady buy a candy bar," said Estelle.
"Do you see her?"

D.R. hadn't noticed the old lady, but now he looked
over toward the magazine stand. They watched as she
stooped over to put the candy in her shopping bag.
The bag was so full of stuff she had to shift the parcels
on top just to make room for the candy. Estelle held
her breath for fear the bag would tear and spill its
contents all over the floor. But it held, and after a
good deal of ruffling and shuffling and hassling with her

umbrella and pocketbook, the old lady finally got herself together enough to pick up the shopping bag and walk around the corner toward the loading zones.

"Wasn't she beautiful?" said Estelle.

"She was very far out," said D.R. "Estelle, listen. We've got to talk."

"What do you want to talk about, D.R.?"

"I don't know," said D.R. He had to clear his throat. He cleared it twice, but it was still raspy when he said, "It just seems like everything's getting weird, that's all. I feel totally weird."

"Maybe it's something you ate," said Estelle.

"It's not anything I ate. It's this sense I've got. It's this feeling."

"You sound very far away," said Estelle. "Is this a long-distance call?"

"You're the one who sounds far away," said D.R.

"I sound far away?" said Estelle.

"Yes. You're talking to me very weird."

"I'm talking to you weird?" said Estelle.

"Yes you are. And you know it too. You're fucking me up is what you're doing."

"I'm fucking you up?" said Estelle.

"*Yes.* I feel entirely fucked up. I feel like I'm going out of my goddamn mind if you want to know the truth. And you're giving me all this shit over the telephone."

"I'm giving you shit?" asked Estelle.

"*Yes!*" D.R. yelled. "Yes! You are."

"Well listen, D.R. Do you mind if I ask you a question?"

"Ask me anything you want to," said D.R.

Estelle said, "Do you think you're giving me shit too, by any chance?"

"If I am I don't mean to," said D.R.

"You mean you don't know if you are or not," said Estelle.

"I mean I don't mean to, if I am. But you mean to. You're really fucking me up."

Estelle said, "What if I told you you were fucking me up just as bad?"

"Well, I'd probably talk to you about it," said D.R. "At least I'm trying to talk to you."

"That's very good of you," said Estelle. "That's very decent. I appreciate it."

"Jesus, Estelle, you're really coming on to me weird, did you know that?"

"I think the whole conversation's weird," said Estelle.

D.R. waited before he spoke again. He cleared his throat, then cleared it again. "Well see if this makes it seem any weirder to you."

"What?" asked Estelle.

"I said see if this makes it seem any weirder to you."

"See what?"

"I haven't said it yet. I'm getting ready to say something."

"Oh," said Estelle. "Excuse me."

D.R. cleared his throat. "I'm thinking the thing to do is for me to go on out to my sister's house by myself. Before I take you."

"What's so weird about that?" asked Estelle.

"Doesn't that seem sort of weird to you?"

"Not really. You want to go check it out, is that right?"

"Yeah. Just check it out. Kind of ease into it with them."

"That seems cool to me," said Estelle. "Why did you think that was so weird?"

"I don't know. Now that I've said it, it doesn't seem so weird any more."

"Is that all you were going to tell me?" asked Estelle. "Is that why you got me on the phone?"

"That's it," said D.R.

"Can I come out of the phone booth now?"

"You're free to go anywhere you like," said D.R.

"Thank you," said Estelle. She hung up then and came out of her booth. But D.R. stayed in his to call his sister Marcella and tell her he was coming out to see her after a while.

 *Arrival*

If your niece is on one arm and your nephew is on the other, does that automatically balance it? Or do their actual weights have to be accounted for? If their weights have to be accounted for, it's hopeless. But if you can go by how it feels, if a nephew automatically balances a niece, out of their own internal, organic, cosmic, natural reasons, then it's cool and doesn't matter if this particular nephew knocks me and my niece and all of us on our asses.

"Herschel you stop that!" Marcella yelled from the kitchen. She was just coming out with a tray of Pepsi-Colas for D.R. and the kids. Herschel had started wrestling with D.R. as soon as he got out of the bus in the driveway. He was nine and about three sizes too big for his age. He wasn't fat, he was just big and husky, in the mold of his father Doyle, who was six feet three. Herschel wrestled with D.R. coming through the house, as he hugged Marcella and gave his niece Debbie a lift and a brief ride across the kitchen, and then he continued to wrestle him right on out the back door and into the yard. When Debbie wanted to join in, D.R. suggested they not wrestle any more, but play the lift-and-swing game like in the old days. That was okay for a minute or two. Herschel swung from the right arm and Debbie swung from the left, and for a minute or two the lift-and-swing game was cool. But then Herschel decided that what he wanted to do was lift and swing and wrestle at the same time, which he proceeded to do by getting a firm lock around D.R.'s waist with his legs as he hung suspended from D.R.'s sagging forearm. That was when Marcella mercifully appeared with the Pepsis.

"You stop that, I said," Marcella snapped at Herschel. Then, her voice softer as she placed the tray on the little green metal table, "Your Uncle David is *tired,* honey. He's been traveling."

"Where have you been traveling?" asked Debbie. Debbie was four. She wore glasses, watched TV and drank a lot of Pepsis.

"Well, all around," said D.R. "East. West. North. South. All around, actually."

"How come you're so tired?" asked Herschel. Herschel had always been D.R.'s big buddy on previous visits. But he was in Little League this year, and was so good at it he'd gotten a little arrogant.

"Well," said D.R. "Let's just say traveling can be pretty hard work sometimes."

"I've traveled, and I don't think it's hard," said Herschel.

"I've traveled all the way to Kentucky," said Debbie.

"That's enough, now," said Marcella. "You kids go on around in front and wait for Daddy."

Debbie leaped at the suggestion. Carrying her Pepsi in both hands she ran around the house yelling "Daddy, Daddy!" Herschel was a little more cool. He went away, but not so far that he couldn't hear what was being said by the grownups.

"Go on," said Marcella. But Herschel sat down where he was and began to play with the ice in his glass.

"Lord I think I'm the one's tired," said Marcella. She filled her glass from the quart-size Pepsi bottle and carried it around to the front of her chair. Slowly she eased herself backward and down, moaning under her breath as if every bone in her body pained her terribly.

Marcella was only twenty-eight, but one of her games was pretending to be about three times that old. She and Doyle had been married nearly ten years, but she didn't look any older than most twenty-eight-year-old women with two children. She was tall and rangy and rather flat-chested. In high school she had been famous for her legs. Girls still played high-school basketball in Kentucky in those days. She had been quite a good athlete, but it was her long, trim legs that made her truly distinctive on the floor. Men had always been hot for Marcella because of her legs although she had never allowed herself to acknowledge that. In the old days in the mountains she had seen herself as a big goof. Now she saw herself as some sort of senior citizen with a sense of humor. She and Doyle only had the two children, but Marcella made it seem as if she was an ancient matriarch of an enormous brood that had used up her life and left her a feeble old crone before her time.

"Lord but it's awful to get old," she said as she settled back in her chair. "I wouldn't ever do it if I was you, David. I declare I wouldn't."

"You always say that," said D.R.

Marcella grunted. In a voice trembling with mock decrepitude she said, "You better listen to an old woman's advice now, child. I declare you better."

She laughed at her role and her lines. Then she took a sip of Pepsi, turned to Divine Right and with a sad expression on her face told him about their Uncle Emmit, who was close to death at the homeplace in Kentucky.

## Emmit's Condition

David I don't know if you remember the Godsey
family or not, but they used to run that little store
where the post office was there at the mouth of Trace
Fork when me and you was kids. Mr. Godsey was the
postmaster in those days. After he died they give it to
Mrs. Godsey, and she's run it and the store ever since,
although the Lord only knows why Trace Fork would
have a post office, they ain't over three families lives
on that creek any more. They've stripped that whole
holler and then auger-mined it and most of the people
that lived there when me and you did's moved away.
But, Mrs. Godsey's there, and it's her that's been
writing me letters about Emmit. She written me twice
in the last two weeks, and I written her once and sent
her our phone number. I told her to call me collect
any time she thinks I need to know something about
Emmit, and so yesterday she called and said the poor
old feller's worse off than ever. She's really a dear
woman, Mrs. Godsey is. She's known us I don't know
how many years. She was Grandma's age. She remem-
bers when Grandma and Granddad first moved to
Trace Fork when they was just a young married
couple. You ought to remember her, David, you used
to go in there and buy candy from her when you
wasn't any bigger than Debbie. Kind of a skinny
woman, with the sweetest little voice you ever heard.
Well, anyway, the poor thing, she's none too well herself, and I don't think she's actually been up to the
homeplace to see Emmit. But she sends her boy
Leonard up, and from what Leonard says, Emmit's so
weak now he barely can get out of bed. Said he can
get up enough to do his cooking, and goes out to feed
his chickens and his rabbits. Emmit keeps rabbits now
Leonard said, and manages to feed 'em. But said he
couldn't garden, and when something goes wrong
around the place he can't fix it, and that he's just going

to have to have some help or be moved out of there, if he lives at all. I told Mrs. Godsey on the phone that we'd try to see about helping him some way, but I swan I don't know of a thing any of us can do. He won't leave the place, he's the contrariest old man that ever was. I'm worried sick about him, and Doyle is too. Mrs. Godsey's letters are in the house. After supper I'll get 'em out and let you read 'em.

## Departure

Ordinarily the talk about their Uncle Emmit would have led D.R. and Marcella on into a general rap about other relatives, and the old days as children in Kentucky. But there were too many distractions for them to go very far with it that afternoon. D.R. was thinking about Estelle waiting at the bus station, and Marcella kept interrupting herself to hassle her children. About fifteen minutes into their conversation Herschel spilled his Pepsi and came demanding more, as Debbie started wailing around in the front yard. Marcella waited for Debbie to come running around the house to be comforted, but when she kept on crying where she was, Marcella jumped to her feet and ran around to see what was the matter. D.R. poured Herschel's glass full of Pepsi and started to refill his own. But then he decided the thing to do was go in and call Estelle and see what was going down back at the old bus station.

"Herschel old friend, why don't you stay here and guard this Pepsi-Cola while I go in the house and use the telephone. Okay?"

"Who are you going to call?" asked Herschel.

"I've got to call a man about a dog."

Herschel said, "You do not."

D.R. said, "I'm going to call the weatherman and ask him to send us some rain."

"You're a turd," said Herschel.

"That's no way to talk to your friend."

"You're not my friend," said Herschel.

D.R. said, "I thought me and you were good old buddies."

"You're a queer," said Herschel. "Why don't you go somewhere and have a car wreck?"

"If I did that we wouldn't be able to wrestle any more, now would we?"

Instantly Herschel leaped onto D.R.'s lap. Together they fell out of the lawn chair onto the ground. D.R. started tickling Herschel in the ribs which made him squeal with laughter, but fight back twice as hard. Herschel crawled onto D.R.'s back as D.R. struggled to his feet. Together they staggered toward the house, scuffling and laughing, both red in the face from the effort.

By the time D.R. and Herschel had wrestled their way back into the house Marcella had evacuated Debbie to the bathroom, where she was having Medi-Quik sprayed on a not very badly damaged knee. Even without Debbie's commotion in the bathroom it would have been impossible to make a phone call with a nine-year-old orangutan on his back, so D.R. told Marcella he was going out to a pay phone to make a long-distance call. Marcella tried to get him to use their house phone, but when D.R. said he wanted to go out she told him about a pay phone over in the shopping center. At the mention of the words "shopping center" Herschel started screaming and yelling for permission to go along. When it was clear he wasn't going to be allowed to he yelled "I hate you" at D.R. and slammed the door as hard as he could. As soon as D.R. got in the bus he fished a roach out of the ashtray, and by the time he found the phone booth in the shopping center he was blessedly stoned.

## A Very Difficult Day

"Hello?"

"Hello, Estelle? This is David Ray Davenport, the famous truth seeker. I'm calling to see if you or any member of your immediate family might have a truth to tell today."

"Where are you?" asked Estelle.

"Ahh," said D.R. "A good question. A very good question. Right now I'd say I'm cruising at about ten thousand feet. And what's that I spy below me there, off to the right, nestled in a little cluster of twenty-one-thousand-dollar suburban houses on the outskirts of Cincinnati? Why, I do believe it's one of those hippie buses, painted up all garish and weird, surrounded by children and a smattering of curious adult on-lookers. But wait! That curious onlooker smashing the headlights with his fists. That's no adult. That's a kid! A two-hundred-pound, nine-year-old kid. And look! Oh my God! The kid! He's gone wild! He's beating the poor hippie about the head and ears, he's hitting him with a Pepsi-Cola bottle. Help, help, someone! Someone call for help!"

"Where are you?" asked Estelle.

"Ma'm, I regret I am unable to give out that kind of information. Heavy stuff is going on. Mad villains are everywhere. Insanity rules, and only a total clamp on all information will save the day. I can, however, reveal this much: my nine-year-old nephew is actually a dwarf with incredible supernatural powers. Only an hour ago, before my very eyes, right in my own hand, by god, he transformed a Pepsi-Cola bottle into a turd. Imagine. A turd. It was awful. It was disgusting. And then, you'll never believe what he did next. There I am sitting in the back yard of this little twenty-one-thousand-dollar suburban home with a big piece of shit in my hand, and he says: you're going to have a car wreck. He lays this curse on me right there, he says, Motherfucker you are about to *crash!* It's been really heavy, ma'm. I've really had a very difficult day.

 ## *The Difficult Day Continues*

"It sounds like it," said Estelle.

D.R. asked Estelle what kind of day she was having.

Estelle thought it over. "Kind of thoughtful," she said.

"Kind of thoughtful, eh?" said D.R.

"Yeah," said Estelle. "I've been doing a lot of thinking."

D.R. asked her what she'd been thinking about.

"Different things."

D.R. asked her to tell him about one of them.

"I guess I've mainly been thinking about us not stopping in Vincennes last night," she said. "Do you remember that?"

"Where?" asked D.R.

"Vincennes. I wanted to stop and get a motel, and rest some. I wanted to take a bath, sleep in a good bed, we talked about it, do you remember?"

"Sure," said D.R. "I remember that. That was in Vincennes."

"Well," said Estelle. "That's what I've been thinking about."

"All day?" D.R. asked.

"Just about," said Estelle.

"What have you been thinking about that for?"

"I don't know," said Estelle. "I guess I just really wanted to stop at a motel in Vincennes. I guess I was just awfully disappointed that you didn't want to, and it's just stayed on my mind."

"I'll be darned."

"You'll be what?" asked Estelle.

"Darned."

"Darned, did you say?"

"Yep," said D.R. "I'll be darned."

"What else will you be besides darned?"

"I don't know," said D.R. "What else is there to be?"

"Quite a lot of things, actually," said Estelle.

"Well," said D.R. "Don't tell me about them."

"I wasn't going to," said Estelle.

"Yes you were," said D.R. "But don't. I don't want to hear about it."

Estelle asked D.R. what he did want to hear about.

"I don't want to hear about a goddamn fucking thing."

"Well, I guess the thing for me to do is hang up, then," said Estelle.

"Where are you, a phone booth?"

"I'm at the ticket counter, D.R., you paged me, remember?"

"Are there people around?"

"A few."

"Can they hear you?"

"Probably."

"There are people around me too," said D.R. "But they can't hear me, and I fucking well can't hear them, and I like that very much."

"Are you in a phone booth?"

"I'm in a fantastic phone booth."

Estelle said, "Well I'm not. And I think I'm probably disturbing the ticket man, although he is certainly being very nice about me using his phone. So I guess that I'm going to do, D.R., is hang up now, and if you come down here after a while I'll see you. Okay?"

"That sounds about right."

"Well good-bye then."

"Yeah. So long, Estelle."

"Good-bye, honey," said Estelle.

D.R. sat in the booth a long time, listening to the dial tone.

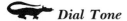 **Dial Tone**

I'm sitting in a phone booth on the sidewalk in a shopping center in Cincinnati, Ohio, listening to the dial tone. I am also counting the little holes in the ear and mouthpiece of the phone but that is only a secondary activity the dial tone is the soundtrack for. As far as I'm concerned, this dial tone is the most important activity going on in this whole shopping center right now, although that dumb fuck in the T-shirt and Bermuda shorts who just now peered in at me as he walked by would no doubt disagree. What that dumb fuck needs is to get his brain reamed out with the dull end of a dial tone some day and maybe he won't be so goddamn nosy. Goddamn nosiness anyhow. I don't give a goddamn what any of 'em out there do, I'm not nosy. As far as I'm concerned it's every bit one enormous colossal fucking goddamn bore. As far as I'm concerned, these sights I'm seeing through all these little windows in my booth are just bad movies projected from somewhere on the other side. I'm in a little room where the walls are movie screens, a very futuristic idea, you dig? Like, you don't go to movies any more. You don't go in some big room with a lot of other people. You just drop your dime in the slot and go in a little one-man booth by yourself and they project weird movies onto the walls, play movies all around you, under your feet, over your head, and what you do is sit on this little seat and pick up the soundtrack over a telephone, and what the soundtrack is today ladies and gentlemen is pure, uninterrupted dial tone.

Yes sir. Stick with us and we'll show an ever-changing panorama to your eyes while your ears are soothed by wonderful dial tone. It's like a long column of dark blue smoke winding through your ear and down all the little avenues of your brain. It curls, it winds, it coils, there's something very snake-like about a dial tone. It's smoky, but there's a lot about it that makes you think of snakes as well. It's like a snake so long its head and tail are completely lost, all you can see is his long smooth body rippling around your brain, sliding in it and through it and up it and down it, along all the secret avenues and hidden passageways and tunnels of your brain. Don't be nervous about this snake. Treat this snake right and he'll do the right things inside your head, watch him and he will show you places in your brain you didn't even know were there. And yet, it's just a sound, an ordinary dial tone on the telephone, it's just a simple soundtrack for the movie about a very angry lady standing around outside the theater, waiting her turn inside.

*Calling the Flash*

It was such a good movie, in fact, D.R. couldn't resist calling the Anaheim Flash and telling him about it. He pressed the lever down, let it up again, put in two nickels, dialed O, and when the operator answered he asked her to put him through collect to the Anaheim Flash in Anaheim, California.

"Where are you now?" asked the Flash.

"I'm at the movies in Cincinnati, Ohio," said D.R.

"Far out," said the Flash. "What's on?"

"Well," said D.R. "Right now it's a short subject about this lady waiting outside a phone booth for this freak to quit talking and come out."

"That sounds like a pretty good movie," said the Flash.

"Listen," said D.R. "You obviously ain't heard the latest yet. Cincinnati is the new film capital of the world. There's been an incredible revolution here. I mean, like, it's so new it's only about half an hour old. I mean man you talk about interface, I mean, like Cincinnati is fucking Frontier City. You know what they got here? This is no shit. They got these little one-man theaters all over town. Pay your dime, go in, sit down, and the whole thing comes alive with movies from every which direction. It's really heavy stuff, man, I mean, like this lady, I mean she's about to go *crazy* right on the fucking sidewalk. It's super far out."

"What about yourself?" asked the Flash.

"You mean me?" said D.R.

"Yeah," said the Flash. "You don't sound too goddamn sane yourself. What are you on, anyway?"

"What am I on?" said D.R.

"Yeah," said the Flash. "It's an ordinary enough question."

"What am I on," said D.R. "I think that what I am on is intensity. Intensity and precision. I feel very intense and precise today."

"Is that what they're dealing in Cincinnati?" asked the Flash.

D.R. laughed. "Yeah. You get it out of the vending machines in these little theaters."

"Well," said the Flash. "It sounds like old Cincinnati is really where it's at."

"Most definitely," said D.R. "Without question. Most definitely."

"Listen," said the Flash. "Where's Estelle?"

"The bus station. Hey Flash, listen: is it cool that I called? I mean, I know this is on your bill. But you got money, right? You still got all your money?"

"Still got it," said the Flash.

"Okay. And you can stake me to this call, right? I mean I don't want to impose it . . ."

"Carte blanche, man," said the Flash. "You sound to me like you need a friend."

D.R. laughed. "Well, we all need friends, Flash. But I'm all right. I've just got stuff on my mind. A lot of new stuff is going on. I mean, two days ago I couldn't even talk. I've been kind of bummed out, but I feel pretty good now. Hey Flash?"

"Yeah, man."

"Listen, I really thank you for the use of that card. It really saved our ass."

"No sweat," said the Flash. "What's Estelle doing at the bus station?"

"Hanging around. Hey Flash, guess what my nephew said this afternoon. He's this nine-year-old jockstrap in the Little League, see, really far-out kid. I come in, our first conversation he says, You're a turd. And then he says, You're a queer, why don't you go out and have a car wreck?"

"Nice kid," said the Flash.

"No man, I mean he's far out. It's pretty wild around here."

"So you've already seen your sister?"

"Yeah, I was out there. Say, man, what time is it anyway?"

"It's eight o'clock in California. Listen, old friend, I'm worried about you. No offense, but it sounds to me like Cincinnati ain't no healthy place for a righteous dude to be."

"Ahh," said D.R. "It's all just a movie. It's just another quadruple feature happening simultaneously all around, it's okay."

"That's what you say," said the Flash. "But that

ain't how you sound. I'm afraid you're not trusting in the Lord enough."

D.R. laughed. The Anaheim Flash asked him what was funny.

"What you said. I heard that as a line of dialogue from the lady in the movie. It's pretty funny."

The Anaheim Flash asked D.R. how the lady was getting along.

"Not too good, I'm afraid. The freak won't get out of the phone booth. She's got her nose up against the screen now, peering right in on him."

"Why don't the freak kiss her?" said the Flash.

"Flash, you're a genius," said D.R. And D.R. puckered up and leaned forward and kissed the movie screen as the woman, horrified, drew away.

"Did he kiss her?" asked the Flash.

But D.R. was laughing too hard to answer. He laughed so hard and so long he finally had to tell the Flash it didn't look like he was going to be able to go on with the conversation. The Flash said he guessed he'd hang up then.

"But listen, man, stay cool, you hear? You take care, and tell Estelle she's much loved, okay? Tell her Angel really wants to hear from her."

"Right," said D.R. "And I thank you for talking to me, I really do."

"Anytime, man," said the Flash.

The Anaheim Flash hung up then, and D.R. went on listening to the dial tone.

 **Doyle**

When D.R. left the phone booth he intended to go directly back downtown to the bus station. But then when he passed Clark Street he figured since he was that close he'd pop in on Marcella and see what those people were up to. When it turned out that what they were up to was supper D.R. didn't see any way to leave gracefully without eating something, especially since Marcella had fixed a place for him and had served smoked ham and chow-chow in celebration of his arrival. The family was already seated at the table in the kitchen when D.R. walked in, except for Marcella who was stirring something on the stove. Doyle was at the head of the table browsing through the *Enquirer* when he looked up and saw D.R. in the doorway.

"Dadburn your hide, where you been?" Doyle shouted. He scooted his chair back and got to his feet so hard the dishes on the table rattled. "I come home early on account of you and there you was out and gone already. How you doing, Buddy, I de*clare* it's mighty good to see you."

Doyle came across the floor like a coal truck and gathered D.R. into his arms. Then he stepped back and took D.R.'s hand in both his own and pumped vigorously up and down.

"I said to Mars I said dadburn the like of him anyhow, me taking off work early to come and see him, and then him not even be here. Where you been, boy, you 'bout to miss your supper."

"Don't listen to him, David," said Marcella. "He's tickled to have you as an excuse to quit early."

"Daddy home early," said Debbie.

Herschel got out of his chair and crossed the room to where the two men were standing. As they talked he tried to worm in among their legs and stand between them.

"Here now, you little sneak, you sit down, we're getting ready to eat."

"I want to sit next to Uncle David," said Herschel.

"You sit where you always sit," said Doyle. "David's place is all laid out."

Herschel made a face of disappointment, but he obeyed his father. He dropped to his hands and knees, crawled under the table and came up on the other side.

"Feistiest thing ever was," Doyle said proudly. "He's turned into a regular devil."

"You ne'en to brag about it," said Marcella.

"I ain't a bragging," said Doyle. "I'm just stating the plain facts. Ain't that right, David?"

"That's right," said D.R. "Doyle's just telling the facts."

"What I want to know is how that bus of yours is running," said Doyle. "I told Mars when you called the other day, I said I bet that boy's got car trouble. She said you'd of said so if you had and you know what I said? I said shoot, the thing about David with his cars is he don't know when he's got trouble and when he ain't."

Doyle broke out laughing at his joke, and D.R. laughed too. Doyle was a mechanic, and partners with his cousin Vernis in a filling station and garage. The year before, when D.R. had stopped off at Marcella's and Doyle's Urge had had a cracked valve and D.R. didn't know it. That anybody could drive a car with a cracked valve and not know it amazed Doyle, and fascinated him at the same time. Doyle had given Urge a valve job for free, and Vernis had banged a few dents out of the body. If they'd known at the time that D.R.'s intention was to use his bus to help Eddie transport about a zillion bricks of marijuana to Chicago they'd have been less generous with their work. But the general freaky appearance of the bus, and, indeed, of Divine Right himself, had disturbed them not at all. Doyle understood that his brother-in-law was some sort of mild outlaw. But he assumed, as Marcella assumed, that whatever it was D.R. was into was only a phase, as Doyle's own youthful outlawry had been a phase, and it never occurred to any of them

to withdraw their affection just because the kid was
in a phase. 'Til Doyle was drafted into the Army,
back in the 1950s, he had terrorized the roads of Eastern Kentucky as a coal truck driver. In the Army he'd
been court-martialed twice for going AWOL, and
general insubordination. He spent eight weeks in the
stockade at Fort Hood, Texas, and described them
later as the best eight weeks of his entire Army career.
Doyle was a settled family man now, a father, a tax-
payer and, as of the previous month, a member of the
Church of God. But there was a natural empathy between him and Divine Right, and in spite of the
widening differences in their lives they remained
among each other's favorite people.

 **Salvation**

When everybody was seated they bowed their heads
while Doyle asked the blessing. D.R. had never heard
his brother-in-law ask the blessing before and he
couldn't resist keeping his eyes open to watch him.
Marcella had been a churchgoer all her life, and the
kids had been going to Sunday School since they could
walk. But the blessing had never been part of meal-
time in their house before, and D.R. was a little as-
tounded. What was surprising was the quality of
Doyle's prayer. It was short and simple, but, for Doyle,
strangely articulate and obviously sincerely felt. He
thanked the Lord for the food they were about to eat,
for the house they lived in and the comforts they enjoyed. He especially thanked Him for David's safe
arrival, and for the privilege of gathering together as
a family once again. Doyle seemed to sense that the
ritual surprised D.R., for when he had said Amen and
Marcella started serving the food, he began talking

about his recent conversion and baptism into the church Marcella had been attending for years.

"Of course," said Doyle, "I'm new in it, there's a lot I don't understand. But as far as feeling good about something, David, I never felt any better about a thing in my whole life than I do this."

"We've already got him taking up the collection," said Marcella.

Doyle laughed. "I'm surprised they trust the likes of me with their money."

D.R. laughed at that, and went on to congratulate Doyle on his decision. "But I have to say I'm pretty surprised," he added.

"Honey, you ain't a bit more surprised than I am, let me tell you. Why sometimes I even forget I've gone and done it. At work I'll rip out a big cuss, and along about four in the afternoon I get to thinking how good a big old beer would taste after work. But then I'll find myself in church on Sunday morning, singing hymns and listening to that little preacher, and it's sort of like waking up out of a dream."

D.R. asked Doyle to tell him how he came to his decision. The question embarrassed Doyle a little, and he took a big mouthful of food to keep from having to answer right away. D.R. watched him as he chewed. Doyle had always been very lean as a young man, but in the last few years he'd begun to accumulate flesh around his middle, and in his neck and cheeks. His face was losing its angularity and taking on a round-ness that made him seem boyish and middle-aged at the same time. Doyle was thirty-four now, but as he bit down on his food the tendons in his big jaw flexed beneath his skin, and for a second the old toughness, and even meanness, of his youth was restored to his face, and for some reason D.R. found that very mov-ing. He loved Doyle. And he loved Marcella. When he wasn't with them he really didn't think about them all that much. But now, sitting with them in their kitchen, sharing food, looking at their faces, at the faces of the children, smelling the raw, familiar odor of their home and hearing the old familiar notes in their strange voices, D.R. suddenly felt a little overwhelmed. It was a rush, a strange high that caused tears to work behind his eyes, and some deep longing to stir inside his chest. If D.R. had been called on to speak just then he wouldn't have been able to. Doyle was having his own difficulties speaking, but at last he swallowed his food and in a low and more serious tone he began to tell about the process of his salvation.

### Doyle's Story

"I think the thing that finally got me serious about it, David, was my brother Clarence getting killed in a rock fall, down home, back in the spring. I don't know if you ever knew Clarence or not . . ."

"I remember him," said D.R. "He used to work at Blue Diamond."

"That's him," Doyle went on. "Older than me, and not so long, as he used to say it. Of course it's been a while since he worked at Blue Diamond. They shut down over there right after we all moved up here. I remember that because Clarence come up here to live a while, but he never liked it enough to stay, and for the last nine, ten year he's been in and out of them little old dog-hole mines, mostly over on Second Creek, and for a while there on Trace Fork 'til they stripped it. He was working for the Combs brothers over on Second Creek last March when a piece of rock fell on him. The whole roof caved in and crushed him, just like that. He never drawed another breath after that rock caught him."

"I didn't know that, Doyle," D.R. said solemnly. "I'm sorry to hear it."

"Well, it was a sad time, I tell you it was," said Doyle. "It like to broke poor Mommy's heart. She was his favorite, you know. He was her first, and he lived there next door to her, and doted on her, and took care of her, him and Carlene. It was just the worst thing that could have happened in Mommy's life, and there it was, him dead just all of a sudden, and there wasn't a thing on earth anybody could do about it except bury him."

"Clarence's funeral was the saddest time," said Marcella.

"Awful sad," said Doyle. "Just awful sad. We went home for it of course. You remember the church there at the mouth of the creek, I guess. I doubt they's over twenty members of that church left around there, so many's moved away. But for Clarence's funeral it was full, people come from far away as Hyden, and Hazard. They was one of his old Army buddies from Pike County heard about it and come. Brother Fugate preached, and there was singing, and old Mr. Stacy got up and preached some too. What was bad about it though, as far as Mommy was concerned, was Clarence never had been saved. And so naturally there was a lot of talk about the rest of us. Mommy cried and cried, and pleaded with me, and my brother Lee. She cried all weekend and pleaded with us to join the church. I don't know if you remember Lee or not, David . . ."

"I remember him," said D.R. "I remember all these people. Brother Fugate baptized me and Marcella right there in Trace Fork, I sure remember him."

"Well," Doyle went on. "You can imagine how it was then. To please Mommy, and ease her all I could, me and Lee promised her we'd think about it. I don't know what Lee's done, I ain't heard from him since the funeral, but I got back up here and that whole

business was all I could think about. But the funny
thing is, although I wouldn't want Mommy to know
this, it really wasn't anything that she said that made
me change my mind."

Doyle paused then to eat some more, and take a
drink of milk.

 ## Doyle's Dreams

"Doyle started having dreams," said Marcella.

"I did," said Doyle. "It was the unusualest thing
that ever was. After we got back from Clarence's
funeral I commenced to dream about him ever night.
And if it wouldn't be him it would be somebody else
that had died. My father, your all's father, or somebody in my acquaintance whose death I knew something about. It was just death ever where I looked,
it was all I could think about. I got afraid I was going
to die, or Marcella, or one of the kids, you can ask
Marcella here, it was really an awful thing to go
through. Nothing like that had ever happened to me
before, and I just couldn't understand it. Ever night
I'd go to bed and lay there all night thinking about
death and dead people and dying and I'd think: well
surely I'll get over this tomorrow. But then when I'd
get to work there it would be, right up in front of my
mind. I couldn't hardly work. Vernis noticed it and
asked me about it. Some of our customers even noticed
something was wrong. This all went on I guess a
month or more 'til finally I just had to do something
about it. And so Marcella called her preacher up and
asked him to come over and talk to me about it."

"He's a real nice man, David," said Marcella. "He's
from Kentucky too, just smart as a tack. You'd really
like him."

"Half of Cincinnati's from Kentucky," said Doyle. "This is briar-hopper country sure enough."

"How well I know," said D.R.

"I'd say it improves the place about five hundred per cent myself," said Marcella, and everybody came out of their seriousness to laugh hard at that.

When they'd hushed, D.R. asked Doyle what he had said to the preacher.

"Shoot. I just told him the truth of it. I told him I thought I was going crazy. I said I was having dreams and couldn't sleep and couldn't work, and terrible headaches. I told him I was afraid I was about to die. But that little preacher was the sweetest to me that you ever saw. I was about half embarrassed to be talking to somebody about that kind of stuff, but I mean he seemed to know what was going on in me even before I told him. He asked me if I was a Christian. I said no. He asked me if I'd like to be one. I said I hadn't thought about it. You know what he did when I said that? He bust out laughing. Just laughed and laughed and laughed, I didn't know what to think. Then he said, oh yes you have. I said what do you mean? He said oh yes you have been thinking about it. Then suddenly he quit laughing and looked me right in the eye and said, what are you afraid to die for? I said ain't everybody? He said we ain't talking about everybody, we're talking about *you*. What are you so scared to die for? What makes you think that's so awful? And just about the time I begun to wonder if he was crazy why he got out his Bible and commenced to read about Jesus, and about dying, and about being reborn, and I begun to see what he meant. He must of talked to me two or three hours that night. And the next night, and the next."

"He stayed 'til two o'clock in the morning one time," said Marcella.

"He can just talk rings around you. He can say stuff you think ain't never been said before, he's really clever. He come over the fourth time on Friday night, and guess what he said. He said he wasn't going to come see me no more. He said if I wanted to know what he had to say he was preaching ever Sunday morning at eleven o'clock, and for me to be there. And I ain't missed a Sunday since. And after three times I confessed, and then about a month ago they baptized me, and I've slept good ever since."

## The Second Departure

When D.R. got ready to leave the house again after supper he didn't tell Marcella and Doyle he was going to the bus station. He said the call he'd tried to put through earlier in the afternoon hadn't happened, and that he wanted to go out to a pay phone and try again. Doyle laughed, thinking he understood: D.R. was going out to call up his sweetheart in California, and he didn't want a bunch of prying kinfolks listening in.

"I don't blame you," said Doyle. "You can't get any privacy with nosy people like Marcella around."

Marcella put her hands on her hips. "I beg your pardon." Then she doubled up her fists and put up her dukes and said she guessed she'd just have to teach Doyle a lesson. Doyle made a fist too, and swung it at Marcella slowly enough for her to grab his arm and commence to bite it. "I'll eat you up if you're not careful," she said.

"Not in front of everybody," said Doyle, and he winked at D.R. as Marcella blushed and tried to kick Doyle in the ass.

"You big goof, you get out of my kitchen."

"Ha," said Doyle, leaping out of the way. "See how mean she is, David? You're going to have to tame down while David's here, Miss Pritchet. Me and David just might beat you up good."

"Shoot," said Marcella. "Kinfolks sticks together where we come from, don't they, David?"

Doyle said, "*Get* her, David. Let's just beat the tar out of her."

Doyle moved toward Marcella then. She squealed and ran to the corner of the kitchen and grabbed the mop. D.R. laughed and for a moment pretended he was going to help Doyle whip Marcella.

But then he backed away and said he better go on and make his telephone call. Doyle walked him to the door.

"You need any money or anything?" said Doyle.

D.R. shook his head. "No. It's cool."

"We'll see you after a while then," said Doyle.

D.R. waved and Doyle closed the door behind him.


## Parking

There were several empty parking places near the entrance to the bus station, but D.R. felt like putting Urge back where he had been that morning, just for old time's sake. He circled the block and pulled into what he thought was the same space, but once he turned the motor off he wasn't so sure that was it. Maybe it's the next one, he told himself, and he backed up one space and turned the motor off again. This one felt a little better, but it still wasn't right. It wasn't balanced. That morning there had been a Fiat in front of Urge and a Ford behind, and D.R. was sorry they had been moved. If the Fiat and the Ford had remained in place they would have balanced it, but with them gone there just wasn't anything out there for a fellow to depend upon. What D.R. really wished for in his heart of hearts was to see a sign that said, "This is where you parked this morning." As it was, there was no indication of any kind that D.R. had ever been on that street before, except the memory of it in his mind which he just didn't feel like trusting at all right now. D.R. moved the bus three more times before he finally just arbitrarily chose two lines to park between. It seemed like a very reckless thing to do, but he was so late getting back to the bus station as it was he really didn't have much choice.

## The Search Imagined

As D.R. pushed through the heavy doors of the terminal he made up a little drama in his mind about how it would be if Estelle was not there waiting for him. He saw himself entering the big waiting room and first looking toward the seats they had occupied that morning. Estelle was not there. The only person in that whole row of seats was a woman with two children, one of them a baby asleep in her lap. D.R. walked by her to the seats they had sat in and paced up and down in front of them, looking at them thinking: *Estelle sat here,* and *I sat there.* He looked at the seats, and all around the big room for some sign of Estelle. He considered asking the woman with the children if she had seen a girl in jeans and a Mexican shirt, but she looked as if she didn't want to be disturbed. Her baby was asleep, and she was half asleep herself. For a second in his fantasy the woman with the children turned into Estelle. She didn't stay Estelle very long but for a moment it was very convincing. She had Estelle's dark, round eyes, and her skin was dark and mellow like Estelle's. She looked up at

D.R. once, sort of blankly, perhaps wearily. Then she was no longer Estelle, which was good because if she had stayed Estelle the fantasy would have ended without the kind of freak out D.R. wanted to go through over his lost love. He glanced at the half-asleep mother again, then walked away quickly to look for Estelle in the coffee shop.

Estelle was not in the coffee shop.

She was not at the ticket counter.

She was not at the magazine stand, or over by the lockers, nor was she outside in the loading zones, leaning against a post. The whole big sleepy bus station yawned Estelle's not being there and closed its eyes again. D.R. tried to wake it up. He tried to force its eyelids open with sticks, and when it yawned he tried to stir it by pouring tar into its mouth. But the mouth slammed shut and swallowed everything that had ever happened until that moment. The hours D.R. and Estelle had been together in that bus station slipped down its long esophagus into subterranean bowels, and no amount of screaming would bring it back again.

D.R. was muttering little fretful cries by the time he went into the phone booth Estelle had occupied. First he went into his own booth, then into hers. But Estelle was not there. He tried calling her, he memorized the number, went back to his booth and dialed. But Estelle didn't answer, and D.R. sat there on the stool muttering little fretful cries. He thought about calling the Anaheim Flash to tell him Estelle was gone, but somehow he didn't have the energy. But then suddenly he did have the energy, and he put in a dime and told the operator to get him the Anaheim Flash in Anaheim, California. The operator got the Flash's number, but a strange woman answered. The Flash was out. D.R. said it was an emergency. The woman asked if she could take a message. No, said D.R. There wasn't any message. But when the woman started to hang up he shouted Wait! Wait! Yes, there is a message. Tell him Estelle's gone. Tell him to find her and take care of her and tell me where she is. The woman said she would give the message to the Flash. D.R. said thank you and hung up, then sat there muttering little fretful cries as he tried to imagine where oh where in the whole wide world Estelle might have gone away to.

The only place left to check out was the ladies' rest room, and D.R. strolled around to it, and began pacing back and forth outside the door. As women went in and out he tried peering through the door but he couldn't see very much, and the women looked at him suspiciously. Then he thought of a scheme. He watched four women go in, then waited until they came out again. One, two, three, four. Obligingly, they came out as they went in, one behind the other, and when number four was out D.R. made his move. He threw open the door and yelled Estelle! He yelled it again, Estelle! Estelle! as he ran the length of the ladies' room, stooping to peer under the stalls. But Estelle wasn't there, and the only thing D.R. could think to do was go in the coffee shop, order a Coke, play a sad hillbilly song on the jukebox and feel his heart break into pieces.

### The Search

But that was all just a little trip in D.R.'s mind as he pushed through the front doors of the terminal. It wasn't real. D.R.'s heart was not really breaking. His head was, but not his heart. His head was shattering into splinters but his heart was beating on nice and strong as always. He went in the station, checked out the waiting room and the coffee shop, glanced around the magazine stand, and out into the loading zones.

He looked around the bus terminal for ten or fifteen minutes, and when Estelle didn't turn up he got in his bus and drove on back out to his sister's house.

## Saturday Morning

Divine Right stayed in Cincinnati all day Saturday and half of Sunday, but only two things of any real interest happened to him. He watched Saturday morning TV cartoons with the kids, and then on Sunday morning received an important message straight from God. More might have happened if D.R. had been open to it. Marcella wanted to get out the family photographs and talk about the old days, and Doyle wanted to take D.R. to his shop and teach him how to give Urge a tune-up. But it was obvious that D.R. was preoccupied and perhaps even upset about something and they didn't want to impose upon him. Marcella had sensed something was wrong when she got her first look at D.R. Friday afternoon. Doyle had felt it too as they were talking during supper. D.R. didn't get back to the house after his second phone call 'til way after everybody else's bedtime and so Marcella let him sleep through breakfast the next morning and Doyle went on to work by himself.

D.R. likely would have slept right on 'til noon if the kids hadn't turned the TV up so loud when the cartoons began. Marcella was outside spraying bug killer on the roses when she heard the noise. She had specifically told the kids to keep the volume down while their uncle was asleep, and when she heard it booming through the windows she got really mad. She rushed in the house, jerked both kids to their feet and was in the process of spanking their asses when Divine Right came into the living room, yawning.

Marcella snapped the television off and ordered the kids to go out in the yard and play. Debbie had begun to cry as soon as her mother burst into the room, and now she was clinging to Marcella's legs, pleading for forgiveness. Herschel almost cried but at the crucial moment he got hold of himself and stomped his foot on the floor instead.

*"Shoot,"* said Herschel. "I wanted to watch Johnny Hero."

"I'm going to Johnny Hero your little butt if you don't get out of here," Marcella snapped. Then, to D.R., "I'm sorry, David. This place is a madhouse this morning."

"That's all right," said D.R. "I feel pretty crazy myself." He was sleepy and groggy but he smiled and gestured with his hands to show that everything really was okay. It wasn't okay with Marcella yet. She was debating whether or not to whip Herschel for stomping the floor, and Debbie was being a perfect nuisance, clawing at her legs.

But the moment passed. Marcella bent over and picked Debbie up, and held her, and Herschel, who had been lurking in the doorway, slunk back in and sat down beside D.R., and very close to him, on the couch. Marcella told D.R. there was coffee made, and juice, and to call her when he was ready for breakfast. D.R. thanked her and said he would. Marcella carried Debbie outside with her, and when the storm door slammed, Herschel ran to the TV and tuned in Johnny Hero again.

 *Johnny Hero*

Last week's episode: Thanks to a timely warning by his ever-watchful guardian, Spider Woman, Johnny

Hero narrowly escaped being buried alive in an ava-
lanche caused by Trickster, the notorious henchman
of the Black Dragon. In a duel fought at the very
entrance to the forbidding Cave of Fear, Johnny sub-
dued Trickster and bound him tightly with silver web
provided by the ever-faithful Spider Woman. Thus
did Johnny Hero overcome another dangerous obstacle in his struggle to liberate the Crystal Crown
from the clutches of the Black Dragon, and lift gloom
from the Land of Mee.

As this week's story begins, we hear Johnny Hero
saying to Spider Woman, "Golly, Spider Woman, it
sure is dark in here."

"Here," says Spider Woman. "Eat this." And she
hands Johnny Hero a magic pearl. Except for the
whites of Johnny's blinking eyes, and a string of magic
pearls glowing like coals around Spider Woman's
neck, it is pitch dark in the cave. Spider Woman is
invisible, but her presence is always known by her
necklace of magic pearls. Moving across the dark now
toward Johnny's eyes is a pearl which seemingly has
detached itself from the string. As Johnny swallows it,
a circle of light slowly illumines the Cave of Fear.

"Wow," says Johnny. "Look at that!"

He points to a pool of water bubbling and steaming
in a shallow depression on the floor of the cave.

"Look!" Johnny exclaims with mounting excitement.
"There's another one! And another! Look! Golly,
Spider Woman, there's pools of steaming water every-
where!"

"Careful," says Spider Woman. "Those pools are
the footprints of the Black Dragon. They look shallow, but actually they're a thousand miles deep."

"Golly," says Johnny. "I sure would hate to . . .
*fall in one!*"

"You'd never be seen again," says Spider Woman.
"No one has ever survived a fall into the dragon's
footprint."

Suddenly Johnny Hero is seized by an idea. "But listen, Spider Woman. If those are the Black Dragon's footprints, I bet we could follow them *right to the dragon's lair!*"

Spider Woman is slow to reply. When she does, you can tell by the heaviness in her voice that she is troubled.

"That's right, Johnny. But there's just one thing."

"What's that, Spider Woman?"

"I can go with you no further. If you follow the footprints to the dragon's lair, you must go on alone."

"Alone!" Johnny exclaims. "But Spider Woman. Why?"

"I cannot explain now," says Spider Woman. "Are you willing to go on alone?"

"Golly," says Johnny. "I've *got* to go on. There's no one to take back the Crystal Crown and lift gloom from the Land of Mee but me."

"Very well," says Spider Woman. "But there are many perils along the way. You'll need these pearls."

With invisible hands Spider Woman removes the necklace of magic pearls from her neck and hands it to Johnny Hero. Johnny looks at them in astonishment.

"But Spider Woman! I shouldn't have these pearls!"

"Do as I say!" snaps Spider Woman. "There isn't much time."

Reluctantly Johnny accepts the magic pearls.

"I must go," says Spider Woman. "Good luck, and Godspeed."

"Thank you, Spider Woman," says Johnny. "Thanks for everything." Then, his voice trembling, he adds, "I'll never forget you, Spider Woman."

As the wind of Spider Woman's departure ruffles his tousled hair, Johnny Hero puts the string of magic pearls around his neck. With a scornful glance at the steaming pools of evil, he sets off into the cave, making a circle of light wherever he goes in the dark and murky cavern.

## *"I'm Johnny Hero!"*

Herschel leaped to his feet and started running around the living room in circles shouting "I'm Johnny Hero! I'm Johnny Hero!"

D.R. yawned and stretched out on the couch.

"Not me, kid," he said, closing his eyes. "I'm so tired right now I don't even feel like David Ray Davenport."

D.R. slept on the couch all day nearly. After supper he went back to bed again and slept the whole night through.

## The Lord Works in Mysterious Ways

D.R. got up and had breakfast with the family and then lay down on the couch to read the paper while Marcella and Doyle got the kids ready to go to Sunday School. It had been made clear the evening before that D.R. wasn't going to feel like going to church with them, and so they left him alone to read and relax while they got dressed and ready. When the family left, the house fell into such profound silence D.R. dozed off immediately. But then around eleven the phone rang and woke him up and when it turned out to be God Himself calling to summon D.R. to Kentucky, alertness spread through him like a rush.

God was calling in the guise of Mrs. Godsey, Uncle Emmit's neighbor down in Finley County, but Divine Right had no doubt who it really was. Her high, nasal voice was certainly a strange one for such a weighty summons, but the Call was clear and unmistakable: Emmit was dying at the homeplace and D.R. must go to be with him.

Mrs. Godsey told D.R. she hated to worry him, that

it might be a false alarm, but she didn't think so. She said the Lord worked in mysterious ways, that it wasn't given people to understand everything He does, that Emmit might perk up tomorrow and outlive them all, but according to her son Leonard who had been to see Emmit twice the day before, he was twice as bad off as he had been, and that she just had to call Marcella and try to do something about getting somebody to go up and stay with him, or else get an ambulance to haul him out of that holler to the hospital. D.R. told Mrs. Godsey he couldn't get there before late that night, but that he would come on if she thought that was what ought to be done.

Mrs. Godsey said, "What was that, honey? Some fool's eavesdropping and cut out what you said."

"I said, I probably can't get there before late tonight some time, but I'll come on if you think that's what ought to be done."

"Lord, child, it would be just *wonderful* if you would come. It'd be a wonderful blessing for Emmit, he'd just be plum tickled to *death* to see you. And I'd be right pleased to see you myself. Why you must be a great old big boy by now. The last time I saw you, you was the least little old thing that ever was."

When D.R. said yes, he was grown now, Mrs. Godsey said, "My, my, time flies, don't it? Why I remember when your *daddy* was a little towhead, not big as your fist. Running up and down that creek, feisty as he could be. Fine man, your daddy was," said Mrs. Godsey. "I know he would of been proud to see you turn into such a fine young man."

Before D.R. could respond to that, Mrs. Godsey cleared her throat and said, "Well, honey, this is costing money. I guess we better hang up. Me and Leonard'll look for you to come in some time late tonight."

"Or early in the morning," D.R. said. "My old bus doesn't go very fast."

Mrs. Godsey said that would be fine. D.R. told her

to tell Leonard to go tell Emmit that he was on his way to take care of him. Mrs. Godsey said she'd do that.

As she was hanging up she added, "Bless your sweet heart, youngun. It's sure a Christian act for you to come."

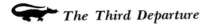 ## The Third Departure

After God hung up D.R. sat a few minutes listening to the dial tone. But then he put the receiver down and went about getting ready to go. There wasn't much to do, actually, except put his clothes on, and leave a note on the desk for Marcella. Someone had left four dollars and some change in an ashtray on the desk. D.R. took it, and added a P.S. to his note explaining that he had. He made himself a smoked-ham sandwich, put some apples and oranges in a sack and took them out to the bus. Urge was in the worst mess he had ever been in, but mechanically he was all set to go. Half an hour after the call from God, Divine Right backed out of his sister's driveway and set out down Clark Creek for Kentucky.

# FIVE

## 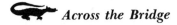 Across the Bridge

There goes D.R. Davenport, David Ray some folks call him, across the bridge into Kentucky, flipping the dial through Bill Monroe and his Bluegrass Boys to the Reverend Archie Turner say'ng Jesus on the mainline, tell him what you need, everybody here loves Jesus say amen. D.R. said amen and roared on across the bluegrass toward the range of hills that stretched across the windshield like the jagged spine of some old dinosaur.

##  Big Hill

In the section of Kentucky where the bluegrass and the eastern mountains meet, near Berea, one of the major landmarks is Big Hill. There are several distinctive hills and knobs and rises in the vicinity, but Big Hill is the dominant land mass for several miles around. For travelers on U.S. 421, the bottom of Big Hill represents the precise dividing line between the flat lands and the branch of the Appalachian Mountains known as the Cumberland Plateau. At the bottom, the traveler headed west is entering the Kentucky bluegrass country. From the top, he faces a range of hills flowing south and east for more than a hundred

177

miles, until they are finally broken by the broad agri-
culture valleys of southwest Virginia and east Tennessee.

Big Hill is a special place upon the ground, and it
was an important feature in the landscape of D.R.'s
mind as well, because it reminded him so much of his
father, and Daniel Boone. The Boone legend in Kentucky, or one version of it anyway, has it that it was
from Big Hill that Boone got his first look at the lush
central Kentucky plain, the fabled garden spot that
had been the object of his fantasy and quest. When
D.R. would ride over Big Hill with his father, his
father never failed to make some reference to Boone
and the Wilderness Road. D.R. had no idea how many
times that might have been, but surely it was in the
thousands. When his father left the coal country of
Kentucky in the fifties and moved the family to Cincinnati, they came home every weekend for the next
year, and almost every weekend for two years after
that. And they always passed over Big Hill on their
way to the homeplace up in Finley County.

His father would say, "Right here now David's where
old Boone got his first look at his new country. Stopped
right over there by that mailbox, could see as far as
he could see." He would grin then, and wait for David
to respond. He made the joke two times every weekend, coming and going, but somehow it was always
funny. David would begin to anticipate it miles before
his father would say it, like a story he knew but never
got tired of hearing. His father would say, "Yes sir, old
Boone leaned his gun against that very mailbox
yonder, and looked all around."

One time when Boone leaned his gun against the
mailbox he found a letter in it from John L. Lewis
that said DON'T COME TO KENTUCKY, BOYS,
THE WORK'S TOO HARD AND THERE'S TOO
DAMN LITTLE PAY. Another time there was a letter
to Daniel from his brother Squire that said, "If you

see a boy named David Ray Collier out in them
woods, you send him home, he's too young to roam."

David said, "There was not."

"Oh yes there was too," said his father.

His father's name was Royce. Royce Collier. And in
those days, before his mother's second marriage to
Wallace Davenport, Collier was David Ray's last
name too.

"Oh yes," said Royce. "Squire sent that very letter
to Daniel Boone. You ask Doyle here if he didn't."

Doyle, the assistant driver and chief mechanic for
the old Pontiac, only twenty-four then, tall and lean,
fresh out of the Army, sitting in the front seat beside
Marcella, would nod and say that it was so, and that if
David didn't believe it he could just ask Royce there.
And round and round it would go, two men supporting
each other's teasing lie, and sometimes it was funny
and David would laugh, and sometimes they would
tease too far and hurt David's feelings, and then he
would sit back into the crowd of cousins in the rear
seat and pout the rest of the way to the homeplace.

### Recollection

That car of Daddy's was an old Pontiac he bought with
the first wages he ever earned in Cincinnati. It had over
a hundred thousand miles on it when he got it, but
he never hesitated to take off in it for Kentucky. The
first year we lived up there we never missed a weekend going home. Fifty-two round trips in a year, over
two hundred miles each way, six, seven, sometimes
eight and nine people in it every run. Every Friday
as soon as Daddy'd get home from work we'd load up
and head out, and drive six straight hours south on
old U.S. 25, through Lexington and Richmond, east

into the hills on 421, then down state route 666 to the homeplace in Finley County. In the wintertime it would be dark before we even set out, but in the summers the light would hold 'til almost Richmond, and I remember the programs that came on the radio about that time of day. My daddy played the guitar some, and he loved hillbilly music, and so at six o'clock he'd tune in the Hillbilly Hit Parade out of WCKY in Cincinnati. I remember it started and ended with somebody's fierce picking of the "Steel Guitar Rag," and then when it was over Wayne Rainey and Lonnie Glossen would come on, trying to sell harmonica instruction courses. Wayne and Lonnie were good musicians too, and when they'd get wound up Daddy would get excited and start to sing along with them, and bounce around in his seat and beat on the steering wheel with his hand. He'd cut up like that for miles and miles. He'd tickle us all so much we'd forget how uncomfortable we were, piled on top of one another in the back seat of that old car. On Fridays you wouldn't mind being uncomfortable because you knew you were on your way to someplace you really wanted to be a lot, but on Sundays you'd feel so blue about having to leave the homeplace to go back to Cincinnati there wasn't any way in the world to get comfortable and Daddy would have to stop every hour or so and let people out to stretch. We hated it, coming back, but then it was only five more days 'til we'd go down home again, and we cheered outselves up with that thought. The five days would drag by but finally Friday would get there. Daddy would come in from work, clean up a little and then there we'd be, on the road again. About six hours later we'd turn off at Mrs. Godsey's store and drive up Trace Fork to the homeplace.

It would be midnight by the time we'd get there and Grandma and Granddad would be in bed asleep. Granddad never let anything keep him from getting his sleep, but if Grandma was feeling well she'd get up and come in the kitchen and hug us all and start taking cornbread and beans and cold mashed potatoes out of the oven and setting them on the table. Daddy would say here now Mommy, you quit that, we've all done and eat. But Grandma would keep hauling out the food and before long we'd all be seated at the table, me and Daddy and Marcella and Doyle and usually some of Doyle's kinfolks would be with us and they'd sit down too and there we'd all be, in the middle of the night at Grandma's house, eating cold beans and potatoes and blackberry jam on that good cold cornbread.

Then it wouldn't seem like half an hour 'til there we'd be again, sitting at the table, Granddad with us this time, the beans and potatoes hot now, the pork hot, the beets hot, the cornbread hot, the cobbler hot, and the milk cold as ice from sitting all night in the spring house. That would be Saturday dinner. Sunday dinner was always chicken and gravy and cole slaw with beans and potatoes, a big pone of biscuit instead of cornbread, and ice tea for those that didn't want milk.

Sunday dinner was considered the best meal of the week at the homeplace but I never did like it after we moved away because it was after Sunday dinner that we always had to load up in the Pontiac again and go back to Cincinnati. I was always too sad to eat much on Sundays, and what little I would eat I'd usually throw up as soon as we got back on the road. At dinnertime on Saturday I'd eat like a starved horse thinking: twenty-four hours. Twenty-four whole hours to romp around the pasture and the woods, then in the evenings to hang around with my grandfather while he went about his chores. On Saturday that twenty-four hours stretched away forever, but when it was over and it was time to leave it would all seem like some strange little fifteen-second dream.

When it was time to go, Grandma and Granddad would follow us out to the car and stand around while we got in. Then Daddy would start the motor, back up to the coal pile, fight the steering wheel 'til the wheels turned, then ease forward down the lane, pausing in front of Grandma and Granddad for a final good-bye. I always wanted to cry at that point but I never did, except once as we were leaving, at the last second, as a surprise, Grandma tossed a Payday candy bar to me through the window and hit me in the eye. I let out a terrific squawl, and cried 'til it was time to get out of the car and puke. I held my eye and screeched like I was mortally wounded, but the thing nobody knew was that I wasn't really crying about being hit in the eye at all. All that was just an excuse for this other kind of crying I wanted to do, which I did plenty of on that occasion. I suffered pretty bad that trip 'til we got back down around Big Hill and Daddy started carrying on about Daniel Boone again. Daddy always made me laugh on Big Hill, and passing over it tonight I could feel that old familiar laugh sensation start to rumble in my guts again.

**Crossroads**

Traffic seemed fairly normal the first hour or so past Berea. But once he turned off 421 onto 666, D.R. went almost twenty miles without seeing another car and he began to wonder if he had got on the wrong road somehow. He wasn't lost exactly but he was afraid he might be, and at night in the mountains on the Wilderness Road it amounts to the same thing. He drove on a while longer, looking for signs, but he couldn't find any and the road got narrower and narrower. To be on the safe side D.R. turned around and retraced his path to a crossroads where there was a sign that said 666. It was a confusing intersection and he sat there a minute studying the sign, making sure it referred to the road he was on. Two other county roads came into 666 from each side near a sharp curve, and in the dark you couldn't see very far down any of them. The only marker was the 666 sign, which as D.R. read it seemed to refer to the middle road. He looked at the sign and the middle road, and finally set out down it into the night again.

But ten or fifteen miles later D.R. grew so doubtful that it was right he stopped and backtracked again. It just couldn't be the right road. The farther he went the narrower it got, and there wasn't a house or a road-sign on it. D.R. went back to the crossroads, pulled off into the gravel and looked around inside the bus for a road map of Kentucky.

There wasn't one, of course. There must have been a dozen road maps scattered around, including one of the Eastern United States that showed the freeways in Kentucky. But for driving on the local roads away from the traffic mainstream there wasn't a map in the bus that showed the way and that pissed D.R. off and scared him at the same time.

His first impulse was to blame Estelle. At about the moment he realized he wasn't going to find a Kentucky road map he came across Estelle's knitting bag in a pile of stuff behind the driver's seat. In his mind the knitting bag, and its owner, seemed to be responsible for there being no Kentucky road maps. In a fury he grabbed the bag and flung it out Urge's side door. Some of the yarn fell out and tangled up around D.R.'s feet. In trying to get it off he tied his hands up in it for a second and that almost drove him crazy. He screamed through his teeth and started flinging things left and right. When he came to something that felt like Estelle's he tried to throw it out the door, but most of it caught on the door facing and piled up at the foot

of the bed. D.R. picked up his cassette recorder and
almost threw it too, but he caught himself and turned
it on instead. The voice of the Greek filled the bus
and flowed out into the night, uttering for the first
time in the history of the Kentucky mountains the
names of Ouspensky and Gurdjieff. D.R. shouted *"Fuck
Ouspensky and Gurdjieff,"* and threw the recorder hard
against the back of the bus. The Greek groaned and
spoke like Donald Duck for a second, then died.

The search for the map was so frustrating it automatically turned into a search for dope. D.R. didn't
remember for sure if he even had any, and the stupidity
of not having any compounded the stupidity of not
knowing where it was if he did have any. That too
seemed like Estelle's fault and he screamed at her as
loud as he could and called her a stupid bitch. D.R.
was so furious he leaped into the driver's seat and
roared off down one of the three roads without bothering to close Urge's side door. Shit was falling out and
crashing on the road but D.R. didn't give a goddamn.
He didn't know which road he was on but he didn't
give a goddamn about that either. When he'd gone ten
miles and hadn't found a 666 sign he turned around
and roared back to the crossroads, right on through
it and down the other road across the way. He didn't
find any signs on that road either. He was on his way
back to the crossroads to set fire to Urge and commit
suicide when a rear tire hit a chughole so hard it
knocked something loose and caused the motor and
headlights to quit, right there in the middle of dark
nowhere. D.R. didn't even get out to see what was
wrong. He just sat there behind the wheel staring
through the windshield at the black shapes of mountains all around.

## ![alligator] *Fess Parker*

But of course it wasn't *total* dark around. Total dark
is a very extreme condition, and while D.R.'s condition was fast approaching the extreme, one speck of
light still shone in his dark night.

It wasn't a star, and it wasn't the moon, and it wasn't
some camper's fire.

The light, off to D.R.'s left front, half a mile away,
was an old Fess Parker movie playing on a drive-in
theater screen.

The screen was so small at that distance that it took
D.R. a long time to even notice it. And when he did
notice it, he assumed it was just another of those vague
and restless shapes that sometimes floated up behind
his eyes when his head was weird.

But now when D.R. closed his eyes, the movie went
away.

And when he opened them again, there Fess was,
dressed in buckskin, chopping down a tree somewhere
in the woods.

The movie was *Bold Frontiersman,* in which Fess
played a frontier hero struggling to establish a clearing
in the wilderness so he could bring his woman there
to live. The reason the movie was so suspenseful and
made such a demand upon Fess's acting talents was
Fess had an evil twin brother named Rance who was
a land speculator back in the settlements, and who
did a lot of bad shit with the Indians. Fess played the
character of Rance as well as the character of Dan,
the frontiersman. Rance's scheme was to let Dan go
do all the shit work in the woods, then use the Indians
and the fact that he and Dan were look-alikes to cheat
Dan not only out of his land, but out of his wife as
well. Of course Fess, which is to say, Dan, didn't know
anything about this evil scheme, and of course D.R.
didn't know anything about it either. All D.R. knew
was that Fess was over there working his ass off at the

drive-in, and that if he, D.R., could make it there before the show was over, he might find somebody to give him a ride to the nearest town. With that thought in mind, and warmed considerably by it, D.R. got out of Urge and started walking down the road toward Fess Parker's clearing in the trees.

## The Monster's Eye

So there goes D.R. Ravenport, walking all alone into the night, with nothing but a Fess Parker flick to lead him on.

And now even Fess has disappeared!

Gone!

Dark!

Where did the movie go?

There it is. There's old Fess, still steadfastly hacking at the trees. It was only a slight depression in the road that interrupted D.R.'s line of sight. The movie was there again, in place like some friendly planet, and Fess was in place too and doing his thing.

But wait!

Now the road is curving, bending to the right, away from Fess Parker on the screen! D.R. can't see but he can feel it, a gradual curve, long and easy, winding off to who knows where in that infinity of black? No way to tell where the road goes to. Nothing out in front for him to guide on. The screen's the only star that D.R. trusts to show the way. It scares D.R. but abruptly he makes his decision: to leave the road and strike out cross-country toward the show.

There goes D.R. again, down a sharp embankment, then up the other side. Through matted underbrush and ripping thorns and tangles of low grapevines and thickets that feel like laurel. By the time D.R. is back on higher ground and can see the show again, his hands and arms and face and neck are laced with scratches, and his lungs feel as if they've been inhaling fire.

It's a freaky feeling, standing out there in the middle of the boondocks, in the middle of the night, in the middle of a Fess Parker movie, breathing hard. It's so freaky the only thing that's holding D.R.'s head together is the growing image on the drive-in screen. It's twice as big as it was when he was back on the road. The trees are twice as big, Fess is twice as big. He's making progress, D.R. is getting there. With heart uplifted and his strength renewed, he faces toward the movie and plunges on.

Down another slope, through a fence this time, a barbed-wire fence that bites him in the ass as he climbs through. Then a creek, a kind of swamp really, with reeds and vines and gnarled, exposed roots of looming sycamores for D.R. to crawl among. The roots feel like giant claws, they feel like scaly feet of some enormous swamp beast as old as the swamp itself. Puffing, D.R. thinks: when I get to the high ground. When I get where I can see the show again.

Where's the goddamn high ground? D.R. wonders.

Where's the goddamn . . .

Suddenly D.R. freezes. Something's coming! He hears it plainly, some *thing!* Dragging through the leaves! Quickly D.R. squirms across the roots and huddles at the base of a giant sycamore. But the sound comes on toward him, closer. Then D.R. sees: *its eye!* Gleaming! Not fifteen yards away, a monster, coming straight for Divine Right through the night!

 *The Miner*

"I thought you was a cow," said the man with the light on his cap. It was a coal miner's hat, with a burning carbide lamp on the front. "I heard you way back yonder and told myself, I said that's somebody's old cow got out."

D.R. was standing up now, brushing his clothes off with his hand. "I thought you was a monster," he said.

The Miner laughed. "Well now, I could have thought the same thing about you. But I've walked this path many a time at night and I learned a long time ago it's always better to tell yourself it's a cow instead of a booger."

The Miner laughed some more, and D.R. managed a little chuckle himself, though it was mainly for the Miner's benefit, rather than anything he genuinely felt. They were standing on a narrow dirt path that ran along the creek opposite the sycamore roots. When the Miner set out walking again and D.R. fell in behind him, the Miner talked on as if it was a common thing to run into strange people on the path at night. He was perfectly at ease and confident in his direction, and when D.R.'s fright had fully passed away, D.R. was glad to be beside him.

"What are you doing out here tonight anyway?" asked the Miner.

"I'm trying to get to my uncle's place in Finley County," D.R. said. "But my bus quit on me up the road aways. I thought I might find some help over at that drive-in movie."

"You a bus driver?" asked the Miner.

"It's a van," said D.R. "One of those Volkswagen vans."

"I've seen them," said the Miner. "They've got a lot of them up in Dayton."

D.R. asked the Miner if he lived in Dayton.

"Off and on," he said. "I use to work at Frigidaire but they laid me off last year and I ain't been back. I told my wife I said if I'm going to be unemployed I'm going to be unemployed someplace I care about living. So we come on home. We're staying with her people on Lower Elk right now. That's off the Poor Valley road, near the Crab Orchard."

"I see," said D.R.

As they walked on in silence D.R. tried to get a better look at his companion. He was about D.R.'s height, but much stockier. The light from his forehead was like a jet. From the side it was hard to see his face in any detail. When the Miner's face first materialized out of the dark and scared D.R. so, it was from the front that D.R. saw it, and although he hadn't taken in any detail then either, it had appeared to him a very old face, weathered and deeply lined about the eyes. He had looked vaguely like an old Chinaman, but now from the side he did not look like an old Chinaman at all. He looked very young, in fact, and he certainly walked young. They'd only walked a quarter of a mile together but already D.R. was having to work at it to keep up. After they walked on in silence for perhaps another quarter mile, he asked the Miner where he was going.

"To join the Happy Pappys if they'll have me," said the Miner. "They might not have me. It's hard to get much out of them people in town, except appointments."

D.R. asked him what the Happy Pappys were.

The Miner snorted, and spat into the weeds beside the path. For the first time, D.R. realized that he was chewing tobacco. "Standing around for a dollar and a half an hour, mostly," he said. "Make work for them has got children at home." The Miner spat again, then asked D.R. if he lived in Finley County.

"I used to," said D.R.

"Who's your people?"

D.R. said, "The Colliers. From over on Trace Fork."

"I know Trace Fork," said the Miner. "Toward Blue Diamond, over yonder past Hardly. Collier, you say."

D.R. said, "My father was a Collier. My mother married a Davenport, and took me with her."

"Well, I'm glad to know you, Collier," said the Miner. "My name's Virgil Amburgey."

The Miner had got D.R.'s last name wrong, but D.R. didn't feel like correcting him. They were at the blacktop road now, leaving the path behind. They stopped long enough to shake hands. Then they set out walking again, and a while later they came to Urge, sitting like a shadow by the road.

## Monkeying Around

In D.R.'s mind the bus was a total wreck and he was ready to leave it and go on to town with Virgil and find a mechanic who could fix it for him. But Virgil said let's take a look at it since we're here. About two minutes after he lifted the hood and shined his light on the problem he had Urge's motor and the head-lights working as well as they ever had.

"How did you do that?" asked D.R.

"Oh," said Virgil. "I just said a little prayer and monkeyed with it." He laughed then and settled back in his seat as D.R. put Urge in gear and pulled back onto the blacktop.

## The Miner's Rap

"Yeah," said Virgil. "It's mighty hard times around here these days. If it wasn't for food stamps and the Happy Pappys some folks would starve plum to death, that ain't no lie. A lot of 'em are hungry like it is. Of course I've seen it when it was worse, and a man's got to count his blessings I reckon. My daddy mined coal

in this country in the nineteen twenties, no union or
nothing in here then, and you talk about mean times,
them times was *mean*. Of course they's not enough
union left worth speaking about, but what I mean is,
now, you take this Happy Pappy program. Take all
this welfare stuff. It ain't nothing but a sop to keep
the people from acting up. That's all in the world it is,
and yet everybody wants to make so much out of it.
Everybody give the President so much credit for coming
in here and setting it up. All that President was doing
was laying out a sop to try to keep the lid on things.
And I mean to tell you, buddy, the lid was about to
pop around here a year or two ago. It was like a time
of war nearly. People hungry, out of work, losing
their hospital cards, getting their pensions cut, little
old younguns going around with worms in their
bellies, some of 'em half naked in the wintertime, I
mean they wasn't nothing else *to* do but go to war. Big
gangs of men roving up and down the highways, stopping cars, shooting, getting shot at. They was a tipple
burnt ever day for two straight weeks up in your
county, two or three railroad bridges went up, people's
cars and houses dynamited.

"And so the President comes in with all this give-
away. Of course now he did have to do something let's
give the devil his due. And the people did get a little
something to eat out of it which they had to have, and
here I am on my way to get on the Happy Pappys if
they'll have me. But what I mean is, everybody talked
about how *good* it was of the President to do that, how
*kind* it was of him to send in the food stamps and start
the Happy Pappys. Oh he was smart, you ne'en to
doubt it. One day they was about to revolute, the next
day they're glad to draw a dollar and a half an hour.
And top it all, here comes the President's wife down in
a jet plane to show how concerned her and her husband was for all the hungry people. They lined up by
the thousands just to get a look at her ride by in a big

car. Parked up yonder in front of the courthouse, got up on a truck bed and made a little speech about how beautiful these old hills are. And how fine the people are, how rugged and independent and so forth all the hillbillies are. And her supposed to be so beautiful. I didn't think she was so beautiful. Why that woman was so bow-legged she couldn't hem a hog up in a pen. I felt about half sorry, I declare I did. Me on welfare, her richer'n Jay Goo, and I felt sorry for her because her legs was bowed. A man's got to be about half crazy to go around thinking like that, I'll swear it."

Virgil leaned his head out the window to spit again. This time he let go of his whole plug. He hawked and spat and dredged a mouthful of phlegm out of his throat and when he'd let that go too he cleared his throat and continued.

"And so what comes next but the strip mining. I mean we had some of it right along, but after that woman come in here and made her speech, seemed like it just broke out all over. Whole mountain ranges chewed up and spit right out in the river. They've done destroyed your county, Collier. Finley County's bad hit, you won't recognize that place. They say they's a strip-mine bench through the Rockhouse drainage over eighty miles long, and getting longer ever day. What's worse, it's a-coming right my way. Man have a house and a barn, some pasture in the valley, they come right over it, the law says that's just fine. Law says a operator got a deed to the mineral, it don't matter what he does or who he does it to, it's legal to take that mineral out any way he wants to. They gouged a woman's baby right out of the grave over in Knott County, and her a-looking. Said her husband had already been took to jail for brandishing a rifle at a bulldozer operator. Then they gouged up their baby right out of the grave, flung it end over end into the sky, the mother a-looking. My wife's people got sixty acres on Lower Elk. Lived there thirty years. Got cows, good garden and a spring, man can live good there if he's willing to work. But they's this outfit owns the coal rights undereneath, and they're on their way to get it. Eighty miles long, that bench is. Reminds me of a big sarpent sneaking through the hills, big old eighty miles long snake killing everything in its path. It's that way everywhere around here. Some folks call it the end of time but me, I just call it a bunch of goddamn criminals out tearing up the world.

## The Miner Drives

D.R. was fascinated by all the things the Miner was saying, but after about half an hour on 421 again he started getting so sleepy he barely could keep his eyes open. He drove through the narrow curving part of the road that had caused him to turn back before, but once into the long valley beyond the narrows, Urge's front wheels started dropping off the blacktop every mile or two, and finally D.R. had to tell the Miner they would have to stop so he could nap awhile, unless he would like to drive. The Miner said he'd be glad to try, but he was a little nervous about operating a car with such funny gears. He offered to just sit and wait while D.R. got some sleep, but when D.R. thought about it that seemed pretty silly, so he pulled off the road and spent a few minutes teaching the Miner about Urge's gears. When he said he thought he had it, D.R. told him it was all his, and he crawled through the junk scattered on the floor of the bus, stretched out on the mattress and fell asleep immediately.

## The Beast of the Sea

Or thought he did anyhow. It sure was wild not to know for sure. Half of D.R. was very deep asleep. It was his other half he wasn't sure about. He didn't know if what he felt around him as he lay there on the mattress, and saw, quite clearly, through the windows by the road outside, was in the actual, waking world or just a dream his sleeping half was having. D.R. felt his body rolling back and forth from side to side as Urge leaned into the curves, then straightened up again. He heard Urge's motor whirring underneath, and smelled the odor of Estelle in the mattress he was lying on. That was what he felt and heard and smelled. What he saw through the windows was the dark, lit by eerie light from slag heaps burning in a dozen different places. He saw sulphuric smoke rise from scattered fires and spread across the landscape of the night. He saw hulks of abandoned automobiles strewn about like monster corpses on some prehistoric battlefield, and he saw coal tipples by the highway like preying creatures frozen by the sudden glare of light. Animals darted off the highway as the bus approached, then gathered on the pavement when they'd gone by to stare with shining, yellow eyes. In one place the road was lined with monsters grinning wickedly. Some were merely bloody heads impaled on fence posts, or hanging by the hair from limbs of trees. Some stuck out their tongues that turned to snakes that hissed and snapped and bit as they drove by. He saw a beast from the depths of the sea, covered with weeds and ancient slime except for its head, which was adorned with jewels that glistened in the light from its own winking eyes. On the beast's head were seven horns, and crowning each horn in rays of light was Estelle's face, distorted by a grin so evil and so know-

ing D.R. shuddered and pressed his face into the
mattress thinking surely I'll wake up now, surely this
is just another dream.

 ### *In the Flesh*

But it was not a dream. Those were really beasts outside the windows, and that was really David, sleeping
there beside him on the bed. D.R. felt as if his blood
was full of methedrine. Something racing through
his mind increased its speed so much it disappeared
completely out of sight. The half of D.R. that was
sleeping was a separate, living person! It was really
David, sound asleep beside him, like a child. Surely
it's a dream, he thought. Surely that's me sleeping,
and all of this I'm seeing is a dream. D.R. leaned up
on his elbow and looked around. He breathed deeply,
and smelled and listened. Urge's motor whirred beneath him, Estelle's odor rose into his nostrils from
the bed. The Miner was up front at the steering wheel,
guiding Urge around the curves, shifting gears from
time to time, driving slowly. The world inside the bus
was still in place. And David was a living person in it
with him, lying there before him in the flesh.

Is he really in the flesh? D.R. wondered. Is that
*really* David there beside me, or are we somehow mixed
up in each other's dreams?

Touch him, D.R. thought. Touch his face and feel
if he is breathing.

Don't touch him! D.R. told himself. Let him lie
there, *don't!*

With the tips of his fingers D.R. touched David just
below the lobe of his left ear. David stirred and
smiled with pleasure, he yawned and stretched and
opened wide his eyes. When D.R. started whimpering

David touched his finger to his lips and whispered *shhhhhh*. He was sitting up now, looking deeply into D.R.'s face. Moving very slowly, David leaned and placed his head on D.R.'s shoulder. Don't be afraid, he whispered. I love you, and you mustn't be afraid. David kissed him then, he kissed him on the neck and lightly on the corner of his mouth. Then he took D.R. by the shoulders and pressing tried to stretch him out full length upon the mattress.

"No."

"Shhhhhh," David whispered.

"I don't care. I don't feel like lying down."

"What's that you say?" the Miner called out through the car.

"I said I don't much feel like lying down."

"Well," said the Miner. "It's just as well. I'll be getting out in another mile or two."

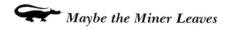 *Maybe the Miner Leaves*

At a junction where the road to Blaine came into 666, the Miner stopped the bus and got out, and D.R. crawled forward to sit behind the wheel. He offered to drive Virgil the three miles on into Blaine, but the Miner said he believed he'd rather walk. Light was in the sky now, but it was still a long time 'til the Miner's appointment at the welfare office, and he was just as glad to have three miles to walk to pass the time away. He thanked D.R. for the ride, and D.R. thanked him for getting the bus to run again, and driving as far as he had. They shook hands, and the Miner set out walking down the road toward Blaine.

 *Tears*

As soon as Virgil was out of sight D.R. started crying. He couldn't help himself, the tears came pouring out, and when David came up front and put his arm around him D.R. yielded. David was very cool. He didn't say a word. He just sat there with his arms around D.R. and let him weep into his shoulder as long as he had tears.

## Maybe the Miner Leaves

After a while D.R. realized he was on the bed again, and that the bus was moving. He didn't remember leaving the front seat, but what was more confusing, it seemed dark outside again. D.R. rolled to the edge of the mattress and looked up through the window at the sky. The clouds were there, but the sky was dark as midnight, there wasn't even a speck of moon to give them light. When D.R. looked toward the front of the bus to remark about the light, he saw the Miner sitting behind the wheel, and David in the other seat beside him. D.R. almost yelled then, but before he could the bus slowed down and stopped at the junction where the road to Blaine came into 666.

"Now I'll be glad to drive you into town," D.R. heard David say.

"Naw," said the Miner. "It'll be a while 'til I meet them people, I'll just walk and pass the time away."

"Well," said David. "I sure do thank you for driving as far as you did. And getting this old bus back on the road."

The Miner spat and grunted and waved his hand at David. He was outside now, leaning against the door, talking to David through the window. D.R. lay very still upon the mattress, terrified that the Miner was going to turn his head and discover him hiding in the shadows of the bus, or that David would suddenly tell the Miner he was back there, then turn around to stare at him and laugh.

"You'll be home 'fore you know it, now," said the Miner. "Go through Hardly up yonder, there where they've got the stock sale, and you're what you might say in the *su*-burbs of Trace Fork, and Rockhouse Creek."

"Oh, I know Hardly," David said. "I use to go up there on Saturdays with my grandfather, and watch him trade."

"Well, it's still there," said the Miner. "You'll be there by the time you shift this thing down into high gear."

The Miner and David shook hands through the window. Then the Miner stepped back and with a stroke by the heel of his hand he got his carbide lamp burning again. As soon as he put his hat back on his head his face and body disappeared behind the light. All D.R. could see was the spewing flame, which grew smaller and smaller as the Miner walked away, until finally it was swallowed by the night.

*Hardly*

By the time they got to Hardly, three miles down the road from Godsey's store, it was light enough outside to see the barns and houses they drove by. As far as D.R. could tell. Hardly hadn't changed a bit since he used to come there to the stock sales as a child. Mooney's store and filling station were on the left exactly as they had always been, and beside them Harold Campbell's Feed and Grain. On the right were the rows of stock pens, and the old run-down house at the end where missionary ladies used to sell second-hand clothes. Across the road from the second-hand store was Mable's Place, and beside it, set back from the road aways, was the old flat-roofed, red-brick-sided Pentecostal Church of God. The place was so still that hour of day it looked more like a movie set of Hardly than actually Hardly itself.

David said, "Let's stop and get out and walk around awhile."

D.R. was sitting in the front again, huddled against the door with one foot drawn back upon the seat. Without looking at David, D.R. shook his head sullenly.

"Come on," said David. "Just for the hell of it. There's nobody out there."

But D.R. didn't want to, and David didn't want to push. He drove on, and a few minutes later pulled up in front of Godsey's store at the mouth of Trace Fork.

## A Sense of Danger

D.R. stayed in the car while David went up on the store porch to talk to Mrs. Godsey. The store wasn't open at that hour, but Mrs. Godsey lived in the rooms behind it and David knocked on the door 'til she came through and answered. When she opened the door, and then stepped out onto the porch to talk to David, D.R. hunkered down low in his seat to keep her from seeing him, but not so low that he couldn't watch them by peeping through the lower corner of the windshield. Mrs. Godsey was scary-looking. Dressed in a long, white robe, and holding a Bible in her hand, she looked like some prophet fresh out of the Old Testament. Her hair was long and white too, gathered behind her head in a bun. Though her face was lined with age, her voice and gestures were as vigorous as David's as they talked.

"Leonard went up and told Emmit you were coming," said Mrs. Godsey.

"Well, good," said David. "What did Emmit think about that?"

"Lord, honey, it like to tickled him to death nearly. He couldn't even believe it at first, and then when he did believe it, big tears come into his eyes. Leonard thinks it's just wonderful of you to come back home like this, David. And I do too. I told Leonard, I said God's the one doing it. There's not a doubt in my mind but what God's the one led you to come home to take care of that man. I did think Emmit was going to pass away, but now I don't think he is. God wouldn't of sent you down here if He meant for Emmit to die."

"Well, I hope you're right," said David. "I sure hope we can do something for Uncle Emmit."

David and Mrs. Godsey moved away to the far side of the porch then, and in quieter tones began talking to each other about death and heaven and God. D.R. sat up a little straighter in his seat and strained to listen, but they were too far away now to understand, except for the three words which ran through their conversation like a refrain.

"Death," said Mrs. Godsey, and David smiled and said "Yes ma'm, and God and heaven too."

David appeared to be enjoying himself immensely. Although his back was to D.R., he could tell by David's gestures that he was exuberant and full of himself as he talked. Leaning casually against the store wall, his shoulder braced against a metal sign advertising Carter's Little Liver Pills, he said, "Death. Death and heaven for sure."

Mrs. Godsey nodded and said, "That's right, honey. And God too. We mustn't never leave out God."

As she said it, Mrs. Godsey glanced past David's

shoulder, across the porch and right through Urge's windshield. She scared D.R. so bad with her look he fell down across the front seats and lay there shaking 'til David came back after a while and told him to get out of the bus.

"Come on," said David. "We have to walk the rest of the way, we don't have all day."

D.R. asked how come.

"Mrs. Godsey said you can't get a car up Trace Fork any more. We have to walk."

D.R. said he wasn't going.

"Sure you are," said David. "Come on. It's only a mile to the homeplace."

D.R. said he refused to leave the bus 'til he had some kind of protection. David looked at him and asked what he was talking about.

"You and Mrs. Godsey were up there talking about me," said D.R.

David laughed. He'd been standing outside the bus, but now he got in and established himself in the driver's seat. "That's a very wierd thing to say, D.R."

"I don't care if it is," said D.R. "It's true."

"You don't know that," said David. "And even if it is, what difference does it make?"

"Mrs. Godsey wants to see me dead!" said D.R.

David looked at him, then shook his head as if in profound sadness. "Well," he said. "Personally, I think we ought to quit thinking about ourselves and put our minds on Emmit. He's the one we've come down here to help."

"He's probably in on it too," D.R. whimpered. "And you are too, and I know that Miner was."

David stared at D.R. this time, grinning. "You want to know what I think?"

D.R. waited for him to say.

"I think you're stoned on your ass." He laughed then, but D.R. was not amused.

"All I know," said D.R., "is I don't trust you for a minute, and I'm not getting out of this bus 'til I feel protected from all this bullshit going on."

There was a little silence between them then, and in it David's tone and manner changed. When he spoke again his voice had a new edge, a touch of cold impatience. "Let me ask you a question," he said.

D.R. waited for him to ask it.

"How'd you like it if I went in and got Mrs. Godsey, and told her to come out and talk to you about the bullshit. How would that be? I'll go in and tell her you're feeling a little bad out here, and ask . . . "

D.R. didn't wait for him to finish. He had seen the evil in David's eyes, he knew for sure now that David was in on it, and that he must run to get away or he would die. Without looking at David again he flung the door open, leaped out and took off running, with David chasing after, close behind.

 *Discovery*

D.R. ran across the old, decaying bridge where Trace Fork met the larger Rockhouse Creek. Both streams were yellow now, and acid-filled, and rusty from the mining that had killed the hills and waters all around. He ran across the bridge, then half a mile up the broken road without stopping until he fell down behind a rusted hulk that used to be a '47 Ford. There was a house nearby that D.R. might have hidden in to rest awhile, an old four-room shack with the roof caved in, half-hidden by the weeds. But he was scared to go to places he couldn't make out clearly with his eyes. He knew that David was hiding somewhere close around. He hadn't seen him since the second curve above the bridge when D.R. plunged into the creek and up the embankment on the other side. But he could feel him. He felt David's presence in the very weeds and mud and slimy yellow water of the stream. For a long time he lay low behind the car, breathing, trying to orient himself in the broken world around.

It was possible that D.R. was already on the lower end of his grandfather's old farm. But Trace Fork had been so disfigured by the strip mining, he didn't see a feature on the landscape that he recognized. The ridges where the Trace Fork waters gathered were so uniformly scarred they looked like rims of craters on the moon. The guts of entire mountains had been ripped out and strewn like so much worthless slop. Every roll and fold, every feature of the drainage that might have formed a context and established where the homeplace was, had been torn away by bulldozers or smothered by fathoms of overburden. A slope that might have been the lower pasture on the homeplace was littered by shattered rocks and jagged ends of broken trees sticking up like legs of mules slaughtered in some awful no-man's land. It was an overwhelming thing to look at, and D.R. would have lain there longer, gazing, if David hadn't called out for him then.

"Wait!" he yelled. "Wait up, D.R., I want to talk to you."

The voice came from the direction of the old house. It was as if the house itself had yelled, its vacant windows eyes of some old dead man, its door a toothless mouth that never closed.

"Wait up for me, okay?"

Faster than his mind could follow, D.R. started crawling, slithering on his belly like a worm through weeds and briars and piles of ancient trash along the creek. He was crying now. He tried to fight it but the tears insisted, flowing in little channels down his face. Behind a mound of old boards and rotted beams and lengths of rusty, coiling cable, D.R. stopped to rest and catch his breath. David was thrashing in the weeds behind him, coming closer, but D.R. was too worn out and tight with fear to move, except for his hands, which on their own began to dig, burrowing in the ground beneath the junk.

The earth and rotting wood were dry and so crumbly to the touch he pulled it loose in double-handfuls and pushed the matter to the side. Whole sections of decayed boards fell to his clawing hands until he had made a place large enough to worm his body through. Pushing with his toes, he squirmed beneath the pile of old debris until he came to the very center of the mound.

And then beyond it!

Down!

Down into the earth itself this time.

An opening.

D.R. lay across an opening in the ground.

A mine!

He had crawled into the drift mouth of an old abandoned coal mine, covered over by the remnants of its tipple. His head was in it now, and now his neck and shoulders, he could smell it, he felt the dark space opening out around, the coolness, he felt the wind from deep inside the earth, and water. Face down in dark water,

jewels

lost cities

ancient bison,

cold.

 *The Journey*

He watches: rails, posts, some roof-bolts in the ceiling. Sees: his father and his uncles, digging coal. Who fishes? Trailing bison through cold water, who bites?

*He* bites. Feels it lift him, pulling soaring through the walls, down avenues and passageways of old forgotten halls.

And far below he sees the bison. Far below he sees the jewels. Far below the ancient cities where the ancient dragon rules.

Gently now the hero's falling. Secretly he folds his hands. Warm among the echoes, calling, D.R. comes to rest upon the sand.

## The Sand Room

D.R. rolled over and buried his face in the sand. He felt it scrape the crusted mud and sweat and slime and blood from his face and neck, his forehead and his hair. He was bathing. He was a snake shedding old and stiffened skin. Grinning, he sat up and peeled off his matted shirt. When he pressed his chest into the sand again, it felt like touching breasts with some warm woman. Smiling in the deepest pleasure he sank both arms into the sand and when he pulled them out he scraped the sand up into piles like breasts and then lay down upon them. Exalted now, he leaped to his feet and wrestled off the remnants of his clothes. Falling forward naked he spread-eagled himself upon the clean invisible sand, embraced it close with every surface of his body. He rolled and rolled again, then wiggled, pulling through it like some amphibious creature joyous to be on land. When he was tired he stopped and nestled wiggling 'til he'd formed impressions for each contour of his body. Sand was under every arch, his lower back, the hollow of his knees, relieving every tired place in him, sending streams of rest through every isthmus, his mind as dark and peaceful now as the inmost silent chamber of the mine.

## The Light

And there beyond the Sand Room was the light.

It filled his eyes.

He closed his eyes and watched it go away.

He opened them and there it was again, a field of light, a glitter and a shine that poured down from a heaven up above.

D.R. felt his lungs go dry, then swell again with moist air and radiance from the light.

He stood.

And then he ran.

Across the sand, and then an ancient oceanbed of stone.

Soundless motions rose and fell behind him in the shadows of the monuments, all towers of vegetation turned to stone.

*I'm near it now.*

It streams.

It falls, a column made of light that's shaped like stone.

The light's a mass of molded stone, hanging in a chamber like a frozen waterfall.

It's a stalactite shaped like some cathedral spire, hanging upside down, a perfect pearl of stone with light inside, shining out through jewels that cling like beads of moisture on a melting tower of ice. Above, it widens and is lost in the high and vaulted ceiling of the chamber. Below it narrows to a tip that points into a pool of water beneath the rocky ledge where I now stand. It shines so bright above it blinds me to look up, but in front, and down along the falling spire, its light is soft, a comfort to my eyes, tinted by the jewels to soothing amber.

I gaze into the amber without blinking. It bathes me in its glow, its love so sweet a sudden sense of evil can't intrude.

Evil tries. It makes a scraping sound behind me, and it hisses. But the love of this pure light won't let me turn away. It bangs and clamors for attention, but my eyes will not be moved from this pure love they finally see.

I feel it, closer, my skin is warned and thrilled by some enormous hostile force behind. My flesh responds in tingling fear, my body feels its threat and pressure, but my eyes are bathed in love and soothed by light, and in my breast is perfect adoration.

There is David, lurking in the shadows of the ledge. He pulls my flesh around and makes me see his eyes shining in the murky darkness of his lair. My stomach turns, my hair feels wild, but my adoration of the light remains serene. It's only David's eyes, and lower forehead. The rest is monster, the mouth of dragon teeth, the chin and jaws receding to a short, thick neck and back of horns and scales and fur.

Oh it's true all right.

He's the monster-guardian of the light.

*Leave fear to the flesh.* The flesh is better terrified, stronger for the wars. Scared flesh attacks, a quick advance into the very teeth of monsters of the deep, throwing dust into their eyes swinging wildly human fingernails as claws. Oh yes, my brother and my friend. It's joined now. Slink back goddamn you, hide back in your lair. My flesh is eager and it's time, old friend. I'm here.

 **Combat**

The dragon drew away when D.R. rushed him, but then came biting back and swiping with his claws. The dragon's rush maneuvered D.R. toward the wall, then pinned him there with furious snapping of his

knife-like teeth 'til D.R. fell and rolled beneath the
claws and came up past the monster, running for the
edge. The monster howled in rage and turned but
D.R. had already leaped and gained a foothold on the
stalactite, and broken off a slender, jagged spire. He
started to climb up the stalactite then, but the dragon
slithered onto it above and trapped him on the lower,
thinning levels of the shaft. D.R. braced his feet in
solid clefts and held his weapon ready in his hands.
When the dragon reached down to claw him D.R.
stabbed it through the scales and made it scream in
furious pain and slither lower to bring his teeth in
range. It bit and clawed but each time D.R. struck it
back, drawing blood from wounds in the monster's
face and head and paws. The dragon's tail extended
back across the ledge, its endless body still wound
deep among the shadowed labyrinths above. The
monster's writhing pushed small stones and grains of
dust off the ledge into the pool below, making the
green water come alive with squirming creatures.
Tails and fins cut the surface, long snake-like tenta-
cles reached into the air and felt along the edges of
the pool. The monster coiled along the folds and
clefts of the stalactite up above, pressing down and
down. D.R. fought back as long as he had room to
stand, but the monster pressed him down and down
and he retreated until there was only the smooth, thin
tip of the stalactite left between him and the pool.
The dragon swiped at D.R. with his claw, then swiftly
struck again and caught him hard upon the shoulder.
D.R. thrust his weapon, but already the chamber was
turning, he was falling, he felt the water close around
him and the creature's thrashing as he sank deep, deep,
the monster's head behind him, biting for his legs.
D.R. felt the teeth sink in, then something stirring,
burning in his veins, a stinging venom. D.R. twisted
and tried to pull away but the monster held him fast
between its teeth and dragged him down and down

and down. D.R.'s legs were numb now but there was strength yet in his back and arms. He saw the monster clearly in the light of his spire gave off, and he maneuvered 'til he had a proper angle. With both hands he swung the spire and stabbed the monster in the eye. He stabbed again, and sunk the spire so deep into the second eye he couldn't pull it out again. Black blood spurted and darkened the churning water as D.R.'s own mind darkened into sleep. In his death throes the dragon plunged, carrying D.R.'s body and its own down through endless fathoms of the deep.

# SIX

### Let Every Soul Be Subject
### Unto the Higher Powers

Mrs. Godsey was in the post office in the far corner of her store, sorting through the Tuesday morning mail. As if people had known it would be a puny delivery that morning, only Mrs. Thornton was there waiting for Mrs. Godsey to hand the letters out. Most days the store was half full of people waiting on their mail, five, six, sometimes as many as a dozen of them, sitting in chairs or leaning against the soft-drink cooler, waiting and talking while Mrs. Godsey organized the mail for distribution. But this morning there was only Mrs. Thornton, and to Mrs. Godsey's mind that was just as well. The only mail in the whole batch that was in the least bit personal was a post card to Wendell Hall from his daughter in Detroit, and she was asking for money. Mrs. Back's copy of *The Upper Room* came, and Barry Berry got a statement from the Famous Writer's School. Old Mr. McClanahan got a brown envelope from the Social Security Administration but you could tell just by looking that it didn't have a check in it. Circulars, statements, bills, and fourteen identical blue envelopes with white writing on it, promotional literature from the Stewart Kesey Soap Company in Chicago addressed to "Boxholder," Trace Fork, Kentucky, and that was it, as sorry a batch of mail as Mrs. Godsey had seen in all the years she'd been postmistress.

"I declare it looks like that Charlene would write

*213*

me," said Mrs. Thornton. "I written her twice this last month and nary a peep have I heard. I begun thinking she don't much care about her old momma any more."

Mrs. Thornton wiped a tear from her eyes with the cuff of her long sleeve.

"Now honey, you know that ain't so," said Mrs. Godsey as she came out of the little cage that was the post office. "You know it ain't like Charlene not to write."

"Sometimes I believe it is," said Mrs. Thornton. "Sometimes I know for sure it is."

Mrs. Godsey sighed. She wanted to commiserate with Mrs. Thornton about Charlene, and maybe pick up some late news on her in the process. But sorting the mail, as little as it had been, had given her such a headache the world was starting to spin before her eyes. She sat down on the bench facing Mrs. Thornton's chair, and appeared to go instantly to sleep. But in a little bit she opened her eyes and looked up at Mrs. Thornton and said, "Honey, I wonder if you'd do me a favor."

"Why sure," said Mrs. Thornton. "You just tell me what it is."

"Get me a R.C. out of the cooler, and some of them Goody Powders off the shelf. My poor old head feels like it's about to come apart."

Mrs. Thornton was a big woman and she had to struggle to get to her feet. She was sweating just sitting there and as she walked to the cooler Mrs. Godsey invited her to help herself to a soft drink, on the house. Mrs. Thornton said she didn't think she wanted anything right then. But once she peered into the cooler and saw the bottles standing cold and luscious in the dark water she changed her mind and took out a Dr. Pepper for herself. She opened them and got a package of Goody's off the shelf.

"I don't know what I'd do without my Goody's," said Mrs. Godsey as she fumbled with the wrapper.

"Them and R.C.'s is about all that'll keep me going any more."

Mrs. Thornton took a drink of Dr. Pepper.

"They say Joyce Jennings is taking tranquilizers now," she said. "They say since Billy Joe left she can't get any rest a-tall without taking one of them pills."

"I never knowed Joyce to get any rest even when Billy Joe was home," said Mrs. Godsey. "I never knowed her to be home any night of the week before one and two o'clock in the morning."

Mrs. Thornton sighed and dabbed her eyes again. "It's her poor old mother I feel sorry for. I declare but children is a trial. They're nothing but a burden to be borne."

Mrs. Godsey nodded. "About the only one I ever knowed that wasn't is my Leonard," she said.

"He's the exception all right," said Mrs. Thornton. "Him and Roxie's both good. You're lucky to have them, Mrs. Godsey. You are, now."

Mrs. Godsey was having trouble taking the cellophane off her package of Goody's. She'd been picking at it ever since Mrs. Thornton handed it to her, but her hands were so stiff and arthritic she hadn't made a tear in it yet.

"Honey, let me undo that for you," said Mrs. Thornton.

"Never mind," said Mrs. Godsey. "I may be old but I ain't plum helpless yet."

The ladies hushed talking until Mrs. Godsey got the wrapper off the package. There were four doses in it, each folded in a paper. Mrs. Godsey took out a dose, laid the box aside, then, very carefully, she poured the white powder into her R.C. Cola.

"I used to just dump it out on my tongue," said Mrs. Godsey. "But here lately it gags me to do that, so I just mix it in a dope now, and sort of sip on it as I go along. I think it's better that way. Seems to stay with me longer."

"When I was in the hospital they fed me through the veins," said Mrs. Thornton. "I laid over there three weeks and never got a bite to eat. I hated it. I've done and told Wheeler he ne'en to expect to ever take me to a hospital again. I told him I'd as soon pass out right there at the house as put up with that outfit over in town."

"I'm just like you, honey," said Mrs. Godsey. "I've got terrible things wrong with me, but I ain't about to go to no hospital for them. I told Leonard if I get down sick to just prop me up in bed, give me some sassafrass tea and let the Lord take care of the rest."

"Amen to that," said Mrs. Thornton. "The Lord's better'n any doctor *I* ever had anything to do with."

"What people don't understand is that you've got to trust the Lord before He can do you any good," said Mrs. Godsey.

"But people ain't willing to do that any more," said Mrs. Thornton. "That's what's wrong with the world."

*"Let every soul be subject unto the higher powers!"* Mrs. Godsey quoted. *"For there is no power but of God: the powers that be are ordained of God.* That's scripture, sister. Romans thirteen, one."

"People just won't accept it," said Mrs. Thornton. "People just turns away."

"They turn away from God and toward Satan," said Mrs. Godsey. "Old Satan's got a arm-lock right around ever one of their necks."

"That's the pure truth," said Mrs. Thornton. "That's the pure truth if it was ever told."

After a little pause for a sip of their drinks, Mrs. Thornton said, "But you know, Mrs. Godsey, if there *is* anybody that ought to be in a hospital it's surely poor old Emmit Collier. I think it's just pitiful, him a laying up there on that old hillside by himself. Me and Wheeler was talking about him just yesterday, wondering what anybody could do."

"Why honey," said Mrs. Godsey. "You're behind the times."

Mrs. Thornton's face said what do you mean?

"Emmit ain't by himself no more."

"You don't mean he's died!" gasped Mrs. Thornton.

Mrs. Godsey grinned. "Oh no," she said. "His nephew David come in and's gone up there to stay with him. Drove in from Cincinnati yesterday in the paintedest-up old bus-of-a-thing you ever saw. Went right straight on up there to take care of him."

"Well I'll swan," said Mrs. Thornton.

"His bus is out behind the house right now."

"Well I'll swan. Now what nephew would that be, honey? It ain't Jenny's boy is it?"

"Jenny's boy'd be too young, honey. He's Royce's. You remember Royce."

"Got killed in a car wreck," said Mrs. Thornton.

"That's right. It was his woman Eva that took up with that Davenport everybody hated so bad."

"Why yes. I remember that family. Their girl went to school to my brother-in-law's wife Rona, when she taught over yonder at Hemlock."

"That's Marcella," said Mrs. Godsey.

"Well now," said Mrs. Thornton. "I remember Marcella real good, but I declare I can't picture a boy."

"He's nearly grown now," said Mrs. Godsey. "I wouldn't of recognized him if he hadn't told me who he was. You'd think he was one of them hip-eyes on television, to look at him. Kind of queer-acting but I tell you now. That child sure meant business about taking care of his uncle. I called up there to Cincinnati Sunday to say how sick Emmit was, and he answered and said he'd come as soon as he could. Just like that. Stopped in here a few minutes, then took off up that creek lickety-split. His bus is out behind the house right now. Leonard pushed it around there."

Mrs. Godsey took a sip of her R.C.

"I tell you now, honey," she went on, "I've been praying for Emmit. I've been asking a blessing for him ever since he come down sick, and I declare if it don't look like the Lord's done sent him one."

"I hope it's so," said Mrs. Thornton. "I say God bless the boy if he don't do no more than make Emmit feel like somebody cares a little something about him."

"That's right," said Mrs. Godsey, and she started to get up then. Struggling to rise, she said, "Well youngun, I don't mean to run you off, but it's my nap time, and I'm going to go in yonder and lay down in the bed awhile."

"I don't blame you," said Mrs. Thornton, and she started getting up too. "I've got to get on home myself. Wheeler'll probably kill me for being gone this long."

Mrs. Thornton was as fat as Mrs. Godsey was old, and it took them equally long to work out of their seats and stand. When they'd made it, Mrs. Godsey said, "You come back to see me, now, you hear?"

"I will," said Mrs. Thornton. "And you come up and see us some time."

"Ohh, I don't know," said Mrs. Godsey. "I guess I'm too old to be out gadding about."

Mrs. Thornton said, "Psshht. You tell that Leonard I said for him to load you in the back of that truck of his'n and haul you up to our house for dinner next Sunday."

Mrs. Godsey laughed and said she'd tell him.

"Where's Leonard at, anyhow?" said Mrs. Thornton. "I've been wanting to ask him something."

"I don't know where he's at today," said Mrs. Godsey. "But he's on the Grand Jury next week."

"The Grand Jury!" exclaimed Mrs. Thornton.

"Yep. Two weeks of it, starting Monday."

"Lordy," said Mrs. Thornton. "He'll come back thinking he's a big shot."

The women laughed again and waved as Mrs. Godsey went through the curtain that separated her house from the store. Mrs. Thornton picked up the empty soft-drink bottles, put them in a case beside the cooler and then went out the door.

## Dragon Tracks

Emmit says, drink this, it's good old 'sang tea, it'll make your insides feel good.

He says, I'm going out to look at the stars, bud. Come on out if you feel like it.

How did I get here? D.R. thought, and Emmit answered: Oh, I might of helped you a little. Cleaned you up some, anyway. Come on out and look at the stars.

D.R. would have taken him up on that if there hadn't been so much work to do. He was helping his dead grandmother with her wash day. And it would be a while before he was free.

His grandmother pulled a pair of overalls out of the churning water and started them through the black and white rubber wringers. He caught the overalls as they came through and guided them into the tub of warm rinse water sitting on the bench beside the old machine, flat

Flat and stiff they floated like a dead man 'til D.R. punched them loose with his stir stick. He punched until their life came back, until they spread out soaking in the water, until the soap was rinsed away and it was time,

and it was time to send them through the wringer once again, then hang them on the line outside to dry.

Let me do it.

Let me do it, D.R. said.

Let me

Get away, said his grandmother. You can't even reach the line.

She filled the clothesline full, twenty yards of overalls and work shirts, sheets and towels and socks and underwear, a few dresses of her own, his own small clothes sprinkled in between. They hung there all afternoon, flapping in the wind like ghosts of an entire family.

Emmit coughed into the curtain of the dream. D.R. heard him in the kitchen, building a fire in the coal stove. He could tell by the way Emmit handled the stove lids he was being as quiet as he could to keep from disturbing him. But it was morning now and D.R. was awake before Emmit was. It was too dark yet to see but he heard him putting his clothes on across the room. He heard the spring on the screen door whine when he went outside to pee. Then he heard him in the kitchen building a fire and putting water on to boil, and D.R. lay there watching the room take shape as the dark gave way to the growth of light in the window.

Here he comes.

He walks

Stoop-shouldered, bent and drawn

Through the curtain Emmit walks, carrying a steaming cup in his hand. He stops at the window to look out and to scratch himself deep down in his pants somewhere, way down along his thigh needs scratching and Emmit gives it a good one before he goes on over to sit down on the bed and sip from his hot cup.

How did I get here? D.R. thinks, and Emmit answers: Oh, I guess I helped you a little. Cleaned you up some anyway. The amazing

The amazing thing about Emmit is his beard. The whole shaggy mass of hair, all over his head. It falls across his forehead and down across his ears, sticking out in little tufts. His beard starts at his ears and covers his entire face except for his eyes and nose and cheekbones, a great thick Santa beard that hangs down like a waterfall across his mouth.

But the rim of his cup finds his mouth in there somewhere and he drinks.

A little. Cleaned you up some, anyway.

And Emmit wipes his mouth and drinks again.

I'm awake, D.R. says.

Emmit raises

Emmit lifts his head like a bird alerted.

He raises his bearded head and looks at his nephew in the big bed across the room.

He looks. For a long time he looks, and doesn't speak.

But then he lifts his cup in a neat salute and says you had a right smart of sleep, old bud, how long

How long have I been sleeping? D.R. asks.

About a day.

Then silence. Do I remember coming here?

But there is just the silence of the old decaying room at early morning, no motion and no swirl. Just still and cool, the old uncle sitting on one bed, the young nephew lying in the other, craving something to drink now, feeling the pulse begin to quicken as he comes again into the world.

He says, I believe I'll have me a cup of that tea, Uncle Emmit.

And Emmit says this just hot water I'm drinking, but I'll go fix you some tea.

I can

I can do it.

But Emmit is up

He's already up and gone to the kitchen to stir the fire and heat a pot of water while he dies.

D.R. saw that he was dying as soon as they went outside. They shouldn't have even tried it, but they were getting used to one another now as they drank, the pulse was quickening and Emmit wanted to go. He wanted to show D.R. how little there was left of what there used to be, and how many new things he had started. He was raising rabbits now. And building worm-pits in the barn, and repairing the barn itself and he wanted to show his nephew that. They walked down the porch steps together and a few steps out the path that crossed the yard and led up to the barn. But then Emmit stopped and shook his head and said he just couldn't go any farther. He couldn't get his breath and his head was swimming. Handing D.R. his cup, Emmit turned and went back and sat down on the bottom step, then leaned against the steps above, fighting to take a breath. Right there in front of D.R.'s eyes.

Right there before his eyes, Emmit was dying.

D.R. started to ask what he should do but Emmit waved his hand and shook his head. He knew what D.R. was about to say and he didn't

hear it

Hear what? What old voice, old time

For sure, Emmit didn't want the boy to say anything he would have to answer, for he was barely breathing now, working hard for every little bit of air he got.

D.R. laid his uncle down and helped him stretch out on his back. He started to take his shoes off for him but Emmit pulled his feet away. He didn't want to be fooled with.

Leave me alone.

He wheezed and strained and bit for air and tried to ass himself up the steps, the second,

third

Moving and breathing a little now, some air was coming in.

D.R. put his arm around his uncle's waist and pulled Emmit's arm around his neck and half-carried him up the steps across the porch and to the bedroom. That one, Emmit said.

That one, over there. The bed D.R. just got out of. They were changing places, passing one another, going opposite ways, and the pulse of things was clicking right along.

I'll be okay, just let me catch my breath, he said. He reached for the sheet and quilt and pulled them over his shoulders and closed his eyes and sank into the pillow, and D.R. took off running.

Running, down the path below the house, through some half-dead trees. Downhill he ran this time, past blasted rock and broken trees and piles of rusted trash along the ruined roadside.

Past what was left of people living there and

mining

old hulks of cars and shells of houses

past the fallen tipple he had crawled back under

past the door of one old house whose mouth yelled
wait! Wait up, D.R.!

Down Trace Fork all the way across the bridge

and there he was again, and again in early morning,
pounding on the store door. And who should answer

Who should answer but Mrs. Godsey, her Bible in
her hand, all smiling, glad to see him, then frightened
by his story.

And Leonard came a running.

And D.R. and Leonard took off running up the
Trace Fork road, leading an old gray horse that pulled
a wooden sled on runners through the breaks and
holes and my how fast it all was moving once it started.

Breathless they stopped at the foot of the little slope
in front of Emmit's house, a slope that in the old days
was a grassy yard that D.R. played on. Even ruined

Even ruined it was recognizable

But not at all familiar, up

Up the final yards to find Emmit on the floor,
tangled in his quilt and dying, his head pointed toward
the kitchen, barely breathing, Leonard

Leonard grabbed the quilt and all the bedding

He grabbed the quilts and blankets off both beds
and ran outside to pile them

He piled them on the sled while D.R. lifted

D.R. lifted Emmit by the shoulders. His eyes were
open, seeing, but he didn't look at D.R. He was looking around his bedroom, this old room

this old house

this bedroom of this ruined house, taking in its
details for what his instinct knew would be his final
time

Breathe, Emmit. Suck you in a big lungful.

Emmit heaved, he bit

Emmit heaved and bit and suddenly raised his head
and sniffed and got some air. In, out, he breathed and
breathed, and by the time they got him on the sled
he had voice enough to argue.

I don't want to go to no hospital.

Well you're going to one whether you like it or not.
I should have taken you in a month ago.

Who was that?

It was Leonard.

It's me, said Leonard.

Goddamn you for taking me, said Emmit. And he
looked at D.R. and said goddamn you too.

Oh it was moving swiftly now. Oh it was happening
fast. Is this how fast it goes? It's so clear, so vivid, is
this how fast it happens? Emmit's final hours on earth
were sweeping through D.R. like some fire, consuming

him, filling all his cracks and empty spaces with its rush and flow and go.

There's so much *work,* so much to suddenly *do.*

quick

Off this mountain, into Urge

What's this you're a putting me in? Emmit wanted to know.

It's a bus, said D.R. I've come from California in it. It's got a bed and everything. Emmit said

He said goddamn you both for taking me.

The doctor said what's wrong? He said, what's wrong, old timer, can't you breathe?

But Emmit wasn't saying. He was captured.

He was a prisoner now, he reserved the right to hold his silence, to keep all that he knew to himself, goddamn them all

goddamn.

And he said no more, except madly, through drugs and semi-sleep and through the haze of death.

Emmit never said another word he meant to say the three more days he lived.

 *Dear Estelle*

Estelle.
  Dear Estelle.
  Estelle, honey.
  Dear Estelle, I'm sitting by my uncle's bedside in the hospital in Blaine, Kentucky. This sweet little hospital where believe it or not I was born about five hundred years ago.
  And my poor old uncle is dying and I am tending to him while he does.
  It's after midnight now. We've been here since this morning, and it's a strange
  Dear Estelle, I'm sitting by my uncle's bedside in the hospital now. We've been here over twelve hours, and it looks like he's going to die.
  Estelle

*Water-Time!*

Emmit was having to pee every ten or fifteen minutes now. Or at least he thought he had to, and each time he thought he had to D.R. had to help him up because Emmit didn't know himself until he sat up, and even if he did know he couldn't say so because he was so far gone in his mind. Drinking and pissing was the treatment. That was it, all right. Flush him out. He was drowning in his own fluids, and the only thing to do was fill him up and pour him out and that was D.R.'s job.
  He yelled, water-time! it's water-time! and D.R. looked to see if he wanted to take some in or let it out. Supporting Emmit with one arm, holding the glass in the other, D.R. offered the water.

And then felt Emmit peeing on the floor.

Later, after he'd peed into the jar, Emmit turned the glass up and tried to drink it.

*His eyes are yellow as lampshades now,* D.R. wrote to Estelle. *I wonder what crazy point of view goes on behind them.*

## Mystery Man

Several times throughout the day and far into the night, Leonard came and went, came and went.

Emmit yelled at him, "You're a mystery man, what are you doing here? Who's in charge?"

"I'm Leonard," said Leonard. "I'm your friend. I'm your neighbor. I'm taking care of your rabbits while you're sick, do you remember them?"

"Kill 'em!," Emmit shouted. "I want all them rabbits dead, do you hear me?"

Then it was water-time again, and Leonard went outside while D.R. helped his uncle up, and held the jar.

When he came back in, Leonard asked D.R. if there was anything he could do.

"I'll stay with him the rest of the night if you want me to."

"Nah," said D.R. "I'm okay. I sleep a little, off and on. If you take care of his place, I'll hold this end down just fine."

"Okay," said Leonard. "But you'll need to eat." And he handed D.R. a ten-dollar bill.

"I think we ought to call Marcella," said D.R.

"Momma already has," Leonard said. "She called her this morning, soon as we brought him in."

D.R. nodded. For some reason he and Leonard

shook hands. They said good-night. As Leonard was on his way out, two orderlies came into Emmit's room, to shave him.

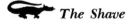 **The Shave**

D.R. started to argue with the orderlies about that, but when they explained that the doctor wanted it done D.R. said, "Okay. But you guys go take a coffee break, and let me do it."

The orderlies looked at one another. Then they shrugged and handed D.R. their tools and went away.

Scissors.

Comb.

Razor, shaving cream.

"I'm going to give you a haircut and a shave, Emmit, what do you think about that?"

"Hunh?"

"I said I'm going to trim you up a little. Cut your hair, shave all that beard off."

"You do and I'll chase you from star to star."

"You can't catch me, Emmit," D.R. laughed. "I'm one of them crabs, I'm on the moon, too fast for you to catch."

"I'm a lizard," Emmit answered. "I'll chase you from star to star to star."

"Yes, but I run sideways," D.R. said. "You know you can't catch somebody running sideways."

"You'll see," said Emmit. "You'll see how far your threats and bribes will stretch from star to star."

Emmit's eyes closed then, he fell into a fifteen-minute dream, and swiftly D.R. cut his hair.

And when he had cut his hair he began to trim the beard away.

Scissors.

Comb.

And scissors, comb.

The hair came off in locks, and then the razor.

As he worked, D.R. was amazed to watch his father's face take shape before him. The mouth, the little cleft in the chin. They'd looked so much alike, Emmit and D.R.'s father. Royce. Somewhere there was a picture of them together in their Army uniforms, taken about 1944, both home on furlough before going overseas, sitting on the front porch of the homeplace, their arms around each other and their cheeks together, mugging for the camera like two lovers. And they looked so much alike you couldn't tell them apart except that Emmit had on paratroop boots and Royce didn't. A few months later Emmit jumped into Holland, around Eindhoven, with the 101st Airborne, and got wounded there. A head wound.

The scar is probably right down there in his hair, D.R. thought.

But he had finished with the hair. There was just the remaining beard now. As Emmit slept D.R. covered his face with lather and carefully shaved him, stroke by stroke, pausing now and then to feel the smooth, clean skin as he cleared it of the stubble.

Emmit felt his face. He rubbed his cheek with his hand, then both cheeks at once with both his hands, and finished smiling.

"Did you do that?" he asked.

"Yep."

"Are you the one in charge here?"

D.R. said he was.

"I wonder, then, if I might dream the sky away?"

"You can dream away the sky and fill the gap with blossoms, Emmit. You can do anything you feel of a mind to do, old friend."

"I'll dream the sky away and think about the honey pond and the fritter tree," said Emmit. "That's a land, you know."

D.R. nodded. "I might dream along with you after a while. I'm getting kind of sleepy."

"Don't go to sleep!" Emmit whispered. "Don't go to sleep!"

D.R. asked why not.

"It would violate the custom," Emmit said.

"What custom are you talking about?" D.R. asked.

"A trustworthy man on guard!" said Emmit, and for the first time since they'd been there, he laughed.

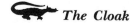 ## The Cloak

D.R. tried to tell Estelle about it, the shave, and Emmit's face, so much like his father's. But that was too particular, too precise a thing for him to have words for now. What he did have words for was an image of how it felt to be there in that hospital like he was. He told Estelle: One of the men in Emmit's ward has been here four months now, and another almost three, and I know that to them a day and a half can't seem like a very long time. But it's been some kind of infinity for me. I haven't slept at all except little naps in my chair, and once last night for about an hour lying on a gurney in the hall. It's very informal here at night. It's a small place, and nobody ever comes on heavy much. You can stretch out wherever you can at night and nobody seems to mind. I have the keenest sense of this place as a secret city hidden from the world. And all the people in it are stoned on suffering. Some of the suffering is birth and some of it is death, and endless different places in between. After a day and a half here, round the clock, I feel as if we've been here all our lives, together, as if we're all warm and comfortable inside this strange, big cloak. It's like I'm *wearing* this hospital as a robe, as if its atmosphere and its routines, night and day and day and night, people coming and going, the change of shifts, the long passing of the night and then the day, is all some kind of magnificent garment I've put on. And Emmit is in it wih me. We're all in it, the doctors, patients, nurses, visitors, secretaries, orderlies, everybody, and it's as if we all *like* being here in one another's company, collectively.

My job is to get liquids into Emmit, and then help him get them out again. His throat is so messed up and his breathing, and now, since they've doped him up, his senses as well, that he can't even handle as much as a spoonful of water at a time. He has to take it in drops. So what I do is sink a straw into a glass of water, or juice, or Coke, then cap it with my finger, hold the straw to his lips, then take away my finger to let it run into his mouth and down his throat. About once a minute I do that. It's like feeding some little animal with a nipple. I manage less than a glassful an hour, but still it adds up because his kidneys continue to function, and Doctor Robinette says that's the key to any chance that Emmit has, which isn't very much of a chance no matter what we do. But it doesn't matter. I just keep dipping it up and dropping it into his mouth, strawful after strawful, and then a little while later here it'll come, it'll be water-time, Emmit will yell out water-time! it's water-time! and I'll tug him to a sitting position and help him leak it out. Then I'll lay him down again and go on dipping in and letting out.

How many times? D.R. wondered. The thousands, surely. Maybe millions. Maybe billions, who knows? Maybe this has been going on and on for years.

If you don't count the times, how can you know how many?

How can you count the stars?

He was outside on the front steps now, breathing

in and looking at the stars. When Leonard had come in the afternoon he had left D.R. a half-pint whiskey bottle with about three drinks left in it, and about midnight D.R. stepped outside and downed them. Emmit had fallen into one of his rare sleeps just before midnight, and the hospital was quieting, quieting down. The lobby was half-lit and silent, except for Mrs. Hubbard shuffling papers behind the admissions desk. Dear Mrs. Hubbard. This was their second night together. It was like some kind of combat tour they'd been on, and it had drawn them close. He's very nice, Mrs. Hubbard thought. She hadn't paid much attention to him the night before, but tonight she thought: he seems like a very nice young man, taking care of his old uncle like that. Not many people take that kind of care of dying old folks. Most just dump them on the hospital to live or die and here's one sure to die, and soon, and yet that young man is caring for him as if it was his own life at stake. The first night she hadn't offered him any coffee from her electric coffee pot, but tonight she did, a couple of times, because tonight they're both into it together, staying up, awake, together on the graveyard shift. D.R. drank two cups of Mrs. Hubbard's coffee, and then later went outside and sipped the whiskey Leonard left him, and as he looked up at the stars, and smelled the coal dust in the air and listened to the trains clanging across the river in the yards, he thought about how kind all the people were. Leonard, Mrs. Hubbard, Doctor Robinette. This big cloak, he thought. This marvelous garment. As he walked back inside, D.R. picked up a corner of the garment and settled it about Mrs. Hubbard's shoulders. She smiled at him and said there'd be more coffee later on.

## Bad News

At nine thirty the next morning D.R. called Marcella from the drug store on Main Street.

"It's bad news, ain't it?" Marcella said.

"I'm afraid so," said D.R.

He could hear Marcella crying. Not much, a sudden flash of tears, then sniffles.

"How long's he been gone, David?"

"Just a few minutes. He died at fifteen after nine."

"Well, honey," Marcella said tearfully. "You've done a wonderful thing, being there with Emmit. I know Daddy would appreciate it if he was living. And Grandma would."

Marcella hushed a minute 'til she had better control of her voice. Then she asked David when he figured the funeral would be.

"I thought about two tomorrow afternoon, Marcella. There won't be that many people to come, and we might as well get it over with."

"I think that's right," said Marcella. "What we'll do is leave here real early in the morning and be there around one, does that sound okay?"

"That's just fine," said D.R. "I'll take care of the arrangements. And Leonard'll help me. He's really a fine man, Marcella. I never would have got through all this without him."

"I know he is," Marcella said. "And you are too, honey. You've done a wonderful job with everything."

D.R. shook his head, as if Marcella could see him.

And then, as if she had, Marcella hushed and told D.R. good-bye. They hung up then, and D.R. went to Olney's Funeral Home to buy a casket for Emmit.

 **Mr. Olney**

Mr. Olney didn't recognize D.R. but when D.R. introduced himself, he remembered. He had buried D.R.'s father and both his grandparents, and now there was Emmit's body, following theirs through the same treatment in the same treatment rooms. D.R. knew there wasn't any way it could have turned out different, but still he resented Mr. Olney for having that power over what was left of Emmit, and he didn't bother to hide his resentment when he spoke.

"How much is this one?" D.R. asked.

When Mr. Olney said eleven hundred dollars D.R. laughed and asked to see the cheapest thing he had. Mr. Olney took him to the far corner of the casket room and showed him one that cost two hundred and twenty dollars. Without bothering to examine it, D.R. said he'd take it.

Then they talked about the burial clothes. There was a blue suit for thirty-five dollars, with a shirt and tie for free, said Mr. Olney. But D.R. said he couldn't afford that much. He asked Mr. Olney if he could help dig the grave and get the suit half-price. Mr. Olney said he believed he could manage that, and suddenly D.R. was sorry he had acted weird toward Mr. Olney a while ago. He's just an old undertaker, D.R. thought.

Be kind to the old and dead.

I'll be old myself before long.

I'll be dead myself, some day.

**The Graveyard**

Oh far out, far out, far out. It happens with such speed, it swooshes by with such haste. There he was

already, him and Leonard, helping two guys from
Olney's Funeral Home dig poor Emmit's grave. There
in the family graveyard, one corner of it buried by
overburden from the mining on the slopes above, rocks
as big as people's heads scattered among the graves.
One headstone, D.R.'s great-uncle Daniel who had
died in 1952, had been knocked over and broken
straight across the middle by a rock from the mining
up above. The graveyard was at the edge of the pasture, when there had been a pasture. D.R. used to
pass it all the time, going to get the cow, out walking
with his grandfather on Sunday afternoons, or just in
the pasture by himself at any odd time, for no reason.
D.R. had been visiting that graveyard of his ancestors
as long as he could remember, and now here he was
again, helping to dig this time. How strange that was.
How swiftly it moved along.

Leonard finished his turn digging and sat down
beside Royce's grave to smoke a cigarette. Royce was
buried just uphill from where Emmit was going to
lie. Royce Collier, his gravestone said. Among The
Angels Now. Beside Royce were his sister Blanche,
and his father, who'd outlived him, and beyond his
father, his mother, who'd outlived them both. D.R.'s
mother wasn't in the Collier graveyard. She had died
a Davenport in Illinois somewhere. Leonard sat near
where she might have been if fate had willed it so,
and smoking he looked up the hill toward the curve
of the slope and told D.R. how the strippers had
come, from left to right, peeling the trees off first,
then the cut, then the blasting and finally the exposed coal seam. The only image D.R. could get was
of road builders indiscriminately hacking through the
pasture, and Leonard said that was pretty close to
how it was.

D.R. asked Leonard if the overburden above the
cemetery was stable, if rain would loosen it and let it

slip on down across the graves. Leonard said there was a chance of it. He said that down behind the main house it was definitely going to slip some more but up there, maybe not.

What if it does, D.R. thought.

What difference would it make?

In the corner of the cemetery where the slide had broken through the picket fence, D.R. picked up a piece of shale that had some fossils in it, little shells of ancient creatures that millenia ago had been alive. Buried all this time and now uprooted, D.R. thought. He thought of his father's bones, and his grandfather's.

And he thought of his own bones too. His living hand held the ancient shale. Some day that hand itself would fossilize, and what difference does it make how deep it's buried down.

Down, they went down with Emmit's grave. Down, down. Three feet. Four. Four and six inches. Five. Right on through suppertime, into the evening they dug, taking turns, resting, going on again.

D.R.'s hands were blistered when at five feet eight inches Leonard said boys that's good enough, let's quit.

 **The Grave**

On their way down the hill Leonard stopped off at the homeplace to show D.R. how to feed and water Emmit's rabbits and chickens. There were forty some rabbits in eleven hutches, and about a dozen banty chicks to feed, a half-hour chore even when you knew what you were doing. D.R. worked along with Leonard, and listened, he wanted to learn this work.

But his mind was still full of Emmit's grave.

When Leonard invited D.R. home with him to eat

supper D.R. said he didn't much feel like eating. He wanted to stay on the hill by himself awhile, and Leonard understood. As soon as Leonard was out of sight downhill, D.R. went back around the hillside to the grave.

A grave.

That is a grave.

That dark, opening.

The dark is a hole in the ground for Emmit's body. It's Emmit's body's home now. We're going to put it in a box and put the box in that hole tomorrow afternoon and cover it with dirt and leave it there for years and years and years. Worms are going to eat his flesh and devour the casket, and in time even his bones will turn to dust. We're going to plant Emmit here tomorrow like a seed.

He's worm-food now.

D.R. was sitting on the mound of dirt they'd thrown up, looking at the hole. Above him was his father's grave, and all around were other graves of long-dead people who had sired him, and it was dark and overhead some early stars were shining as they had the night before, how many nights before? In the ground, D.R. thought.

In the ground.

And then out loud he said it: "In the ground."

And without really deciding to in his mind, D.R. scooted to the edge, then bracing across the corner of the grave he lowered himself into it, and lay down on his back and closed his eyes.

This is Emmit's wake, he thought.

This is Emmit's wake. I am waking here for Emmit. I'm awake.

And suddenly D.R. felt Emmit in the air around him, he was flying through the cool night air, and walking on the broken slopes above.

That's silly, D.R. thought. He's not flying. He's not walking.

He's not even Emmit any more. Emmit's lost his name now. Gone free of names.

And in the cooling dark, feeling the walls of earth on either side, D.R. wondered what that could feel like, what it could possibly feel like to have no name.

To not be David.

To not be Collier. Or Davenport or Divine Right, or even D.R. No name, he thought.

No name, no name. I've joined the earth and turned to no-name stone downhill from the bones of my father.

Father.

I remember you, my father, lying through this wall of earth above my head. You played the guitar and sang and drove us around. I remember seeing you carrying groceries on your shoulder in a box, and one time on the courthouse lawn in Hyden eating crackers and sardines and drinking Pepsi-Cola, the two of us there together. Now you are bones and I am bones, and let the dead bones lie. Old fish that used to swim here have no names. Old cows that used to pasture here forgotten, without names. And people that used to live here, Indians in the rockhouses, digging hominy holes, dead, and only remnants of their living here remain. And no names. A few names fading in the headstones maybe, stones already sinking, leaning, eager to lie down. I am lying down.

Down, down in Emmit's bed, trading places with him as a wake.

 *The Morning*

But then the night and then how soon the daylight comes, how endless are the details of the work. It's busy, busy, it's ritual time, it's tending to the dead.

D.R. rolled out of bed—Emmit's bed, the big one—at six A.M., and by six thirty he was sitting in Leonard's kitchen, his wife Roxie's kitchen, eating eggs and ham and biscuits covered by thick gravy.

"You just help yourself now, David," Roxie said. "You eat anything you can reach, and what you can't reach just ask for it, you make yourself right at home."

D.R. ate. He ate, and ate. He ate like some great tanker taking on a load of fuel, while in the next room Leonard was tying his tie.

Leonard looked strange in a suit, and yet it belonged on him too. He was tall and roughly cut, big-boned and lean, a powerful man. Leonard was in his fifties, a grandfather as a matter of fact. But nobody ever deferred to Leonard because of that. People deferred to him but it wasn't because they thought he was old or beyond his prime. He was right in his prime, and so was Roxie. She was large and getting round, but she was some years younger than Leonard, barely forty. She was only seventeen when Leonard married her, and eighteen when she had her first child. Their children were all grown now, four of them, three already married, living in Indiana and Illinois. Their youngest son Glenn had left home back in the winter, to join the Army. He was over in Vietnam now. When D.R. finished breakfast, Leonard told him to come in the bedroom and try on Glenn's high-school graduation suit.

"Why that's a perfect fit," said Leonard.

"Close to it," D.R. said.

"Why yes," said Roxie. "That suit looks fine on you."

Wearing their suits and ties, Leonard and D.R. went up to the church then to talk to Reverend Bagby about the funeral.

## Funeral Plans

Mrs. Thornton's niece Dorothy would sing "Abide With Me," and Mrs. Bagby would play the piano. The message would be short, said Reverend Bagby. It was hot, and there was the work of getting the casket up on the hill to bury. At the graveside there would be a prayer, and then the lowering of the casket into the grave. And that would be all. It sounded just right to D.R. He liked Reverend Bagby. There was something a little foreign about him, something a little too educated maybe in the way he used his eyes. But he certainly wasn't faking his attitudes and D.R. liked him for that. He liked Mrs. Bagby. He liked Leonard and he liked Roxie. D.R. tried to hide it as best he could, but the truth of the matter was, he was really enjoying this day so far. There was something in this day that was filling D.R. with a vast, private joy.

## Reunion

About an hour before the service, Marcella and her family arrived. How good, just plain *good* it was to see her, and Doyle, and Herschel and little Debbie. Doyle grabbed D.R.'s hand and shook it as Marcella gave him a powerful hug, and Herschel began tugging at his coat pocket. Debbie hung back, and D.R. lifted her into the air as a reward for being demure. Lift me! Lift me! Herschel shouted, and Doyle took him by the hand and led him off to one side to explain why he ought not be yelling like that. Leonard stood among the people as a greeter. It was proper that he do so. Everybody felt it, and in their separate ways

they thanked him for it. Doyle held his hand out to
Leonard and said you may not remember me, Leonard, but I'm Doyle.

Leonard said, "Why Doyle, I remember you good.
You fixed a car of mine one time, an old Mercury,
don't you remember that?"

Doyle looked a little puzzled, then embarrassed.
"Why, yes. Now I'd plum forgot all about that," he
said. "Maroon car. Put a new coil in it for you, down
there by your all's store."

When Doyle mentioned the store, Marcella interrupted the men to ask Leonard how his mother was.

"She don't change, Marcella," said Leonard, grinning and shaking his head. "I swear, but she ain't a
bit different from when you all used to live here."

"Well, I've been talking to her on the phone a lot
lately, but it's been *so* long since I've seen her."

"Well now, she'll be here after a while. And she's
going to be really tickled to see all you people again."

And a few minutes later, there she was, old Mrs.
Godsey, with a hat on now, a great, white, wide-
brimmed hat, and a kind of cream-colored dress that
reached to her ankles nearly. Her daughter-in-law
Roxie was walking with her, holding her by the arm.
But when she saw Marcella the old woman moved out
by herself and stepped toward Marcella with her arm
stretched out to shake hands. Only instead of shaking
hands she hugged her, and the two women pressed
their cheeks together briefly, then stood back to look
at one another.

"And these are my children," said Marcella. "This
is Debbie. And that's Herschel. Herschel, come and
say hello to Mrs. Godsey. She's an old neighbor-friend
of ours."

"Mrs. Godsey knew your mother when she wasn't as
old as you are," D.R. said to Herschel. "What do you
think about that?"

Herschel didn't think much about it one way or another, but he shook hands anyway, and then retreated behind his father.

The people talked about Emmit then, going over some of the details of his last days at the homeplace, and the experience of the hospital. Leonard said, "I tried for a month to get him to go to the hospital, but he wouldn't have a thing to do with such an idea."

"And then here comes this boy along, and packs him off the first day," said Mrs. Godsey. And she patted D.R. on the shoulder.

"He didn't like me for it, either," said D.R. "He cussed me and Leonard all the way to Blaine, and up two flights of stairs."

"But it had to be done," said Leonard. "It just *had* to be done."

## The Funeral

Everyone hushed talking when Mr. Olney drove up in the hearse. As Ray and Chester, the two fellows who'd helped dig the grave the day before, unloaded the casket, Mr. Olney came over to the shade of the big elm tree where the people were standing and solemnly shook everybody's hand. What D.R. realized then that he had only sensed the day before was that Mr. Olney was a very sick man himself, pitiful-looking. D.R. shook his hand warmly today, and in some strange way he felt responsible for him. Mr. Olney seemed to have a burden D.R. wanted to relieve him of, and he studied the old undertaker as he walked into the church behind Ray and Chester, who were wheeling the casket in.

Ray and Chester came back out in a minute to get the flowers they'd brought in the hearse. The flowers had been delivered to the funeral home. Six wreaths: from Marcella and her family, Leonard and his family, Mrs. Godsey, the Thorntons, Reverend Bagby on behalf of the congregation (although only five people in the congregation came to the funeral), and one wreath that was signed, simply, "hospital staff." Ray and Chester took the flowers in and arranged them in front of the casket and at the ends, and then as a final act they opened half the coffin lid and the people who had gathered in the church filed by for one last look at Emmit, lying on the light-blue pillow, hardly recognizable without his beard, and in the suit and shirt and tie they'd dressed him in. His lips were puckered unnaturally, but the whole thing was so unlike Emmit that detail didn't matter much. The people filed by, some of them sniffling, and then they all sat down in the front two rows, fourteen people counting children and the Reverend and Mrs. Bagby and Ray and Chester and Mr. Olney and the Thornton girl who was going to sing "Abide With Me."

Mrs. Bagby played the piano softly for a while.

And then her husband, who was not a tall man, but who made a strong impression with his voice, stood up and opened the Bible to Ecclesiastes, chapter three. Sweetly, and yet with power and resonance in his voice, he said that for everything there is a season, and a time for every purpose under the heaven. There is a time to be born and a time to die. A time to plant and a time to pluck up that which is planted. A time to kill, and a time to heal. A time to break down and a time to build up. A time to weep and a time to laugh. A time to mourn and a time to dance. A time to cast away stones and a time to gather stones together. A time to embrace and a time to refrain from embracing. There is a time to get and a time to lose, a time to keep and a time to cast away. A time to rend, a time to sew, a time to keep silence,

And let us keep silence now.

And Reverend Bagby presided over a silent prayer with his arm upraised and his hand outstretched, 'til finally someone among the people said amen.

Reverend Bagby began to talk about Emmit then, but personal remarks about him were only a part of what he had to say. He gave a little of Emmit's biography. He said that he was born there on Trace Fork, that he'd grown up there, and had gone to Finley County High School. He said that he'd served in World War Two, and been wounded, and that after the war he'd gone into the coal business for a while. He talked about Emmit living a few years in Louisville, and about his year in the Veteran's Hospital and then his return to Trace Fork when his father passed away. But the remarks about him personally were only little decorations on a larger statement he was trying to make that D.R. listened to very carefully. It wasn't a logical statement, it was better than that. He began with the reading from Ecclesiastes, and then allowed his words to spread up and outward into a kind of song. Half the time he spoke with his eyes closed. And now and then he'd stop suddenly, hushed by some inner command, and in the church a silence would build that he in turn would use to build his song upon, reaching higher and higher and lower and lower, sometimes bridging the high and the low by lapsing into an unknown tongue, not much, and never for very long, just little shines of the pure language of glossolalia, fah lan tah, mah nah lah, fa lan tah.

And D.R. listened.

He heard a sweet voice sing "Abide With Me."

And then he helped them carry Emmit in his coffin outside to where the sled was waiting.

And he walked with Leonard leading the horse up Trace Fork, the others coming behind, not the old folks, not Mrs. Godsey nor Mr. Olney, just those who could make it in the sun over the broken road and then across the broken hillside up the rugged slope past yellow, yellow earth of the churned-up land.

He helped them lower the coffin down into the grave.

And he walked with Marcella and Doyle and Leonard and the others back down to the homeplace. Mrs. Thornton had stopped off there on the way up the creek, cleaning up, and someone had brought food, big plates of fried chicken and beans and potatoes and pies and cakes, and suddenly everybody was eating. Eating and laughing and talking, the whole thing suddenly a social occasion, a big party that in spite of all was a very happy time. Marcella and her family stayed all night with D.R. there in the old house, where they'd both lived at different times as children. Doyle and the kids went to bed fairly early that evening, but D.R. and Marcella stayed up far into the night, talking about their family, and the old days.

# SEVEN

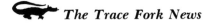 *The Trace Fork News*

by Barry Berry
(reprinted from the Blaine *Herald*)

Well, I know a lot of you were disappointed that
there wasn't any news last week. It didn't mean that
nothing was going on. Something's always going on
around Trace Fork and up and down Rockhouse
Creek, but I just felt too bad last week to write it up.
I've had a virus going on ten days now. I don't know
what it was, but it sure makes you feel awful when you
get it. I'm not plum over it yet but I do feel some
better this week although I'm still not up to making
a full report. This time next week I intend to be well
enough to write half the paper full, but I'm going to
take it kind of easy this week because I sure don't want
any relapse of whatever it was that I've been down
with.

Dolly Huff told me that Mr. and Mrs. Dwayne Hol-
comb were down from LaPorte, Indiana over the
weekend visiting her mother, who is 88 years old.

Aunt Eunice Bartlett and her son Denver went to
Lexington to visit Ira Combs, who had surgery on his
leg. They report the operation was a success and that
Ira should be home in a week or two. Denver drove his
new Chevrolet.

Mr. and Mrs. Joseph Cooney have also been to Lexington lately. Their daughter Sarah finished nurse's

251

training at Good Samaritan Hospital and her parents went down to the graduation. Sarah is a registered nurse now. Seems like only yesterday she was here in high school, cheerleading. Congratulations, Sarah. Why don't you come on back home and be a nurse in one of our fine mountain hospitals? We need good nurses and doctors. We need all of our young people to come back home to live.

But it seems like there's just not enough opportunity here for young people any more. I'd hate to know the figures on just how many of our fine young people have moved away in the last few years.

Mr. and Mrs. Elmer Hampton from Cutshin in Leslie County visited his sister, Mrs. Ruth Gordon on Ten Mile Creek two weekends ago.

Phyllis and William Sims have a new baby girl. Her name is Janell. Congratulations, Phyllis and William.

I didn't get to go to church the last two Sundays but Brother Bagby says attendance has been real good.

Hagen Banks made the honor roll at Morehead University the last semester. His mother, Theda, said this was the third straight semester Hagen made the honor roll. Hagen is going to summer school so he can finish college in three years. He is studying to be a biology teacher.

Sammy Kirk has been home on furlough from Fort Knox the past couple of weeks, but he has to leave Saturday for Vietnam. I know his mother, Mrs. Cinda Banks, will hate to see him go so bad. Readers will remember that it has only been a little over a year since Cinda lost her husband Arlis in a mining accident. May the Lord watch over Sammy and return him safely to us as soon as possible.

Our community was saddened last week when Emmit Collier died. Most people didn't even know that Emmit was all that sick, 'til they took him to the hospital in Blaine. Leonard Godsey, who was a good friend of Emmit's, said he was bad sick for a month or more, and that he tried to get Emmit to go to the hospital, but he wouldn't. Emmit lived by himself up at the head of Trace Fork and didn't get out much. I didn't get to go to the funeral but everybody that went said it was real nice. Brother Bagby officiated, and Dorothy Thornton sang. They buried Emmit in the family cemetery up on the old Collier homeplace. The road up Trace Fork's so bad any more they had to haul the casket up in a sled.

Relatives at the funeral included Emmit's niece Marcella, and her husband Doyle Maggard, and their children, all from Cincinnati, plus Marcella's brother, David Ray, who was already here visiting.

Lee Sergeant said that his neighbor, Mrs. Lois Pope's application for a Black Lung pension on her husband, the late Kermit Pope, has been approved, and that Mrs. Pope will soon begin to receive the monthly benefits. As far as I know, Mrs. Pope is the first in this end of the country to have her Black Lung application approved. But there are many more who ought to receive those benefits if justice is to be done to all those whose health was destroyed working in the mines.

Well, that's all for this week. My head's starting to hurt again so I'm going to quit and go out on the porch awhile.

 **Dear Flash**

Well, man, it's far out. In the last ten days me and Estelle split up, I've gone crazy and an uncle of mine here in Kentucky has died. I tended to him the best I could but he died, and we buried him on the hillside last Saturday afternoon. I helped dig his grave.

And now I'm living here in his house, an old house my grandfather built about 1920, a house my father grew up in, and that I lived in a while myself when I was a boy. It's an amazing scene. This hill, and all the hills around here, were strip-mined a couple of years ago. I mean, man, they've been destroyed. Bulldozers pushed the tops of the mountains into the valleys so they could scoop the coal up with machines. About eighty per cent of my grandfather's farm here is under mud now, and out behind the house there's this incredible big mound of mud, this big wall of it, about fifteen feet high, waiting on a rain to loosen it enough to flow right on through this very kitchen. I wish you could see it.

In fact, consider coming to see it. I'm going to stay on here a while and look after things and get myself together a little. The Lord has sent me to a cool place at last. I haven't ridden in a car in almost a week now. The theme here is staying put. Being still. No freeways, please. No wheels, except maybe one at a time, on a wheelbarrow. About all I want to do at this point is rest and be real quiet, and what I'm finding is that the best way to do both those things is to work hard. I've been working full days since my uncle's funeral. If you feel like resting and being quiet, come on down here and work with me a while. You can shovel rabbit shit while I water the garden.

If you can't swing that, do two other things for me. Send me some money, and find out where Estelle is. I don't need a lot, and I don't need it all at once, and whatever you send, from now on, I intend to pay you back. (I mean, like, how many freaks mooching off you intend to pay you back, Flash? This may be the start of some whole new trend.) If you could send me two hundred dollars now, and a hundred dollars a month 'til further notice, I'd be cool. I can live on a hundred a month here easy. Food for the rabbits and myself is the only really big expense. (My inheritance includes forty-seven rabbits, all hopping around and eating and shitting in hutches out behind the barn.

They're part of my uncle's scheme to save the world with rabbit shit, which I will describe for you in full detail in another letter. It's very far out.) If I stay the rest of the summer, I'll owe you four hundred dollars by fall. But even if I wind up staying a whole year I'd only owe you about fourteen hundred next summer. I'll figure out something else by then. What I need to do now is get some money coming in so I won't have to sweat it for a while, so please let me know pretty soon if you'll be able to carry me for a while.

Estelle. I don't know what to say, where to begin. We got really fucked up in Cincinnati. Or at least I did. It was heavy, I was heavy, and it got heavier and heavier 'til I really couldn't carry it any more. It's much better now. I'm much better. At least I think I am. I feel like I am. And what I want to do is get hold of her and tell her that. And a whole bunch of other stuff too. So please try to scout her out for me Flash, get an address or a phone number and send it to me as soon as you can. Maybe Angel's heard from her. I'm sure she didn't go back to her parents' place in Grayling, although maybe she did at that. I'm sending a letter to her, in care of you. As soon as you get an address please forward it to her *immediately,* and then let me know.

Well, old hoss, many thanks to you. I'm not rapping with anybody here much, except a little with this one guy, Leonard, who was a friend of my uncle's and who comes up to help me now and then. So I'll be laying some letters on you for a while, probably. And if you feel like it, lay some on me in return.

Peace.
D.R.

 *Dear Estelle*

I've written you about fifty pages of letter since I've seen you but it's too big a mess to send. Some time I want to read those pages to you, or let you read them, and I'd like to talk to you a long time about what's in them. Some amazing things have happened since I didn't see you in Cincinnati any more and it's probably been the same for you. It seems like adventures keep on happening to me and you, and most of the people we know, even when we don't particularly want to have adventures for a while.

What I want us to do, Estelle, is get together and talk it over. I want you to come here where I am, and be with me a good, long while, and let's get into it again and see what happens this time. That's what I want us to do. If it's necessary, and you want it that way, I'll come wherever you are. I want to hang around here awhile, but I want to see you more than I want to stay here, so if you want me to come where you are, just say so.

But let me tell you a little about this place, Estelle. Let me tell you how it is here.

Mainly, it's very quiet. It's not so lovely to look at because this is coal-mining country, and the hills have been pretty much fucked over, but in its way this is the loveliest place to be that I've found in a long time. Of course I always thought it was lovely. I used to be around here a lot when I was a kid, and I've got a lot of sweet kid memories of how it was in those years. But the way it's lovely now doesn't have anything to do with memory. I'm surprised that it's that way. It seems very far out to be looking at this place from such a different angle. But I'm not spending much time on my surprise. I'm too involved in this other loveliness that's here that I can't describe very well, but that I feel really strongly.

What's here is an old house, and an old barn, both of them ruined. There's a small garden that's not ruined, and water piped down from a spring. There's some chickens, and there's just one hell of a lot of rabbits living in hutches out by the barn. Most people would consider this a pretty grim and worthless place, but it holds a very large value for me that I haven't got completely figured out yet, but that emotionally I feel like I've got a pretty good grip on. There's no electricity, and you can't get a car up here, but those are both pluses as far as I'm concerned. I'm writing to you right now by the light of a coal-oil lamp, and that's a plus. In a few minutes I'm going to go out on the front porch and sit in my uncle's rocking chair and look at the stars and feel the cool and enjoy this quiet Kentucky evening and that's a plus for sure.

But the really big plus would be if you were here with me. I want you to be. At the least, I want you to write to me and tell me where you are and that you're okay. I'll worry about you 'til you do. I'm pretty bored with worrying about myself so much, but I'll worry about you 'til I hear that you're okay. So please write to me just as soon as you possibly can.

Love,<br>D.R.

 **People at the Store**

When D.R. went in the store to mail the letters to Estelle and the Anaheim Flash, Mrs. Thornton saw him and headed him off at the bread rack.

"Well I'll swan," she said. "Look who finally came down off the hill."

"Hello, Mrs. Thornton."

"Hello yourself is what I say," said Mrs. Thornton. "What have you been doing all week, anyhow, hibernating?"

D.R. laughed and blushed a little and scratched his head. "No ma'm. I've been working pretty hard."

"I'll bet you have," said Mrs. Thornton. "Sorting through Emmit's stuff I bet, God rest him."

"Yes ma'm. Trying to clean up a little. And keep his animals fed. There's a lot of work to do up there."

"I know just what you mean," said Mrs. Thornton. "It took us over a month to go through Wheeler's daddy's things when he died. We couldn't figure out what to do with it all."

"Is that him?" said a man's voice behind Mrs. Thornton.

'This is him," said Mrs. Thornton. "And then to D.R. she said, "We've been talking about you, youngun. Come over here and meet some people."

The man who had spoken was a pale and nearly bald fellow sitting in a wheelchair. Grinning, he rolled himself outside of the little circle of chairs where the other people were sitting and came forward to meet D.R. and Mrs. Thornton.

"I'm Barry Berry," the man said. "I'm proud to make your acquaintance."

"Barry's the news correspondent for the county paper," said Mrs. Thornton. "He was asking me questions about you. I don't guess you've seen this week's paper yet have you?"

"No ma'm, I haven't," said D.R.

"Barry wrote you up," said Mrs. Thornton, and turning then she called out to Mrs. Godsey, who was in the post-office cage in the far corner of the store, "Is they a copy of the paper around anywhere, Mrs. Godsey?"

"Is they what, honey?" Mrs. Godsey called back. She was reading someone's post card and did not look up when she replied.

"The paper. David ain't seen Barry's article in it yet."

"I've got one in yonder," said Mrs. Godsey, still

without looking up. "I'll get it for him when I get done here."

"Mrs. Godsey'll show you her'n after awhile," said Mrs. Thornton.

"I'd like to see it," said D.R.

"Well," said Barry. "It wasn't much, actually. I've been down with some kind of virus lately, and I didn't write much last week. It was just a little mention about Emmit was all. I sure was sorry to hear about Emmit, I'm going to miss him a lot."

"You know," Barry went on, "I don't guess I saw Emmit more than once or twice a year the last five or six years he lived, but I tell you, I was always mindful of him living up there on that hill. I use to know about everybody that lived on Trace Fork. I watched 'em move out one by one, 'til they wasn't a soul living up there except Emmit. Of course it's all ruined up in there now. But it seemed like as long as Emmit stayed on, the place wasn't plum dead yet. I'd been wanting to get up to see Emmit for a long time, but I just never got around to it. Of course, if I'd of known he wasn't going to be with us right on and on, I'd have made myself get around to it. But there you are."

"It really is a shame," said Mrs. Thornton. "I mean, me and Wheeler talked about going to visit Emmit too, but we just kept putting it off. It's funny, how you'll put off things you intend to do, and put 'em off and keep on putting 'em off. And then all of a sudden it's too late to do it even if you tried. I feel bad about it, I declare I do."

"We all could have done better by Emmit than what we did," said Barry. "We sure could have been better neighbors than what we was."

D.R. said, "Well, the thing for you all to do is come up and visit me some time. It looks like I'll be staying around awhile."

Mrs. Thornton and Barry both looked a little startled. "Are you really?" said Mrs. Thornton.

'Yep," said D.R. "I thought I would. A month or two, anyhow. Maybe even longer."

Mrs. Thornton said, "Well I'll swan. Now that really is news," and turning around again she called out to Mrs. Godsey, "Did you hear that?"

"Hear what, honey?"

"David said he's going to live at the Collier place awhile. Said he was going to stay on up there a month or more."

"Oh yes," said Mrs. Godsey. "Leonard told me that a day or two ago."

"Well it sure is news to me," said Mrs. Thornton, and she turned to gush about it some more to Barry and D.R.

But Barry had led D.R. over to the circle of chairs to introduce him to the other people in the store. There were two, Mrs. Whitaker, who was so shy she could only nod and say hello to D.R., and Mr. McClanahan, who was not at all shy, but who was old and could barely hear.

"Do what?" he yelled, cupping his hand to his ear.

"I said this is Emmit Collier's nephew," said Barry. "David's his name."

*"Cecil Agnew!"* the old man shouted. "Who? What did you say?"

*"Emmit Collier!"* Barry yelled. *"That died the other day. This is his nephew."*

Mr. McClanahan heard the word "died" and suddenly it all came together in his mind. He shifted his cane to his left hand and with his right he reached out and grabbed D.R. by the leg, just above the knee, and squeezed hard.

But when he spoke, he still addressed himself to Barry.

"I knew this boy's grandfather," said Mr. McClanahan. "Me and him use to log together. Hard worker. Knew his father, too. That was a good family of people."

"David here's going to live a while at the old home-place," Barry said.

"Do which?"

"I said, David's going to live a while up there where Emmit did. He's taking care of the place."

Mr. McClanahan shook his head. "Trace Fork used to be full of people," he said. "But they ain't nobody lives up there now that Emmit's dead."

Barry smiled and nodded and let it go at that.

And about that time Elmer the mailman came in with the morning delivery. D.R. excused himself from the conversation and took his letters to Mrs. Godsey, behind the cage.

"He's about to miss the boat ain't he, Mrs. Godsey?" said Elmer as he traded mail sacks with her. "Yes sir. About to miss the last mail boat out of China."

"Oh no," said Mrs. Godsey as she held D.R.'s two letters up to the light. "These letters's going to California, Elmer. We can't slow *this* mail down. Going to, what's this, honey? Anaheim? I can't make that out."

"Flash," said D.R.

"Flash. Now that's a queer name. And what's this one? Esther?"

"Estelle," said D.R. "Estelle Adams."

Mrs. Godsey stamped the postmark on the letters, then sat a minute, thinking. "Adams. That's not Felix Adams's girl from Leatherwood is it? That joined the WAC's here while back? Seems like they sent her to California."

"No ma'm," said D.R. "Estelle's not from around here. She's from Michigan."

"How come you're writing to her in California then?" asked Mrs. Godsey.

D.R. grinned. "Well, I was thinking she might be in California by now."

"But you don't know for sure," said Mrs. Godsey.

"No ma'm, I don't," said D.R.

"Sounds like this girl must be your sweetheart," said Mrs. Godsey.

D.R. laughed. "I guess I don't know that for sure either," he said.

"Well now, she either is or she ain't," said Mrs. Godsey. "Ain't that right, Elmer? Elmer here's a bachelor, but he knows more about women than anybody else around here, don't you, Elmer?"

Elmer took the letters from Mrs. Godsey and stuffed them into the mailbag. When he'd drawn the strings on the bag together again, he looked up and pushed his cap back off his forehead.

"It's like this," said Elmer. "She either is or she ain't unless you're on the outs, and then it all depends. Sometimes one can be your sweetheart but get on the outs with you, and then it's just all hurly-swirly."

Everybody in the store laughed at Elmer then, including Mr. McClanahan who hadn't understood what was said, but who was in the habit of laughing at Elmer every time he saw him at the store.

"Elmer's got more sweethearts than any man around here," said Barry.

"But I hear there's one he likes better than any other," said Mrs. Thornton.

Standing in the door now, about to leave, Elmer said, "If you all don't quit talking about me I won't bring you any more mail."

"You don't ever bring nothing worth reading anyhow," said Barry.

"I bring the Blaine *Herald* once a week," said Elmer.

"Well you *know* they ain't nothing worth reading in that thing," said Barry.

Mrs. Thornton said, "Elmer, if you don't bring me a letter from Charlene pretty soon I'm going to wring both your necks."

"I'll bring you one tomorrow if I have to write it myself," said Elmer.

"I'll be looking for it," said Mrs. Thornton.

"So long," said Barry, and as Elmer went out the door, waving, Mrs. Godsey said, "We'll see you tomorrow, Elmer. You be good now."

 **Credit**

After Mrs. Godsey had sorted the mail and handed it out and chatted with the people awhile, she told D.R. to come with her to the kitchen and she would show him Barry's article in the paper. D.R. followed and when she'd found the paper for him she asked if he wouldn't like to sit down at the table and have a cup of coffee or something while he read. D.R. said he'd like that fine, and before long he had finished reading the article and Mrs. Godsey had joined him at the table with an R.C. Cola of her own.

"That's a nice thing Barry wrote," said D.R.

"He's awful good at it," said Mrs. Godsey. "Barry's wrote books and everything."

"Has he really?"

"I don't think any of them's been printed. But he's writing one now that he says is sure to be printed, because he's made arrangements with the newspaper in town to have it done."

"That's very far out," said D.R.

"It's what, honey?"

"That's unusual. I'm impressed."

"Lord, honey, that Barry's a genius," said Mrs. Godsey. "He used to be a house painter 'til he fell and paralyzed hisself. That's when he took up writing. He's a pure genius at it, everybody thinks so."

Mrs. Godsey took a drink of her R.C.

"Leonard told me you quizzed him about getting credit here at the store," she said.

"Yes ma'm, I wanted to ask you about it."

"Nothing to ask," said Mrs. Godsey. "Emmit had credit with me for years. He never missed paying a one of his bills, and I know you wouldn't either. You're welcome to anything in my store that you want."

"Now I appreciate that, Mrs. Godsey," said D.R. "And I appreciate you letting me park my bus out back, too."

"Why, that ain't nothing," said Mrs. Godsey. "I like to look at it setting out there."

"You and Leonard have been a big help to me," said D.R. "I feel like I'm in debt to you both."

"We're glad to help you, honey," said Mrs. Godsey. "We're glad you're going to be with us a while. Leonard is, especially."

"How is Leonard?" said D.R. "I haven't seen him in a day or two."

"Well," said Mrs. Godsey. "I think that old Grand Jury business has thrown him behind in his work pretty bad. He's been to town ever day this week, and has to do it again next week too."

"I hope he comes up to see me when he gets a chance," said D.R. "There's some things I need to ask his advice on."

"You ne'en to worry about Leonard coming up," said Mrs. Godsey. "Use to, they wasn't anything he liked better than to take off up that creek and hang around with Emmit half the day. He'll be up, you ne'en to worry."

D.R. got up to go then. Mrs. Godsey followed him into the store to help him pick out a few groceries and write them into her account book. D.R. bought canned things mostly, corned beef hash, peas, beets, turnip greens, a bag of cookies and a loaf of bread and some milk. Mrs. Godsey put it in a bag for him, and when they had bid each other good day D.R. set out walking back up Trace Fork again.

## Saturday Morning

About six o'clock Saturday morning D.R. heard somebody clamber up the front steps, stomp across the porch then pound on the door like the house was on fire. D.R. was already vaguely awake, but the weight of pure comfort held his body in the bed, and likely it would have lured him back to sleep again if the racket on the porch had not made him bolt up and reach for his pants and shirt.

"Who is it?" he called out.

"It's Leonard," came the reply. "I'm sorry to bother you this early."

D.R. said he'd be right there. Hobbling with one shoe on and one off, and buttoning his shirt as he went, D.R. went out of the bedroom and faced Leonard standing in the kitchen by the door.

"How'd you like to work for me today, David?"

D.R. had never seen Leonard as restless and impatient as he was now. He followed D.R. into the bedroom, then paced out again and walked around and around in the kitchen.

"I'll be glad to try," said D.R. "What doing?"

"Building a hog pen. This goddamn jury business has thrown me plum behind. I thought if you wasn't busy we might try to build that thing today."

"Nah," said D.R. "Nothing up here that can't wait to be done."

"Good," said Leonard. "Come on down and Roxie'll fix you a good breakfast."

"I like it already," said D.R.

And when he got his shoes tied he stood up and followed Leonard out the door.

## Watering

Outside D.R. snapped his fingers and said, "Shit, Leonard. I've got to water the rabbits first."

Leonard looked pained. "Didn't you water 'em last night?"

D.R. shook his head. "They all still had some water in their crocks. I fed 'em. I thought I'd water 'em this morning."

Leonard was plainly pissed off, but all he said was, "Always water your stock at night, son. Don't put that kind of thing off."

Working together, D.R. carrying the bucket and Leonard dipping, they filled the crocks in all eleven hutches in ten minutes and then went on down the hill to Leonard's house for breakfast.

## Breakfast

Roxie fed D.R. another big breakfast of ham and eggs while Leonard loaded his tools into his pickup truck. The barn they were going to build the hog pen onto was half a mile up the road from Leonard's house there behind the store. The barn sat on two acres of bottom land that an in-law of Roxie's had owned 'til he moved to Louisville two years before. The first year he was gone Leonard rented the barn and used it as a storehouse, and then later he bought it. He still used it as a storehouse, but this year Leonard decided to try keeping hogs up there. He had four, penned in a makeshift stall inside. But they were getting so big so fast they needed an outdoor place to be, and that was what he'd ask D.R. to help him build that day.

When he got the tools loaded and the truck turned

and pointed out the driveway, Leonard left the motor
running and went to the back door and asked D.R. if
he was ready.

Roxie said, "Let the boy finish eating, Leonard."

"I'm finished," said D.R. "One more biscuit and I'm
ready to fly!" D.R. wiped the remaining egg yellow off
his plate with a biscuit, stuffed it into his mouth and
washed it down with a drink of coffee as he got out of
his chair. "Mighty good," he said to Roxie and she
smiled at him as he went out the back door after
Leonard, who was already halfway back to his pickup.

## The Plan

Leonard said, "What we want to do now, David,
is fence in this place here where you see it's shady.
This shade now's from the barn, but later on in the
heat of the day those sycamores over there shade this
same spot pretty good too, without keeping the sun
out completely. I've studied this side, there's good sun
late in the morning and then along about the middle
of the afternoon it comes in from the roadside pretty
good. If we do a good job fencing, those hogs'll have
a good place out here.

"What we'll do, David, is just come right out from
the two corners of the barn there, make it square on
that end, come out about twenty feet on this side, and
I figure about twenty-six on that side over there because
of that old stump. It won't be square on this end and
we'll have to dig an extra post hole or two, but that'll
be easier than trying to fight that old stump, and the
hogs'll be glad of the extra room. I don't expect to win
any architect's prize with this pen, but it'll be solid if
we get the posts in good, and that's what we're interested in.

"What I'll do, David, is mark off where we want the posts to go, and work with you a little to get you started. Then while you dig I'll take the truck into Blaine and get the posts and my one-by-sixes, shit I guess I better get nails too. I'm sorry I'm so disorganized this morning, but it's just piled up on me so bad I ain't thinking too straight yet. But we'll get lined out. It's a little after seven now. If we get the holes dug this morning and I get back with the fencing material by dinnertime, we might not be in such bad shape after all. Get those diggers off the truck why don't you, David, and I'll gouge around a little with my spade, and we'll just light right into it and hush talking about it."

## The Work

They dug the first hole six inches from the corner of the barn. Leonard started it by scraping away some surface rocks and digging out some old leaves and crap that had accumulated under the eaves. Then he took the diggers from D.R. and started down. He dropped the diggers hard into the ground, spread the long handles and then lifted out the dirt in bites. The first few inches of the hole were easy, just dirt lying there waiting to be scooped up. But about a foot down the diggers banged into solid rock and Leonard told D.R. to hand him the sledge. It was hard to get at the rock with the sledge because of the narrowness of the hole, but after five or six licks he cracked it enough to get the end of the long crowbar in to work. By the time they'd broken the rock into pieces small enough to pull out, both men were sweating and ready for a little rest. Wiping his forehead, Leonard looked at D.R. and grinned and said, "It ain't like grave-digging, is it?"

D.R. automatically looked at his hands. It had been a week and a day since they had worked with Ray and Chester, digging Emmit's grave. The blisters D.R. had worn that day had all broken and hardened in that time, although after he'd worked with the diggers a while the one on his left palm near the fleshy part of his thumb opened up again and started to bleed.

"Don't force your diggers," Leonard said. "You're banging 'em down a little too hard to suit. Just sort of try to help their own natural weight along a little, if you see what I mean. That's it. Easy-like. That's right. You're getting it."

Leonard worked with D.R. about an hour, sharing the work with him, trading on and off with the various tools. By the third hole they seemed to have worked beyond the shelf of rock that made the first two holes so hard. D.R. dug most of the third one by himself, and was starting into the fourth as Leonard got ready to leave.

"I'll be back by dinnertime," he said. "I'll come and get you and we'll go to the house awhile."

Without breaking his motion D.R. nodded and said good enough, and Leonard drove off to town.

## *Wanting to Quit*

After the sixth hole, D.R. wanted to quit. It wasn't his body that wanted to quit. His hands were hurting a little but his strength was flowing good and his arms and back felt readier to go on with it than when he'd started. It was something else, some longing, some invitation from somewhere deep inside him to lay down the tools and just arbitrarily quit.

Not stop to rest.

Not go sit down by the barn and lean his back against the wall and sip water from the half-gallon Mason jar Leonard had left.

But quit.

For the day.

Just stop right there where he was, ten inches deep into the seventh hole, and go down to the store and hang around awhile, or else on back up to the home-place for the afternoon.

It was like some kind of sour bile swimming through his head. His hands and arms and back worked on well, but his mind, his mind was terribly dissatisfied to be there with nothing to do but observe his arms and hand and back. His mind was a message to him, it was an argument from the very depths of itself to stop this work and, at the very least, take it easy for a while.

Look how much you've already done! it said. Five holes already, look at that! That's a morning's work for any man!

Not for Leonard, D.R. said.

Fuck Leonard! the message said. You've got the whole afternoon to dig these holes. At least go sit down and rest for a couple of hours.

All right, said D.R. Soon as I finish this hole, I will.

And he dropped the diggers hard into the ground.

I'll get a start on number seven and then quit, D.R. said. Let me start number seven and I'll stop awhile.

And he said the same thing when he had finished the seventh hole, and gone on to number eight.

And then nine, and then ten. Let me finish ten, he said. This one more, and then I'll quit for the day.

D.R. finished the tenth hole. He needed the sledge on that one. Eight inches down he came into thick rock, and he needed the sledge and the bar, and the sledge and the bar together, and then the diggers, little pinches of earth and rock at a time. That one hole took him over half an hour of solid work, but he finished it, and was starting the eleventh hole when Leonard came back with the lumber.

"You getting tired?" he said.

Not "Wow! look how much work you did!"

Not, "Congratulations, David, you're the most fantastic hole-digger I ever saw."

Not even, "It looks like you've worked hard while I was gone."

Just, "You getting tired?"

"Not too bad," D.R. said.

"Do that one, and one more while I unload this stuff," said Leonard. "Then we'll go see what Roxie's fixed us to eat."

 **Nails**

Nail hammer *whap whap* nail.

Set it and hit it, drive it *whap* hit it home and nail that board to the post.

Set it in here, David. Throw in some rock, fill it and tamp it, hold on now, let's get 'er straight. Reach me the level there and we'll line this baby up. There. Tamp it down, hand me the end of that one-by-six and you take the yon.

Nail. Hammer *whap whap* and nail. Nail it in and drive it home. This one's warped, David, hold on, let's not get ahead of ourselves. Got yours nailed? Hit it.

Nail. Hammer, *whap*. Nail, *whap,* set, *whap,* hit it and drive it, drive it and pound it

and

Leonard bears his weight down on the loose end 'til the warp comes out and says drive it in now, son, set it and hit it, that's right, we'll teach this wood to bow.

One time, David, I was carpentering with this old one-armed boy over in Owsley County. Fellow by the name of Calhoun. Building a school up there, back before the war. I'd tried mining and didn't like that, so my daddy said why don't you go up to Owsley County and help 'em build that school. The boss of that job was a friend of my daddy's and he took me on. He said I could work a week and if I could drive nails faster than this Calhoun he'd let me stay on. So we worked. Side by side with old Calhoun. Him with just one arm, I figured surely I could outwork a one-armed man. But you ought to of seen him, David. He'd set nails this way: hold the head between his two fingers like this, you see, brace the head against the flat of his hammer, go *stick* like that and set that nail in the wood just pretty as you please. Then he'd rare back with that hammer in that one good hand of his and go *whap* and about two whaps later that nail'd be out of sight. Drive a sixteen-penny nail in three licks when he wanted to. I couldn't keep up with him with two hands. Nobody on that job could.

But the old foreman let me stay on anyhow.

*Whap!* Nail. Set. Hammer. *Whap.*

Sweat.

Sweat all down his neck and off his ears and in his eyes.

Get us another locust post and I'll deepen this next hole a little.

Fill it. Tamp it down. That's right, stomp it right in there good. She level? Read it right, now, we want this fence preee-cise, looking too good to mess it up now. You finish here, David, and I'll go get us another one-by-six.

## *Time*

Nail. Set. Hammer. *Whap.*
  Set. Nail. *Whap.*
  How's your blister, David?
  Not too bad. It's not on my hammer hand.
  We'll get some turpentine on it when we get done
here.
  Done.
  Get done.
  Two o'clock.
  Two ten.
  Nail. Set. Sweat, slick, hand, *whap.*
  And then it was two eleven.

## *Inattention*

But you could see it now. Taking shape. The short
side was completed, and they were halfway across the
long front, nailing to the seventh post. An enclosure
was being made. A wall, the horizontal one-by-sixes
parallel, a perfect shape of empty space between them;
the upright posts their roots into the ground. There
was a texture now; the rough lumber like beard
stubble, splintery to the touch; there was shape and
there was texture and marvelous patterned lines and
angles at the posts. There was aesthetic going on,
and cosmic law. It's measured space, enclosed, D.R.
thought. It's a line upon the earth for the work of
meat production to go on behind. They were agents
of the fence, its architects and builders; they were
building fence, setting limits on the space. The space,
enclosed, was inside time, it's two twenty now . . .

"Yeoww! *Shit!*" and **D.R.** dropped his hammer and grabbed his thumb and danced around in circles.

Leonard looked up and grinned as D.R. cussed.

"Be kinder to yourself," said Leonard. "Always pay attention to your work."

 *Attention*

Attention drove the afternoon along outside of space and time.

It drove the work along like floating free of gravity.

It lifted the work above its own resistance and its friction, like running naked after wearing heavy boots and suits of clothes.

It set the posts and tamped them firm.

It drove the nails unerringly, and ran the one-by-sixes across the front and past the dog-leg by the stump, and pointed then along the final side to link up with the other corner of the barn.

It closed the fence. It held them to their task 'til they had cut a door in the barnwall for the pigs to come out through, and smell out their new universe.

Reluctant, then curious, the pigs came out, cautious, one at a time, then gathered in committee in the corner to inspect D.R.'s and Leonard's work.

They approved.

Grunting, muttering little squeals, they scattered across this unexpected ground, and one pissed on it. D.R. and Leonard laughed at that, and D.R. listened carefully to their laugh. He watched closely as Leonard fed the hogs, and closed them back in their stall for the night.

On their way to the house for supper he paid attention when Leonard said: next winter when we have us some good sausage for breakfast we'll remember this day, David.

That thought thrilled D.R. and he paid attention to the thrill.

He paid attention to Roxie pouring turpentine in the wounds from his day's labor. He noticed how her hands felt on his, he paid attention to her presence, close, and to the food she had prepared.

Roast beef, boiled potatoes, beans, cole slaw heavy with mayonnaise, rhubarb, cornbread, cold milk, and then banana pudding for dessert. D.R. noticed every bite he took, he paid attention to his mouth chewing, he tasted every flavor that there was, and all their exotic mixtures in his mouth. He paid attention to the coffee, and when they had finished supper he experienced himself getting up and saying he guessed he better get on up the hill and get his animals fed—and watered—before it got dark.

He thanked Roxie for the supper, and Leonard thanked D.R. for the work. D.R. paid attention to Leonard's face and voice when he said it. Leonard offered to pay D.R. but D.R. said oh no. I owe you that much.

Leonard said, Well, when I get a little time I'll come up and give you a hand.

I'll be needing it, D.R. said.

Come down and go to church with us tomorrow if you want to, David, said Roxie.

D.R. said he didn't think he would, but he thanked her for inviting him.

We'll see you later then, said Leonard.

Yeah, said D.R. Good-night, you all.

And he left then. He got home with just enough daylight left to do his chores.

## Sunday: The Mine

Walking, body jolting, downhill. It's Sunday morning now and D.R. is on his way to explore the old abandoned coal mine he'd freaked out in his first day back at Trace Fork. Every time he has gone in or out of the hollow he has passed the ruins of the tipple, and it's been on his mind to crawl back in with a light of some kind and get a real look at the place. But 'til this morning he has always been on one specific errand or another, and there has been no chance to stop and look around.

But it's Sunday now, his day of rest and leisure. D.R. slept 'til almost ten, fixed himself some eggs and fried a slice of green tomato for breakfast, and now at about the hour the other people of the community are gathering for Sunday worship at the church, D.R. has set out from the house with this very special destination in mind.

It was an easy entrance this time. The little furrow he had made before was still there, a little tunnel through the rotting wood and dusty earth that led him to the center of the pile of beams and timbers across the drift mouth. Lying in the drift mouth, D.R. felt the cool air from the mine blow across his neck and face and arms. He smelled the coal-ness of the mine, the slate-taste-color flowing from the earth into his nostrils like some subtle gas that soothed and calmed his mind. Cool. Dark. Quiet, except for the sound of his own body crawling now, easing into the hole.

Then, when he was still again, it was utterly quiet, except for the sound of water slowly dripping, and except for the way the very silence was a kind of noise.

He was actually *there,* beneath the mountain, quiet in the bosom of the world. And conscious of it this time, there freely, there simply, without all the smoke and swirl. On his way down the hill to the mine his thought had been that he would go inside, maybe deep inside, and explore by the light of his candle. That impulse was gone now. Within thirty feet of the entrance D.R. found what he had come for. He hadn't known, really, just what he was going there for. But now he knew. It was just to sit a while, at rest in a cool, quiet place. That was all.

D.R. sat holding the candle in his hand, looking around him in the circle of light at the ragged posts on either side that held the roof in place.

The roof was slate, and the color of slate.

The walls were solid coal.

The floor was dusty near the walls, but in the center it was moist, with here and there a pool of water gathered from the dripping above.

He sat a long time without moving. There was the roof above, the floor beneath him, and the walls on either side. And the candle, in the center of the circle of the light.

After a while, without deciding to, D.R. leaned forward and set his candle in the mud beside a little pool near his feet. The reflection in the water was a perfect reproduction of the real, and D.R. marveled at it. One above, one below, the two candles shone together in the vastness of the cavern, and D.R. sat crosslegged on the floor in total fascination.

Behind him in the dark was the entrance to the mine, and the world of day beyond. Behind the candles was the deeper vastness of the mine.

Neither attracted him.

D.R. didn't want to go in motion either way.

He was where he was.

This was his place to be.

And that stayed true even after he blew the candle out.

Without deciding to, D.R. crawled forward and blew the candle out. And then, for longer than he knew, he sat there where he was, within and of the dark.

### Monday: The Scheme

On Monday morning, D.R. went to work expanding Emmit's scheme.

He had tinkered with it and nursed it along, doing chores, in the time he had lived alone as Emmit's successor at the homeplace. But it wasn't until this particular Monday morning that D.R. took up tools to enlarge and make his own mark on the work that Emmit had begun the last year of his life.

It was a scheme to reclaim the soil of the homeplace that had been killed by the mining on the slopes above the farm. Until Emmit started rebuilding the garden soil with rabbit shit behind the barn. The only living spot on the homeplace was the little triangle of green in front of the house, where some grass still grew and the poplar trees and the silver-leaf maple tree had leaves. It was only a matter of time before that little patch would be destroyed too, however, and the old family house along with it. For behind the house was a wall of dried mud and shale and blasted rock high as the roof in places. It had rolled down from the bench above, and then in two wet winters continued to slip until now it looked like a frozen ocean wave, waiting for another winter to melt it and send it flowing through the house and on across the yard toward the road and Trace Fork creek below.

But out near the barn, which stood a little uphill from the house and on a kind of roll in the slope, the overburden had stabilized. It had slipped as far as it was going to, and it was there that Emmit had chosen to make his effort and invest his work the last few months of his life.

The barn had been pushed off its foundation by the wash of overburden, flowing down. A rock big as a car, set rolling by a bulldozer up above, had smashed into the upper end of the barn and ripped a big hole in the wall. But in spite of the damage the barn was still a fairly solid structure, and when the mud had dried and settled Emmit had gone to work behind the barn, spreading all the manure and organic matter he could get, in an effort to create enough new topsoil to make a garden.

There'd been some old rotted manure in the stalls in the barn, left from the days when the Colliers kept cows and a workhorse. Emmit had shoveled it out and scattered some spoiled hay over it, and then worked that into the spot he intended to garden. Emmit's health was starting to fail him even then. That shoveling was among the last heavy work he tried. It was then he got his idea to raise rabbits in hutches as a source of manure for the garden he intended to create below the barn.

A friend of Emmit's on Upper Rockhouse Creek who raised rabbits for meat sold him the buck and the first two does. Emmit built hutches for them out of weather boarding he ripped off the back of the old doomed house he lived in. In a year's time he built eleven hutches from lumber off the house, and his herd grew to nearly fifty rabbits. He fed them commercial rabbit feed that Leonard hauled up the creek in the sled by the hundred-pound bag. It cost him, but the project was important to Emmit and he was willing to pay. Emmit received a disability pension from the government for his war wound, a hundred and forty some dollars every month. His personal expenses were rarely more than half of that, so he could afford his herd of rabbits. Leonard said that Emmit would eat a rabbit now and then, but what he kept them for was the first-class shit they produced. As it accumulated beneath the hutches he spread it on the sterile soil, and in a year's time he had redeemed a patch twenty feet by ten, and it was now growing

short, single rows of lettuce, carrots, turnips, cucum-
bers, potatoes, beans, tomatoes and comfrey, and two
longer rows of beans.

The rabbits were the central project in Emmit's
scheme, but he had other things going too that he
had worked at as he had the time, and strength. He
had a worm pit going by one of the walls inside the
barn. He'd built it when he first got his rabbits, filled
it with manure and stocked it with five thousand red
worms he'd ordered through the mail. A year later
there were so many worms in it he was scooping them
out by the pitchfork full and planting them in the
garden rows to go to work on the mulch of shit and
hay. But as the garden expanded and the rabbit
population increased, Emmit wanted still more worms,
and the extension of the pit was one of the projects he
left unfinished when he died.

D.R. intended to finish that pit, and perhaps build
another one along the facing wall.

It would not be possible to breed too many worms
for the work he had in mind.

He also intended to go on dismantling the old
house, to tear as much of it down for salvage as he
possibly could before the coming winter's rains. Emmit
had only taken boards off as high as he could com-
fortably reach. He had stripped the weather boarding
from the lower portions of the house on three sides.
With a ladder D.R. would be able to get three times
as much lumber as Emmit had before he even touched
the insides of the house. Emmit had worked the lumber with a hammer and a wrecking bar, pulling out the
nails and trimming up their edges with a saw. As he
cleaned the boards he had stacked them neatly in a
corner of the barn. He had scavenged more lumber
than he needed for his hutches. It wasn't clear what he
had intended to do with the extra, but D.R. knew exactly what his own intentions were: he was going to

remodel two of the stalls into a weather-tight room, and live in it that winter.

Two rooms, if he could get them done.

And three rooms, if Estelle would come to live there with him, and help him with the work.

If Estelle would come, they would convert one whole end of the barn into a house, and live there together by the rabbits and the worms and near the garden. They would get up early every morning and work to improve their place. If they wanted to, they could have a hundred hutches full of rabbits, and a million worms a year. They could have five hundred hutches full, and ten million worms at work in their manure, if they wanted to. If they wanted to, they could have a thousand hutches, one standing on every five square yards of that old ruined mountain, shitting pure worm food onto the ground, creating perfect lettuce beds and comfrey stands, and alfalfa fields galore.

They could do that if Estelle would come to live there with him.

They'd do all of that, and more.

If Estelle came.

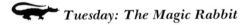 *Tuesday: The Magic Rabbit*

Until the work was done, Tuesday was very much like Monday.

D.R. spent the morning turning under the manure he had spread the day before. He planted the little new ground with worms and humus from the pit, then worked a while tearing boards off the side of the house, dressing them and stacking them in the barn. Already the stack was waist-high and five boards across, enough to begin the work of converting the stalls to rooms. D.R. had an impulse to commence it then and there, but he knew he ought to talk to Leonard first. He could probably bang a room of some sort together by himself; but this was no crude project he had in mind. There are ways to go about certain kinds of work; there are rules in building and D.R. wanted to learn them. He wanted to do a good job, and know something truly useful when he was done. So he left the room alone 'til Leonard could come up to advise him on it, and worked some more in the afternoon on the new worm pit instead.

D.R. worked the whole day through, going from job to job. It tired his body in that satisfying way he'd come to relish the last few days, and after supper he was glad to sit in Emmit's rocking chair on the front porch and rest himself a while. His body sank into the chair and without reluctance let go of the day in anticipation of the night.

But D.R.'s mind wasn't ready for that yet. His mind was still excited, eager for some action, some outlet for the words that had built up through the day and gone unsaid. And so he went in the house and got his tablet and his pen, came back to his chair and wrote another letter to the Flash.

Dear Flash,

Here's what's going on:

Saturday I helped Leonard build a new pen for his hogs.

Sunday I crawled back in an old coal mine and watched a candle burn. Then I sat a long time in the dark, just being quiet.

Yesterday I spread rabbit shit on some old dead ground, and today spaded it in and sprinkled two gallons of red worms on it.

I also ripped a lot of boards off this old house I'm living in, and cleaned them up to use building myself a pad in a corner of the barn.

This house I'm living in is dead.

There are people living who have memories of it, and things that happened here. I remember things, and my sister, and there are a few others scattered around with old home movies in their brains they filmed in years gone by.

But the house itself is dead, and within the year it will be buried by about a million tons of mud and crap piled up behind it.

The barn is where the life is now. The garden is behind it. The worms live inside it in a pit. There's a chicken lot on one side, and on two sides all the rabbits in their hutches that I told you about. They're in those hutches right this minute, Flash, wondering when I'm going to come and live there as their neighbor.

This afternoon I stuck my head in one of the hutches and breathed awhile with the old momma and her litter. She's brown and white and solemn. The babies are about three weeks old, just starting to hop in and out of the nest box on their own, and sniff their mother's solid food. They're getting curious about the larger world. The old momma already knows. She's wise and proud and I think satisfied. We looked deeply into one another's eyes a time or two. I'm her bringer of food. That's my whole function in the world as far as she's concerned. As a matter of fact, it's my function in the world as far as I'm concerned too, except that what I know that she doesn't is that there's this whole larger scheme going on. What I know that she doesn't is that her produce—the manure; those thousands of little pellets that gather beneath her hutch—is food too, in this amazing scheme that my uncle started before he died, and that I'm now in the process of expanding.

It's a business, actually. I mean, just this very second I flashed that this enterprise of mine is actually a business. It's called the Magic Rabbit. The rabbits are my employees. They shit all week, around the clock, and I pay them with food. Our purpose is soil redemption. Salvation! Healing, by miracles, signs and wonders. The theme song of our commercials is "The Old Rugged Barn."

> On a hill far away,
> Stood an old rugged barn,
> The emblem of effort and pride.

Far out!

Come be my partner, Flash. Go find Estelle and bring her with you, and join the Magic Rabbit, Incorporated, and we'll get into soil salvation. First we'll save our own; we'll breed ten thousand rabbits and twenty million worms, and make this dead old hillside bloom. Then if other people feel like they've got a troubled soil, why let them call upon us, and we'll respond, with miracles, signs and wonders.

Faith, brother! Faith and rabbit shit, that's the theme!

> On a hill far away,
> Stood an old rugged barn,
> The emblem of effort and pride.
> How I love that old barn,
> So despised by the world,
> For the weirdness that happens inside.

You've got forty-eight hours to reply to this business proposal, Flash. Refuse it at the peril of your soil.

Your associate,
D.R.

 *Wednesday: Urge's Bath*

When D.R. went off the hill late Wednesday to mail his letter to the Flash he was almost certain there'd be a letter waiting for him at the store. From the Flash, from Marcella, maybe even, by sudden cosmic arrangement, some word from Estelle. A post card, a note, *some*thing, from *some*body.

But there wasn't, and D.R. had to fight his disappointment down.

He bought a Coke from Mrs. Godsey, and after he had drunk it he bought a few more groceries to see him through the remainder of the week. Mrs. Godsey asked D.R. how he was and he said fine, but it was clear to her that he wasn't fine, and Mrs. Godsey found herself worrying about D.R. a little. She tried to think of something to say that might make him feel better, but she didn't have any confidence in any of the words that occurred to her. She wrote his groceries up in the account book, and wished him a good day as he carried them out the door. But that wasn't enough, it wasn't enough at all and she felt bad about D.R. as the screen door slammed behind him.

Before he started back up the hill, D.R. went around in back of Godsey's store to look in Urge a minute. Urge had still not been given a thorough cleaning since he had been in Kentucky. A little at a time, D.R. had been taking stuff out of the bus and either throwing it away or carrying it with him up the hill. But the great bulk of their stuff still had not been touched, and in looking at it now D.R. felt suddenly inspired to pitch in then and there and clean it out once and for all.

As soon as he decided that's what he'd do, he felt instantly better, and better still when he started dumping junk out of the bus left and right. He spread their old stale sleeping bags on top of the bus to air. He dragged the mattress out and laid it on the grass in Leonard's yard. He collected the worst of the actual trash, the empty bottles, old apple cores, old smashed Kentucky Fried Chicken buckets, paper cups, old magazines, and grubby old paper napkins, and threw it all outside in a pile. Beside it he piled an old quilt that had had a chocolate milkshake spilled on it, and a towel too far gone to preserve. A pair of his own worn-out jeans wound up on the pile.

When he started coming to things he wasn't sure what he should do with, he began a separate pile. He found one of Estelle's blue sneakers, worn through at the little toe, laced with binder twine. He found a pair of her cut-off Levis, and three dirty socks. In a pillow case he found two of her special outfits, the gingham frontier dress, and the tie-dyed jumpsuit she'd made out of a mechanic's coveralls. He found their kitchen stuff in a box lined with the green sports section of *The San Francisco Chronicle*. The pots and pans and skillet and plastic plates and bowls were piled in with the Mazola Corn Oil, a box of salt, some spices in little cans, brown sugar in a jar, some old rice. He found their mangled copy of *The Whole Earth Catalog*, the paperback of *Stranger In a Strange Land* that Estelle had made so many notes in. And then, way back under the bed, face down on the floor, opened at the hexagram called Youthful Folly, D.R. found their *I Ching*.

Far out.

The *Ching*.

It was like running into an old friend. D.R. picked it up and dusted it off, and sat for a while holding it in his hand. He had been wishing for the *Ching*. It was time for him to start consulting it again. And maybe he could find some shit to order from the *Catalog*, too. The found books pleased D.R. enormously, and lifted him past the little desire that had begun to build in him to stop working on the bus and go flake out somewhere. D.R. was suddenly filled with tenderness and affection for Urge, and he went the whole way with his cleaning job.

When he had emptied the bus completely, he went to Roxie's house and borrowed a broom, and swept

everywhere in the bus the broom could touch. Roxie
showed him where the outdoor faucet was, and Leonard's hose. D.R. took the sleeping bags off the top,
spread them out beside the mattress, and moved Urge
until the hose could reach. And then he washed him
good, all over, inside and out, with soap and warm
water from Roxie's kitchen, and then a cold rinse with
the hose. It was the first bath Urge had had since
the west coast, and you could tell by the sound of the
motor how much the old bus dug it. When he went
back in the store to get some cardboard boxes, Mrs.
Godsey told him he could store anything he wanted
to in her basement. D.R. spent the rest of the afternoon sorting through the stuff that he would keep,
getting it into boxes, four of them, and then stacking
the boxes on the floor of Mrs. Godsey's basement.

Leonard came home from another day with the
Grand Jury in town as D.R. was finishing up and
asked if he would like to stick around for supper. D.R.
said no thanks. He had a whole new fund of energy
now, and he wanted to get back up on the hill with it,
and use it well. He gathered up his books and his
groceries and set out whistling, back up Trace Fork
again.

## Keeping Still

That evening after supper, D.R. went out on the
front porch to sit a while, and in the final hour of
light that day he threw the *I Ching*. He had always
been ceremonious when he cast the *Ching;* but that
evening the sense of ceremony and ritual came more
naturally to him than it ever had before. There were
no trappings. No candles or bells or incense, none of
that. There was only D.R. on the front porch of the

house, sitting on the floor with his feet two steps
down, the book beside him on the floor, and the coins
lying loosely in his hand. He was sitting quietly,
waiting for the spirit to move him, and the spirit was
taking its time. It wanted D.R. to really settle now, to
fit into his natural place, within the flow and motion
all around. The day was ending, the night was on its
way. The air was fresh and thick with the settling
evening dew. Over by the silver-leaf maple tree some
lightning bugs were blinking. And above them in the
sky the first stars of the evening were popping out.
Day and night were trading times and places, easing
into one another's spheres around the world.

And D.R. sat very still and allowed a similar change
to happen inside him.

Beginning in his mind, then flowing down along
his spine and outward through his body, the change
came slowly over him. His hands waited for it to be
complete. Then, on their own, unhurried, they began
to toss the coins. Six times they shook and dropped
the coins, and the reading materialized:

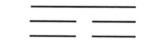

Ken/Keeping Still, Mountain

"The image of this hexagram is the mountain, the
youngest of heaven and earth. The male principle is
at the top, because it strives upward by nature; the
female principle is below, since the direction of its
movement is downward. Thus there is rest because
the movement has come to its normal end.

"The hexagram signifies the end and the beginning
of all movement. The back is named because in the

back are located all the nerve fibers that mediate movement. If the movement of these spinal nerves is brought to a standstill, the ego, with its restlessness, disappears as it were. When a man has thus become calm, he may turn to the outside world. He no longer sees in it the struggle and tumult of individual beings, and therefore he has that true peace of mind which is needed for understanding the great laws of the universe and for acting in harmony with them. Whoever acts from these deep levels makes no mistakes."

D.R. read the passage two more times before he closed the *Ching* and laid it on the floor beside him. It was dark by now, and he was feeling sleepy. It occurred to him to go for a walk, maybe stroll up to the barn and stand around the hutches for a while. The rabbits seemed to like it when he did that. But the chickens didn't, and anyway it was time for working people to be in bed asleep, for the coming day. So he went in, and by the light of the oil lamp undressed, and lay down across the big bed where Emmit used to sleep. D.R. was so far gone by then he wasn't sure if that was him blowing the oil lamp out, or someone else that he was only dreaming.

### Thursday: A Letter

By morning, though, D.R. was thoroughly animated again, restless and filled with an energy that just *knew* there'd be a letter for him in the mail that day. He felt it so strongly he couldn't get his mind on any work he tried around the place. At ten thirty he gave up trying and took off half-running down the hill to the store.

And sure enough, waiting at the post office was a letter from the Anaheim Flash.

Divine Right,

1. Man, you have blown me out.   2. The telephone is more civilized than letters.   3. Letter-writing closes up my centers.   4. Estelle has been at Angel's place the last couple of weeks.   5. She may not be there now. 6. But I sent your letter on to Angel's place anyhow. 7. That's all I know.   8. Here's 200 bucks.   9. Don't spend it all in one place.   10. And for Christ's sake, use the phone next time.

(signed) A. Flash, Esquire

Right on, said D.R. to himself.

And he left the store and the people there and went around to Roxie's house to place a collect call to the Flash in California.

 *Phone Call*

"Yal-low?"

"Flash, this is D.R."

"Stop right there," said the Flash. "Before you say another word, I want you to tell me a phone number where I can call you. I would of called you days ago . . . "

"Where's Estelle?" D.R. interrupted.

"Tell me your phone number and I'll answer that question."

D.R. told the Flash Leonard's phone number. There was a little silence while he wrote it down.

"That's better," said the Flash. "People might as well be lost in outer space without a phone number. Estelle's up near San Francisco."

*"Where?"*

"She's with these friends of Angel's in the mountains, south of San Francisco."

"What the hell's she doing in San Francisco?"

"What are you doing in Kentucky?" asked the Flash. "What am I doing in Anaheim? It shifts, friend. It shifts and moves around. You should know."

"But San Francisco . . . "

"She's not in San Francisco," said the Flash. "She's in the Santa Cruz mountains south of there."

"Did Angel tell you that?" D.R. asked. "When have you talked to Angel?"

"Yesterday, the day before yesterday, and about a week ago. I would of called you if I'd had your number. Always have a telephone number, D.R. It facilitates communication."

"So go on with it. What did Angel say?"

"She said Estelle had split. She said Estelle stayed with them two weeks, and day before yesterday took off, hitchhiking south. Angel told her to stop off and stay a few days with these friends of hers who live in this dome in the mountains. Estelle said she'd probably do that, and if she did, then we can find her."

"What about my letter?"

"It got there the day Estelle left. Angel read it, and that's why she called me."

"I'm sorry she's hitchhiking," said D.R.

"Angel said that was what she wanted to do. Besides, she was broke."

"Oh shit. Did she say how she was, how she felt?"

"She's kind of down. I'm not supposed to tell you that, so don't tell Angel I told you. She's already convinced you're a rat, I don't want her to think I'm one too."

"Jesus. Did she say what was wrong?"

"No. But listen, dad: don't sweat it. The Anaheim Flash is swinging into action. If my little scheme works out, you'll be talking to Estelle this afternoon."

"This after*noon?*"

"I'm going to set it up. There's no phone in this dome she's supposed to be visiting. But I know a guy up there, in Menlo Park, and he'll fetch her to a phone if he can find her. Then you two can hate each other voice to voice. Or groove, or whatever weird thing it is you all are trying to get on. What the hell *is* going on, if I may ask?"

D.R. grinned into the telephone. "I've started a new corporation," he said.

"A what?"

"A corporation."

"You're crazy. What are you doing, dealing?"

"I'm president of Magic Rabbit, Incorporated," D.R. said. "You're a vice president and chief cohort."

"The hell I am," said the Flash.

"It's true. I've written you all about it. My truest and grandest scheme."

"Well I'm hot to hear it," said the Flash. "But listen, man: no more letters from me, okay? You got the money, I guess."

"Got it. And many thanks for it, too."

"The interest is six per cent," said the Flash.

"Fair enough," said D.R. "If you get Estelle and me together on the telephone, I'll do better than that. I'll make you a full president of Magic Rabbit."

"Can't beat that," said the Flash. "Hang around that phone now, son. If you don't get a call by tonight, call me back, okay?"

"Will do," said D.R.

When he hung up, D.R. ran out of Roxie's house yelling, "Yip-eee!"

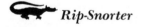 **Rip-Snorter**

Okay folks, hold onto your hats. This is Gurney Norman the author speaking, bringing you the end of this folk tale, and it's a rip-snorter. The guy in Cali-

fornia that the Anaheim Flash sent to fetch Estelle
to the telephone was me. I live here in Menlo Park
not far from Troll's and Marilyn's dome up in the
hills. I've been so pushed for time the last few weeks
I wasn't at all sure I was going to be able to get away
from my writing desk long enough to go and find
Estelle. But I did, and it all worked out okay.

As the Flash indicated, Estelle was a little down.
She'd been pretty blue since she and D.R. split up in
Cincinnati; her trip since then had been pretty much
of a bummer. She was nervous and jumpy, and half-
hostile when she asked me who the hell I was. I said
I was a friend of the Anaheim Flash's, and that he'd
called and asked me to get her to a telephone so she
could call D.R., who was most desperate to hear from
her.

Estelle seemed a little suspicious of the whole thing,
but she went with me to Skylonda, where there was a
phone booth. I loaned her a dime and she went in, and
stayed a long time, talking to D.R. I didn't hear what
they said, but apparently it was a pretty groovy conversation because she came out all smiles, and announced that she was going to Kentucky.

I asked her how.

She said the fastest way possible.

That means through the air, I said, and off we went
to the San Francisco airport, where I bought her a
one-way ticket to Cincinnati, and gave her twenty
dollars for bus fare from there to Blaine, Kentucky,
where D.R. would be waiting. (All of this on the as-
sumption, of course, that I'm to be reimbursed by our
mutual friend and benefactor, the Anaheim Flash.)

By the time the passengers were ready to board the
plane, Estelle had mellowed toward me some. As she
was about to start down the ramp she turned to me and
said, "I really thank you for all your help."

"My pleasure," I said. "All my pleasure."

And indeed it was. With her fellow passengers as an

audience, Estelle put her arms around my neck and gave me this incredible kiss, right on the mouth. Before I could say a word she turned and ran onto the plane, and a few minutes later it was roaring down the runway, then rising in the air.

By the time Estelle's plane was east of the Sierras I was back at my desk again, where D.R. was still in raptures from the phone call. He was so stoned out by the whole thing he gave up all attempts at serious work and spent the afternoon wandering around the home-place in a daze. He forgot supper entirely. After his chores he sat down at the kitchen table and tried to read *Stranger In a Strange Land,* but he couldn't focus on it so he set it aside and picked up the *I Ching* again. Sitting up very straight now and breathing deeply, D.R. cast the coins upon the table and then read them by the light of the coal-oil lamp. He threw a broken line. A solid line. A broken line. A solid line. Another broken line, and then a final solid line.

### Wei Chi/Before Completion

"This hexagram indicates a time when the transition from disorder to order is not yet complete. The change is indeed prepared for, since all the lines in the upper trigram are in relation to those in the lower. However, they are not yet in their places. While the preceding hexagram offers an analogy to autumn, which forms the transition from summer to winter, this hexagram presents a parallel to spring, which leads out of winter's stagnation into the fruitful time of summer. With this hopeful outlook the Book of Changes comes to its close."

And so does *Divine Right's Trip.* D.R. has only one more run to make, to Blaine, in Urge, brightly shining, freshly washed and cleaned-up Urge, to meet Estelle's bus coming in from Lexington late that night.

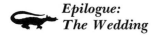 ### *Epilogue: The Wedding*

There are no guarantees, of course.

There are no guarantees.

But if it could work.

If it looks like it's worth the risk.

The leap.

If there's even a chance for the two of them there, then what D.R. and Estelle will do is have a most marvelous wedding.

One day late in the summer, or early in the fall.

All day long, from morning to night, a celebration.

And all the people they know and love will come.

The Flash will come.

He will have to come because he's the presiding minister.

All the way from California, driving his silver Lotus.

The Flash in his silver jumpsuit.

The Flash with his silver hair.

The Flash with his silver eyebrows, and little silver ring in the side of his nose.

Silver boots, with pointy silver toes, and silver buttons down the sides.

And buttons on his jumpsuit, silver.

And silver scarf and silver gloves and sunglasses, on both sides, silver.

The Flash had his silver helmet with him too, but as he parked the Lotus among the throng of other cars and buses and pickup trucks in front of Godsey's store he thought: I better not overdo my silver bit. So he left the helmet on the seat and clambered out, uncoiling his five-foot-four-inch frame as Barry Berry came rolling by in his wheelchair.

"My name's Barry Berry," Barry said. "I'm a neighbor to the bride and groom."

"I'm the Anaheim Flash," said the Flash. "I'm the preacher for this occasion." And he got behind Barry's chair and pushed him up the Trace Fork road behind a band of freaks and weirdos, strewing colored ribbons in the weeds.

"Good morning!" Barry called out as they rolled by. "My name's Barry Berry."

"Morning," said J.D. "I'm J.D."

And Pam said she was Pam.

Barry shook hands with them every one, Diane and Jerry and Amy and Barbara and Dudley and John and B. Anne and Peter and Laura and Soni and Doug and Terry and Francine and Bernie, all friends of D.R.'s and Estelle's who had journeyed from the west coast to Kentucky for the wedding day, where Shera was filming it all.

Shera had moved down the road aways from the party to catch the new arrivals coming up.

She filmed the Flash and Barry Berry.

And Dick Raymond escorting Mrs. Godsey up the road.

She filmed them all passing, and then from low in the yard she filmed Angel's band of Oregonians, Ken and Fay and Babbs and Gretch and Hassler and Paula and Zodiac and Sky and Hagen and some others, decorating the front porch steps as an altar where the bride and groom would stand.

She filmed Reverend Bagby and some men from the church building a table across the yard, fifteen sawhorses covered with boards, and then the women, working behind, spreading sheets as tablecloths, and tacking on red and blue crepe.

Nearby was a people pile, eleven guests, weary from

travel, all in a heap and trying to sleep while the Captain, an utter freak in purple velvet and long mustache and a conductor's hat too small for his shaggy head held a tape recorder mike in front of their mouths and asked them to speak their names.

"It's for the archives," said the Captain. "The bride and groom are going to start an archives."

"I'm Fred," said Fred.

"I'm George," said George. And Mike and Evelyn and Steamboat and Stewart and Lois and Steve and Holly and Lloyd and Sarah all said who they were too. The Captain recorded them, then wandered on through the crowd, catching sound as he went.

He recorded the Scott boys, Henry and Tommy from Second Creek, making bird sounds with their mouths.

He recorded the musicians warming up, Dorothy Thornton with her dulcimer, Cecil and Claudine Turner with guitar and mandolin, and Terry sitting in with his new sitar, leading now as they break into an old Mac Wiseman song called "Rainbow In the Valley."

Some women were walking past the musicians, carrying dishes to the table, talking as they worked. One was Marilyn, of Troll and Marilyn, big and beautiful and pregnant, saying, "It'll be a natural childbirth. I'm going to have it at home."

"I had all my younguns at home," said Mrs. Thornton. "Tended by a granny-woman. Old Aunt Dicey Pace from Turkey Creek. She's dead now, bless her soul."

The Captain recorded that, and at the Kool-Aid table he recorded Elmer the mailman rapping with a leather and denim freak from San Diego.

"I think ginseng is the answer to about half of mankind's problems," the freak said.

"Shoot," said Elmer. "My daddy picked 'sang for

a living, when I was a boy. It's as native to these hills as it is to over yonder in China."

The Captain recorded that, and he recorded Maybeline Monday from the Organic Sunflower Commune in California, telling Mrs. Jennings of Jennings Branch that she was doing her own weaving now. And making quilts, and canning her own vegetables.

"We live in a commune, on the land, you see. We're opposed to the nuclear family."

"Lord, child," said Mrs. Jennings. "I've been weaving since I was nine years old. And ever quilt in our old house is handmade. I had thirteen brothers and sisters, and then nine younguns of my own. We all live over yonder on Jennings Branch, you ought to come see us before you leave."

The Captain was getting it all. Armed with a fresh cassette, he moved to the shady side of the house where Swami High-Time from Santa Cruz, carrying the Book of Tao, was into a heavy theological rap with Mrs. Godsey, who as usual held her Bible in her hand.

"A double-minded man is unstable in all his ways," she said. "That's scripture, brother. James one, eight."

The Swami smiled and nodded and turned to chapter twenty-one in the Book of Tao. "The surest test if a man be sane is if he accepts life whole, as it is," he read.

And just as he finished reading, the Anaheim Flash came up and said, "Excuse me, folks. But I couldn't help overhear that little exchange. That's interesting scripture you're into there, and what I'm wondering is, would you be interested in reading those passages in the wedding after a while."

"Wow, man," said the Swami. "Far out."

But Mrs. Godsey shook her head. "I've got to go in the kitchen here and help out," she said. "Get Brother Bagby to read my part."

As the Captain was getting that, the Flash reached

out and touched the microphone. "That's a nice piece of equipment you've got there," he said.

"I'm taping for the archives," said the Captain. "The bride and groom are going to start an archives, and I'm out gathering sound."

"I can dig it," said the Flash. "Archives are the minestrone of history, and history is the spaghetti of cosmic time."

"I was going to ask you about time," said the Captain. "I mean, just for the record, how do you feel about it?"

The Flash motioned for the Captain to follow him. "Come over here and I'll show you," he said. And he took the Captain back over to where the musicians had assembled.

There were twice as many now as there had been before. An entire rock band, the Anonymous Artists of America, had just arrived by school bus from Colorado, and J.D. and Steamboat had joined in with autoharp and drums. Two chicks that no one knew came in with another banjo and a flute, and at the last minute before the music got really going Elmer and the leather and denim freak took places at the edge of the group, playing spoons and combs. There were at least two dozen musicians by now and their exotic sound, which Adrienne had already dubbed Hillbilly Hindu Rock, lured Chloe and a string of dancers wearing tie-dyed leotards out of the house and down the steps, a winding snake of movement through the crowd. Florrie and Annie and Gloria and Paul and Sarah and Sue and Susan and Terry and Diana and Maxine and Marian followed Chloe as she circled around the charcoal pit where Leonard and Doyle and Peter were baking potatoes and barbecuing chickens. They wound past the long, white table where Roxie and Marcella and Mrs. Thornton and Tandy and Rhonda Craft and Hattie and Cynnie and Jennifer were setting out bowls

of beans and corn and pickled beets and kraut and
casseroles and pies and cakes and puddings and plates
of biscuits and cornbread with jams and jellies, fruit
jello and salads. The dancers writhed as they moved
through the crowd toward some square-dances Wheeler
had formed. The rising tempo of the music whirled the
dancers around and around and around and around,
and finally the square-dancers couldn't resist it any
longer. Ken and Gwynne and Mae and Maude and
Thelma and Sol and Mary Jane and Holly and Larry
and Buster and Phil and Virgil and Ruby and Pat and
Warren all found places in the circle and whirled
around and around as other people watching began to
clap and stamp their feet and finally to form smaller
circles of their own. As the Captain moved in closer to
catch the music the Flash patted him on the back and
grinning said, "*This* is how I feel about time!"

The Flash left the Captain then and went over to
see how Leonard and Doyle and Peter were doing at
the fire.

"About ten minutes," said Leonard. "Ten more
minutes, and the chickens'll all be done."

"That's fine," said the Flash. "We'll be ready." And
he signaled then for the music to slow down.

Down, down. It all slowed down. And when it was
quiet enough for his voice to be heard the Flash called
out, "It's time for the wedding, folks. It's time to
gather around."

Gather around.

Gather around the front porch steps where the altar
had been arranged, a circle of stones that Angel and
her friends had decorated with flowers. As the people
assembled around it Leonard, the best man, pushed
through to stand at the side of Angel, the maid of
honor. He had on his working clothes. He was sweating
hard from his work at the fire and there was a streak
of black across his forehead which Roxie came up to
wipe away. She and Leonard squeezed hands then, and

Leonard took Angel's hand and squeezed it too, and Angel looked up and smiled. People were laughing and chattering as they gathered around, but once the circle was formed and the Flash had come down the steps to stand beside Leonard and Angel, the scene became quiet and still.

At last, when all had settled, D.R. and Estelle came through the screen door, across the porch and down the steps to where they were supposed to stand.

D.R. had his leathers on, leather pants and leather shirt, and coonskin cap with tail.

Estelle had her ankle-length gingham on.

There were no flowers.

Estelle's bouquet was simply D.R.'s hand in her own.

They stood there together, grinning at the people who grinned at them, waiting for the Flash to begin.

The Flash moves now to the third step up so he can see over Leonard's head. He has a book with him, and a large brown bag filled with something which he rests on the step by his foot. The book is the *I Ching*. He opens it to After Completion and clearing his throat he reads:

"The transition from the old to the new time is already accomplished. In principle, everything stands systematized, and it is only in regard to details that success is still to be achieved. In respect to this, however, we must be careful to maintain the right attitude. Everything proceeds as if of its own accord, and this can all too easily tempt us to relax and let things take their course without troubling over details. Such indifference is the root of all evil. Symptoms of decay are bound to be the result. Here we have the rule indicating the usual course of history. But this rule is not an inescapable law. He who understands it is in position to avoid its effects by dint of unremitting perseverance and caution."

The Flash closes the book and places it on a step behind him.

Then he calls upon the Reverend Bagby to read the little passage from the Book of Tao.

"The surest test if a man be sane is if he accepts life whole, as it is," says Reverend Bagby.

And then the Flash calls upon Swami High-Time to read from the Book of James.

"A double-minded man is unstable in all his ways," says Swami High-Time.

As he and Reverend Bagby step back into the crowd, the Flash reaches into his pocket and takes out two rings. He hands one each to Leonard and Angel, who in turn hand them to D.R. and Estelle.

They face each other. They hold out their left hands, and simultaneously slip the rings on one another's fingers.

Then they come together in a kiss and full embrace.

And the Flash says, "As a minister in good standing of the Universal Life Church, I pronounce you guys husband and wife. And I pronounce everybody at this wedding hereby married to one another."

The Flash reaches into the bag at his feet then, and from it he begins to fling rice out over the gathered people.